Operation
Musketeer

Based on a true story

DAVID LEE CORLEY

CONTENTS

NOTE FROM AUTHOR

Although *Operation Musketeer* can be read as a stand-alone novel, it is best understood if read after my novel *Sèvres Protocol* which is Part One of the Suez Crisis.

PROLOGUE

On July 26, 1956, Gamil Abdel Nasser, the president of Egypt, nationalized the Suez Canal. World leaders were shocked by the new president's audacious power play and concerned the international waterway might be in danger of shutting down, cutting off Europe's access to Middle East oil. British and French investors that owned the Suez Canal Company were outraged. Something had to be done.

On October 24, 1956, leaders from Britain, France, and Israel met in secret at a villa in Sèvres, France just outside of Paris. Together they conspired to fabricate a war with Egypt with the objectives of taking control of the Canal and toppling Nasser. The plan required that Israel attack Egypt to put an end to the ongoing Fayeed cross border raids that plagued Israeli settlers and to secure safe passage for Israeli shipping through the Straits of Tiran which was being blockaded by Egyptian naval guns on the southern end of the Sinai Peninsula. As the fighting intensified, the Israelis would advance toward the Canal Zone, threatening international shipping. To protect the Canal, Britain and France would deliver an ultimatum to Israel and Egypt requiring the warring parties to ceasefire and create a sixteen kilometer buffer zone on both sides of the Canal. The Israelis would immediately agree, but the conspirators knew that Nasser could never agree to stop fighting while Israeli troops occupied Egyptian territory. Britain and France would be forced to invade Egypt to protect the Canal and drive a wedge between the two belligerents. The Israeli invasion was called "Operation Kadesh." The British and French invasion was called "Operation Musketeer."

As Operation Kadesh draws to an end with Israeli forces occupying most of the Sinai peninsula, our story begins...

"Small wars can turn into big wars..."

Nikolai Bulganin, Premier of the Soviet Union (1955-1958)

ONE

October 31, 1956 - The Red Sea

The *HMS Newfoundland* was a British Fiji-class cruiser on patrol in the Red Sea, eight miles south of the mouth of the Suez Canal. It was close to midnight and the lookout on the port side was struggling to keep his eyes open. He took a quick sip of tea from his thermos flask. It snapped him awake. He raised his binoculars and gazed into the dark sea. To his surprise, he saw a large object traveling in the opposite direction. He rubbed his eyes and looked again as he turned the focus ring on the binoculars. The dark outline of a ship came into focus. Her running lights were off. He reported it to the watch commander.

The British captain was in his cabin writing a letter to wife when he heard a knock at his door. An ensign informed him that the watch commander was requesting his presence. The captain rose from his desk and followed the ensign to the bridge. "What's happening, Lieutenant?" said the captain to the watch commander.

"The lookout reported a ship heading out of the bay with its running lights off, Captain," said the lieutenant.

The captain picked up a set of binoculars and scanned the horizon until he spotted the dark mass. "Humph. Bring her about and let's have a closer look," he said.

The British cruiser closed to within fifteen hundred

yards and came parallel to the darkened ship – the Egyptian Frigate *Domiat*. It had just left the port of Adabieh on its way to rendezvous with the Egyptian Frigate *Rosetta*. The captain of the *Domiat* was hoping to slip by the British warship unnoticed. "It looks like an Egyptian frigate," said the captain. "She must have just left port."

"Shall I sound general quarters, Captain?" said the Lieutenant.

"No," said the captain. "But have our gun crews direct the main guns toward the ship just in case. I don't want to give away our intent, but I don't want to take any chances either. Send a message to the captain of the *Diana* to cutoff any path of the ship out to sea. I don't want our mouse escaping."

The British captain waited until his gun crews sighted their guns at the dark ship.

"Guns are ready, Captain," said the Lieutenant.

"Good. Signal the ship's captain. He is to heave-to or be fired upon. Make sure the message is in both English and Arabic. I don't want any confusion."

"Yes, sir."

The Lieutenant sent out a radio signal. The *Domiat* signaled its acknowledgement of the order in Arabic. The running lights on the *Domiat* came on and the ship appeared to slow. After a moment, the *Domiat* went dark once again and turned her four inch main guns toward the British cruiser. "Ah, bollicks!" said the British captain. "All guns fire."

The eighteen-gun broadside of six-inch shells rocked the Egyptian frigate with multiple explosions. Even in the dark, the British gunners were so close to their target there was little chance of missing.

The Egyptian crew recovered and returned fire, hitting the *Newfoundland* several times at point-blank-range with their four-inch guns, causing some damage and casualties. The Egyptian frigate was clearly outmatched by the larger

British cruiser. Fires broke out on both the *Domiat* and the *Newfoundland*. Smoke rose into the sky, shrouding the moon and stars, and reducing visibility. Fire crews on both ships battled the flames. The main gun crews reloaded. The anti-aircraft guns and machineguns fired, raking each ship and creating more chaos.

The second volley from *Newfoundland*'s main guns badly damaged the hull of the *Domiat*. "She's listing badly to port, Captain," said the Lieutenant, watching through binoculars.

"Any signal from their bridge?"

"No, sir. Not that I can see."

"What the hell does their captain think he's going to accomplish, aside from killing his crew?" said the British captain. "Continue firing until he surrenders."

"Yes, sir."

The *Newfoundland* continued to fire on the *Domiat*, punching large holes into her hull and taking out her main gun turrets. Fire spread through the frigate and its rate of fire slowed to a sporadic trickle.

The battle was joined by the British destroyer *HMS Diana*. It opened fire as it crossed the bow of the *Domiat*. Multiple five-inch shells from the *Diana's* guns plowed into the frigate's forward hull just above the waterline. The explosions caused the Egyptian ship to heave upward then down into the water, like a breaching whale.

The damage was too much and the Egyptian crew abandoned ship right before the *Domiat* turned on her side and sank. The British ships ceased firing and fished sixty-nine surviving Egyptian sailors out of the sea.

It was a very short battle with a violent ending. Nobody ever discovered why the Egyptian captain thought he could do battle with two British warships larger and more modern than his own. He had died in the battle. "What a waste of men," said the British captain, shaking his head as he watched the drenched and bloodied Egyptian sailors being hauled on board his ship. "Downright insanity."

Washington D.C., USA

Dwight Eisenhower, the President of the United States, sat in the Oval Office Dining Room. He used his fork to pick the flesh off the bones of a sautéed trout as he listened to his three guests: Secretary of State, J. Foster Dulles, CIA Director, Allen Dulles, and Henry Cabot Lodge, U.S. Ambassador to the United Nations. The news wasn't good, and Eisenhower had lost his appetite. What he really wanted was another cigarette but that would have been his sixth in less than an hour. He didn't like the idea of being addicted to anything. It was a weakness. He fingered the lighter his wife had given him and decided to forgo the cigarette until everyone was finished with their meal.

The dining room was understated in its furnishings and decorations. That was the way Eisenhower liked it. It wasn't that he didn't like the White House. He loved it, especially its sense of history and the paintings of past presidents. The eyes of the presidents on the walls reminded him that they too were human and had struggled with hard decisions just as much as he did. But there were times when he found the White House too formal and overwhelming. When he first came into office, almost four years ago, he had ordered the Oval Office dining room to be dressed down and made to feel more casual. It was one of his favorite rooms.

A messenger knocked on the door and entered. He handed Allen Dulles a note. The CIA Director read it and nodded a dismissal without reply to the messenger. The messenger left. "The British cruiser *HMS Newfoundland* and destroyer *HMS Diana* just sank the Egyptian frigate *Domiat* in the Red Sea," he said.

The room fell silent as everyone contemplated the escalations of hostilities in Egypt. "A cruiser and a destroyer against a frigate. I imagine that wasn't much of a battle," said Eisenhower with disgust. *Damn it*, he thought to himself as he set down his fork and lit a cigarette. The first pull of smoke calmed him as he knew it would.

There was only one topic for discussion that day... the Suez Crisis. It seemed to engulf everything. Even the presidential election less than a week away took a backseat to the news from the Middle East. The polls said Eisenhower would win by a large margin, but he wasn't so sure. He didn't trust polls. The voters could change their minds on a whim and the news of another war involving America's allies didn't help his case. But then again, he didn't care much. War was a terrible thing and far more important than his reelection.

Eisenhower felt this was a critical turning point in history. The two great colonial powers, France and Britain fighting to keep their influence as their empires crumbled; Egypt, a former colony struggling to remain free and shed itself of Western authority. He couldn't help but feel sympathy for Egypt. After all, America was once a colony and had similar struggles to free itself from its former master.

The big problem was Sir Anthony Eden, Britain's Prime Minister. He loathed Gamal Abdel Nasser, Egypt's president, and had secretly attempted to have him assassinated several times. Eisenhower was not a fan of Nasser either, but he understood him and respected his right to govern his country as he saw fit. Nasser had been swept into power after a coup, but had submitted to an election by the Egyptian people which he won overwhelmingly. He was a democratically elected leader. He was also a pain in the ass for the Western powers, stirring up the Middle East with his anti-Western politics and calls for pan-Arab unity. He wanted to be the leader of the Arab nations and used the demonizing of the West to solidify his support. The people of the Middle East applauded Nasser for standing up against the great powers, and the Arab leaders praised Nasser in their speeches, even though they privately thought him foolish.

Eisenhower was honest with himself. He was partly to blame for the situation in Egypt. He was deeply concerned about Soviet influence in the Middle East. When Nasser had circumvented the Western weapons embargo by purchasing a large shipment of Soviet arms from Czechoslovakia, Eden had suggested that Britain and America show their displeasure by slowing down the funding of Nassar's pet project, the Aswan Dam. Unlike Eisenhower, who was a career military officer, Eden was an experienced statesman and knew how to press Eisenhower's buttons. Eisenhower was angry with Nasser and agreed to Eden's plan. In response, Nasser nationalized the Suez Canal so he could use the revenue from the ships' tolls to continue funding the dam's construction.

British and French investors owned the rights to operate and collect the revenue from the Suez Canal. The canal was also a strategic international waterway. Both Britain and France were dependent on the canal's continued operation for oil and trade. The idea that the Canal – and with it Britain's financial fate – was now controlled by Nasser sent Eden through the roof.

Eisenhower thought the nationalization of the Canal by Nasser was a mistake and could cripple Egypt's economy for years to come. International investment would be closed off to Egypt until the Western investors in the canal were fairly compensated. But Eisenhower recognized Egypt's right to nationalize assets within its borders even if he thought it a bad idea.

The British and French didn't see it that way. The Canal was an international waterway and it needed to be protected by the Western powers. "First the allied bombings and now the sinking of an Egyptian frigate. This whole thing is spinning out of control. We need to find a way to stop it before it expands," said Eisenhower.

"The international community is mostly against British

and French interference," said ambassador Lodge. "They see it for what it is... an attempt by colonial powers to reinsert themselves into the Middle East. International leaders are applying diplomatic pressure. There is a lot of talk in the UN about sanctions against both Britain and France if they don't stop their attacks against Egypt."

"And what is the UN's feeling about the Israelis?" said Foster Dulles.

"They're condemning the Israelis too, but for different reasons."

"This whole thing smacks of conspiracy," said Allen Dulles. "It's just a little too convenient that the Israelis invade Egypt right after the nationalization of the Canal. They haven't even used the Canal since Egypt banned their ships."

"Maybe that's what they hope to gain," said the Secretary of State, "a relaxation of restrictions on their shipping."

"Maybe... but I think their actions are more about giving Egypt a bloody nose. Make 'em think twice about attacking Israel with their new Soviet weapons," said the president. "But I will admit the Israelis' timing is somewhat suspicious. Allen, what resources does the CIA have in the area?"

"We have four undercover operatives in the embassy in Tel Aviv. But so far they haven't discovered anything that looks like a conspiracy with the British or French. I know Naval Intelligence is also working to find information on the Israelis. I can check with them and see if they've turned up anything."

"Probably not a good idea to have you stepping on the Navy's toes, even for Intelligence. The last thing I need right now is my Intelligence gatherers in a turf fight," said Eisenhower. "I'll ask Admiral Burke myself."

"Of course, Mr. President."

Algiers, Algeria

At French division headquarters in Algiers, the battalion commanders of the 10th Parachute Division stood around General Jacques Massu as he used several maps to explain Operation Musketeer. "Our mission will be peacekeeping by definition but do not let that fool you. We expect there will be plenty of fighting. We have two objectives. First, separate the Israelis and Egyptians so that the fighting can cease. Second, protect the Suez Canal from damage or occupation by either side. The French and British commanders have agreed to a sixteen-mile neutral zone on either side of the Suez Canal. Neither Israeli nor Egyptian forces will be allowed within that zone."

"But the Egyptians already have positions inside the Canal Zone," said Colonel Pierre Chateau-Jobert.

"This is true. They must give them up and move to new positions a minimum of ten miles from the Canal."

"Have they given any indication that they might do that?" said Lieutenant Colonel Marcel Bigeard.

"Just the opposite. The Egyptians are digging in."

"Then there will be a fight?"

"Most likely, yes."

"What are the Intelligence estimates as to the size of the Egyptian forces?" said Bigeard.

"Three hundred thousand all equipped with the latest Soviet weapons."

"And our forces?"

"Eighty thousand including the British."

"We will be outnumbered three to one?" said Bigeard.

"It seems so. However... British and French forces will use both naval and aerial bombardment to soften up the Egyptian positions should they elect not to observe the neutral zone."

"And their air force?" said Bigeard.

"Formidable. They have over two hundred MIG-15s. I have been assured our own air force and the British will annihilate them in the early part of the war."

"And tanks? The Egyptians have over five hundred tanks and armored cars." said Bigeard.

"How are we supposed to deal with that many tanks?" said Chateau-Jobert.

"Once their air force has been destroyed, our air force will be free to deal with their tanks and what remains of their navy," said Massu. "When the proper preparations have been completed, our para forces along with the British commandos will drop deep into the neutral zone and expel whomever is left. At the same time, the British will land a large number of infantry and marine forces at the mouth of the Canal on the Mediterranean side, near Port Said. Our job is to take and hold the key points along the northern sides of the Canal until the British forces can relieve us."

"How long might that be?" said Chateau-Jobert.

"We are estimating eight to ten days," said Massu.

"What about the Israelis?" said Bigeard.

"It seems the Israelis have halted their advance and are defending their current positions, all of which are more than ten miles from the Suez Canal. There should be no need to fight the Israelis. In fact, any combat with the Israelis must be approved directly by me," said Massu.

"What if they fire on us?" said Bigeard.

"They won't," said Massu.

"How can you be sure?" said Chateau-Jobert.

"I have it on good authority and I will leave it at that… and so will you. No combat with the Israelis." Massu snapped.

The commanders exchanged concerned glances with each other. "What about civilians?" said Bigeard.

"You will use your discretion but any person that takes up arms against our forces, whether wearing a uniform or not, will no longer be considered a civilian and should be dealt with accordingly," said Massu. "I do not want things to get out of hand as they did in Philippeville. Keep the civilians in your areas of operation under control. Gentlemen, to be clear... our mission will require us to destroy the Egyptian army and bring Egypt to her knees. Nasser cannot be reasoned with any other way. From this point forward the Suez Canal will be an international passageway protected by both Britain and France."

"And the FLN?" said Bigeard referring to the underground organization fighting for Algerian independence from France.

"Nasser cannot support the FLN if Egypt is left in ruins. The destruction of the FLN is not our main goal in this operation but I think we can all agree it will be a welcome by-product of our victory," said Massu with a knowing smile.

Sinai, Egypt

The still of the night was broken by the groan of heavy engines pushed to their max as a column of Egyptian armored vehicles raced across the desert. Their headlights were off. It was safer that way. The lead driver's eyes had adjusted to the darkness after the first hour. The trick was no light whatsoever, not even inside the armored vehicle. This allowed his pupils to open wide and let in as much light as possible. He saw a surprising amount of detail in the surrounding landscape, more than enough to pilot his vehicle on the dirt road. The drivers of the vehicles behind him only needed to follow the vehicle in front of them.

Riding in the open hatch of the lead armored car was Colonel Hajjar, the armored battalion commander. Nasser had issued the order for all units to advance across the Suez Canal to the Western side where Egyptian forces were gathering to confront a possible British and French invasion. *Advance,* thought Hajjar. *Interesting choice of words. He meant retreat, but Nasser, a colonel himself, had become a politician which made word selection critical. Like the American*

11

*commander at Bastogne had said when his forces were retreating…
we are advancing in the opposite direction. Words were important,
especially when you were losing.*

His battalion of tanks and armored cars was the
rearguard for his division. The rest of the division had
crossed the Suez earlier that night, but not before being
badly mauled by Israeli aircraft armed with rockets and
bombs. The division had lost twenty-two tanks, thirty-five
armored personnel carriers and five SU-100 self-propelled
tank destroyers. Those weapons and the men that operated
them would be missed when the fight for Ports Said and
Fuad started.

Hajjar looked back the way they had come. The sky
was beginning to lighten. The sun would be up soon. He
needed to get his men across the Suez before sunrise…
before the Israeli aircraft returned.

The one good thing about the lightening sky was that
he began to see shapes on the horizon. He recognized
distinct shapes of the mountains to the south of the
column. They were a landmark he knew well. He glanced
at the map in his hand, held below the rim of the hatch.
He flipped on his flashlight, equipped with a red filter over
the lens to make it less noticeable in the darkness. The
map was hard to read as it bounced around from the
rough ride. The armored car's suspension was firm and the
road was filled with ruts and potholes. He steadied his
hand as best he could. He just needed a moment to see
where they were in relation to the landmark and the bridge
that would take them across the Canal. Just a few more
miles to safety. He turned off the flashlight and tucked
both the map and the flashlight into his pocket. "Are you
alright, Corporal?" said Hajjar to the driver. "Our entire
column is depending on your eyes."

"I'm fine, sir. It's getting easier to see," said the driver.

"Yes, but it means the enemy can see us too."

"I didn't think about it that way."

"That's why you are still a corporal."

"Yes, sir."

Several bright flashes to the north lit up the horizon, blinding the driver for a moment. "What the hell was that?" he shouted.

"It's the Israelis. They must have used the old road to get ahead of us," said Hajjar as he slipped beneath the rim and closed the hatch.

"I can't see, sir."

"Don't worry. They'll be plenty of light in a moment."

Shells exploded around the column, lighting up the sky. An armored personnel carrier took a direct hit, killing everyone inside and blocking the vehicles behind it. Fortunately for the Egyptians, they were on a flat part of the road and the vehicles could maneuver around the burning hulk.

Hajjar had a decision to make – fight or flight. If they fought there was no way they would make it across the Suez before daybreak. The Israelis would send in their planes to finish off his column. The Egyptian air force had been decimated over the past forty-eight hours by the British and French bombers and fighters. He knew he could not count on any air support to hold off the Israeli aircraft. His vehicles and men would be sitting ducks. He knew the Israelis probably would not follow his column across the bridge where they was already a large buildup of Egyptian units on the Western side. It wasn't a hard decision. He chose flight. He would save what he could.

"This is Arrow twenty-one, to all units," he said over the radio. "We continue to the bridge at full speed. If a vehicle is hit do not stop to pick up survivors. We must keep moving. Our duty to Egypt is to make it across intact. Out."

More vehicles were hit as the Egyptians continued across the desert floor. Three Russian T-34 tanks were completely destroyed, along with several tank destroyers, armored cars and armored personnel carriers. It was a big loss for Hajjar's battalion. It was unlikely they would be replaced until after the war was concluded. He felt ashamed at leaving the wounded behind. Even though his commission had been purchased by his family, he had fought hard to prove himself worthy to his commanding officers and his men. He hated running from a fight but he knew it was best for his men and for Egypt. As they continued toward the Suez, the Egyptian tank commanders swung their guns and fired wildly at the Israelis. They knew they wouldn't hit anything, but it might slow them down.

It was getting brighter outside. Through the commander's viewing slit in the armored car, he could see the Suez and the bridge leading across it. They were almost there. Just a little farther and he and his men would be safe. There was something else on the horizon in front of the column but he couldn't make it out. It was only when he saw multiple machinegun flashes that he understood that it was a low-flying Israeli Mustang heading straight for the column.

As the first aircraft in a squadron of Mustangs approached the column's lead vehicle the pilot released one of his five hundred pound bombs.

Events slowed. Hajjar knew what was about to happen as he saw the bomb dropping directly toward his armored car. He thought about taking evasive action, but it was too late. He whispered, "God is great." A peace settled over him. He was resolved.

The bomb hit the armored car just below the turret and exploded, killing the entire crew. The impact of the explosion sent the armored car back on its heels flipping it. The burning wreckage tumbled and settled on its side. There wasn't much left.

Cairo, Egypt

"Do you hear that?" said President Nasser, standing by the

window as U.S. Ambassador to Egypt, Raymond Hare was escorted in to his office.

"The jets overhead?" asked Hare.

"British Valiant and Canberra bombers to be exact."

"Yes, Mr. President. I hear them."

"They've been bombing my people since early yesterday morning. And why? Because we were invaded by our Jewish neighbor and refused to let them occupy our country?"

"America agrees the entire series of events is unjust."

"And yet you do nothing?"

"I wouldn't say nothing."

"Your Sixth Fleet sits in the Mediterranean like a bloated whale after eating too many fish, while my people die. The British and French warplanes are destroying my military. Soon, we will have nothing with which to defend ourselves."

"You have the United Nations on your side."

"The United Nations? It will take them a month to decide on the shape of the table they should sit at to discuss the situation. We need action now while we still have a country worth fighting for. Next week will be too late."

"I understand, Mr. President."

"I don't think you do, Ambassador. America's reputation in the Middle East is on the line. You say you want to be the Arab's friend and protect us against the communist threat. But where are you when we truly need you? Cowering behind the U.N."

"America does not cower, President Nasser," said Hare with a sharpness in his voice.

"Excuse my choice of words. I still struggle with your language. What would be the appropriate word for failing to act when action is what is required?"

"Politics, I believe."

Nasser chuckled and said, "Very good, Mr. Ambassador. Very good."

"I don't mean to make light of the situation, Mr. President. Believe me when I tell you little else has been on President Eisenhower's mind these last few days."

"And here I thought he was distracted by his reelection."

"No, sir. He is distracted by the possibility of things escalating."

"Escalating? What more can British and French do, besides invade, which our Intelligence tells us will happen as soon as their troop transport ships arrive?"

"Mr. President, I know you are busy. I have no desire to waste you time. How may I help you?"

"You can convey my request to President Eisenhower that America must honor the Tripartite Declaration and defend Egypt."

"I shall do so, but I believe you already know the answer."

"Britain and France are your allies."

"...and key members of NATO."

"Tell me, Ambassador Hare... How long will NATO last if its members cannot be taken at their word?"

"I understand your point, Mr. President. These are not easy times for Egypt or America but for different reasons."

"Yes, like the fact that Egypt is being attacked and America is not."

"Yes, sir. But you also understand that America's priority is preventing the expansion of Communism and Soviet aggression."

"And I am beginning to wonder if the East would not be better allies than the West!"

Hare held his temper like any good ambassador and waited a long moment before responding, "Is that the message you wish for me to convey to my president?"

It was Nasser's turn to think before responding. "No."

"President Eisenhower understands these are serious times and is doing everything he can to bring about a peaceful conclusion to this situation."

"Everything?"

"Everything within reason."

"I agree these are serious times, Ambassador. One must not go off... how do you say... half-cocked."

"No, sir. That would not be wise."

"But Egypt is running out of time."

"Yes, Mr. President. I will convey your concerns to President Eisenhower."

Nasser , shook Hare's hand. "Thank you, Raymond," he said with disappointment in his voice.

"Of course, Mr. President," said Hare and left.

Military Airfield, Cyprus

It was early morning with French and British warplanes already taking off and landing, one after another. The airfield was bursting at the seams with barely enough room to turn around, let alone find a place to park. Many of the aircraft had been damaged by Egyptian anti-aircraft guns and needed repair. The ground crews did their best to deal with an untenable situation. It looked more like a big city traffic jam than a military airfield.

Behind the airfield was the bivouac area for French and British paratroopers. The two groups were separated. Even though they had recently fought a war together, the paratroopers of both nations were terribly proud and naturally aggressive even with their own allies. It was considered wise to keep them apart.

Unlike the other French units slated to participate in the campaign, the paratroopers had come straight from the battlefield where they had been fighting the Mujahideen in the mountains of Algeria. They were flown to Cyprus so they could rest for a couple days and prepare for the invasion. They were too valuable to let waste away on a ship. They were the best France had to offer.

Tent flaps opened, Colonel Bigeard sat on the edge of

17

his cot smoking a cigarette and sipping his coffee. He was dripping with sweat, having just completed his morning calisthenics routine which included multiple sets of military-style pushups, sit-ups, squats and lunges. He was considered by many to be the fittest soldier in the French army and he planned on staying that way as he aged. *A cot,* he thought. *Ridiculous. I am a para commander. I sleep on the ground when in the field like my men.* His staff had insisted on a cot for their commander's tent. He, above all others, needed to be well rested they reasoned. Their lives depended on his clear thinking. He admitted to himself that it helped him sleep, but he hated the way it looked to his men. *They'll think I am soft.* He was getting older. Now a lieutenant colonel, if he was promoted again to full colonel he would most likely be forced from the field. He loathed the idea. *Commanders need to lead their men from the front not from behind a desk.*

He removed the blankets, lifted the cot and placed it outside his tent. He would have the quartermaster pick it up later. In the meantime, his men would see the discarded luxury and understand what it meant – that the man leading them was one tough son of a bitch.

It was sunrise. Time for breakfast. He walk over to the mess tent where was a large crowd of men waited. They parted like the Red Sea as their commander approached. His staff officers were already seated inside sipping their morning coffee but nobody was eating. They were waiting. More men entered the mess tent.

The cooks had set out seven burlap sacks filled with raw onions. He reached into one of the sacks and found the largest onion. He turned back to his men and took a big bite. Some of the men winced. They knew all too well what it tasted like. The thinking was simple. If you started your day by eating a raw onion it was all downhill from there, no matter what happened. He walked outside the mess tent to finish his onion. One by one his men picked up an onion from the burlap sacks, took their first bite and followed him outside.

He finished the last bite of his onion and took a deep breath. "Sea air. Good for the lungs," he said. "Ten kilometers I think."

Some of the men groaned. He smiled and said, "Come now. It will put hair on your chest."

His men called him Bruno – his old radio call sign from the résistance when he fought against the Nazis. He had fought in three wars and survived two chest wounds that barely missed his heart and would have killed a lesser man. He asked no man under his command to do more than he himself would do. He started to jog through the camp. Without orders to do so, his men followed. How could they not? He was a legend.

The group grew in number until the entire battalion, including the officers, was jogging behind Bruno. Bruno turned onto the dirt road separating the British and the French paratrooper camps. The British lined the road and watched with dismay. These were the French paratroopers that had fought at the Siege of Dien Bien Phu. The British knew of their reputation as being tough, but the French were going to wear themselves out before they went into battle. They should be resting for the sleepless nights ahead. It seemed foolish.

A French staff sergeant began to chant a French cadence. The others joined in with their husky voices. Bruno smiled, honored to lead such men into battle. They were Bruno's boys and everyone knew it.

Suez Canal Zone, Egypt

A British twin-tailed Sea Venom fighter-bomber swooped down to attack a convoy of Egyptian vehicles making a run for a bridge crossing to the Western side of the Suez Canal. The British and French Air Force and Naval aircraft had taken over the air assaults on the Egyptian military forces as the Israeli Air Force was ordered by their commanders to only operate in the Sinai.

The pilot, Lieutenant Commander Wilcox, lined up his aircraft to fly directly over the column of vehicles. Both Wilcox and his observing officer, Lieutenant R.C. Olding, could see the Egyptian soldiers diving out of the vehicles and scrambling for cover on both sides of the road. He unleashed eight sixty-pound rockets and destroyed two trucks and an armored car on his first pass. One of the explosions was spectacular as the truck's cargo of ammunition was ignited. The armored car penetrated the bridge's guardrail and tumbled into the water below, like a meteorite.

Wilcox swung around for another run and fired six hundred rounds from his four Hispano 20-mm cannons, setting several more vehicles on fire and killing anyone stupid enough to have stayed behind. With his munitions expended Wilcox headed for home – the aircraft carrier *HMS Eagle*.

As his aircraft approached the Mediterranean, Wilcox saw multiple puffs of black smoke around his cockpit. Several anti-aircraft rounds hit his plane, tearing holes in his wings and causing the aircraft to become unstable. Just when he thought it was over, a final round entered the bottom of the cockpit under Olding's seat and exited through the canopy. They were both lucky that the round did not explode inside the cockpit as it would surely have killed them both. But when Olding looked down he saw that the round had gone through his right leg leaving a gaping hole. He could see the ground below the aircraft through his leg as it passed over the shoreline. When Wilcox asked if he was okay, the young lieutenant simply responded "I don't think so."

Wilcox could see that the wound was life threatening and that Olding was going into shock. He barked out an order for Olding to remove his belt and wrap it around his leg above his wound. Olding obeyed the order. Wilcox then ordered Olding to help him navigate the plane back to the aircraft carrier. Wilcox knew he had to keep Olding's mind off his wound or the shock could kill him. He continued to make demands of the young lieutenant and the lieutenant did his best to obey each and every command.

Within fifteen minutes, Wilcox, with Olding's help, landed the crippled aircraft on the *Eagle*. A medical crew hoisted Olding out of the cockpit. Wilcox escorted the lieutenant inside and gave him one final demand before he was taken into surgery, "Don't die, Lieutenant. That's an order."

Olding obeyed his commander, but lost his leg.

Israel Field Hospital, Sinai

Brigitte Friang sat by her boyfriend's side as he slept. Tom Coyle had been through a lot, and was lucky to be alive. The plane he was piloting was carrying over a dozen Israeli wounded from a battlefield deep in the Sinai when it crashed in the desert. He and the two survivors of his Spanish crew went for help on foot. After many days, the Israeli army found Coyle wandering at night in the desert. He was badly dehydrated and hallucinating. The two Spaniards had died.

Brigitte, a war correspondent, was informed that Coyle was alive and was being treated in an Israeli field hospital. She came immediately.

Back in Paris, Brigitte had uncovered a copy of a secret agreement called the Protocol of Sèvres. It had been signed by high-ranking officials from Israel, France and Britain – the three nations that had conspired to invade Egypt. The protocol outlined an audacious plan. Israel would be the straw horse and invade Egypt through the Sinai. Then France and Britain would intercede to separate the two warring nations and secure the safety of the Suez

Canal. Egypt would naturally refuse to accept the Anglo-French ultimatum and Britain and France would be forced to invade and occupy the Canal Zone to keep the international waterway safe. The British and French air forces would bomb Egypt until Nasser capitulated or was overthrown by his military. The allies hoped for the latter. A truce would be negotiated that took security and control of the Canal away from Egypt.

Upon discovering the document, Brigitte realized she could never show it to anyone without being accused of treason. But that didn't stop her from using the threat of exposing the document as the means to get what she wanted… a front seat covering the upcoming war.

She had been imbedded with the Israeli paratroopers under the command of Colonel Ariel Sharon. On October 30, 1956, Israelis forces raced across the border and attacked Egypt. The Israelis fought a Blitzkrieg-style campaign, attacking Egyptian strongholds from many sides all at once. Within one week they gained control of the Sinai and were a threat to the Suez Canal, just as the conspirators had planned. Brigitte witnessed the key elements of the operation and had a book full of notes and photographs that she would use to write her stories once the news blackout imposed by the Israelis was lifted.

The Israelis were winding down their offensive and digging in for a ceasefire that they knew would be coming. Brigitte instinctively knew that there would be little happening with the Israelis unless the Egyptians counterattacked, which was highly unlikely. They were too busy retreating back across the Suez to the Western side. The war was being handed off to the British and French. Brigitte needed to embed with the French paratroopers as she had done in Indochina. The French para commander, Colonel Marcel 'Bruno' Bigeard was her close friend and former lover. If she could reach Bruno she would find the second half of her story. But that was easier said than done.

The British Commandos and French paratroopers were on the island of Cyprus preparing for the invasion. Almost the entire island had been taken over by the British and French Air Force and Navy. Commercial flights to the island were almost impossible to book because of the bomber and fighter missions taking precedence over air space. Brigitte would need to find another way onto the island if she was going to make contact with Bruno.

The Israelis were of little help. They were still pretending to be belligerent aggressors with France and Britain playing reluctant peacemakers. Trying to convince them that the world was wise to their conspiracy was like whipping a dead horse. There were no flights, commercial or military, from Israel to Cyprus and nobody was interested in helping a noisy French war correspondent.

While Coyle slept, Brigitte made phone calls to her contacts within the French military and government. Everything had been kept so secret it was difficult to find anyone to help. She finally found a naval commander who told her that the aircraft carrier *Arromanches* was stationed fifty miles off the Egyptian shoreline. If she could get to the aircraft carrier she might be able to hitch a ride on a supply run to Cyprus.

Brigitte went back to say goodbye to Coyle. He was still sleeping and she didn't want to wake him. She didn't want to leave him but she also didn't want to miss out on one of the greatest stories of her career. She wrote him a note, sealed it with a lipstick kiss and tucked into his hand so he was sure to see it when he woke. She kissed him on the forehead, gathered her gear, and left.

Brigitte convinced an Israeli sergeant at the battalion's motor pool to give her a ride to a port on the Mediterranean. She had tried the straightforward approach of telling him the truth and asking nicely for his help. She always preferred the straightforward approach and was pleased and surprised when it worked. A war correspondent often needed special treatment to get a story, and that meant getting people to cooperate. Most people naturally wanted to help journalists; they saw them as allies in uncovering the truth and keeping those in power in line with the will of the people.

When the straightforward approach did not work, Brigitte was not above being manipulative and even deceitful. Deception was a skill journalists nurtured from early on in their careers. The best journalists were devious and dogged, yet principled, and Brigitte was one of the best. She was clever, focused, and very persistent. There were lines she would not cross. She would never out-and-out lie to get what she wanted. She preferred to infer. That way it was up to the person she was trying to deceive to take the bait. By accepting her inference, the person became a co-conspirator in her quest for truth. By her standards that made it okay to deceive when required to uncover the truth. The public knew that deceit was a common method among journalists and it was a generally accepted practice. That made her readers co-conspirators too. In her mind the ends justified the means.

Like most veteran journalists, Brigitte had a bag of tricks of the trade she used to find the truth. Some worked better than others. She worked in a career dominated by men, many of whom did not take her seriously. That was their mistake and she used their ignorance to her advantage.

When dealing with men who refused to help her, she usually tried flirting first. She was attractive and had a great smile. She was also good at cultivating sympathy and was not above shedding a tear if she thought it would work. Most men instinctively wanted to help a damsel in distress and would give in to her requests.

If that didn't work, she usually tried dropping a name. Brigitte was well connected and had developed a large list of powerful contacts. The problem was that many of them both feared and disliked her. She had written a lot of stories that exposed the unbecoming secrets of people in power. But the person she was talking with at any moment usually didn't know she was on the outs with the person whose name she would drop. Her biggest problem was people's ignorance. She was constantly stunned how many people did not know the Prime Minister's name. Dropping names did not always work well.

Her final tool, and usually the most persuasive, was fury beyond reason. Most people just wanted to get on with their lives and didn't want problems. Men were especially vulnerable to a woman on a rant. It was an art developed through years of practice, like learning the cello. She would start off slowly usually transitioning from damsel in distress to female anger unleashed. Her argument would become more and more unhinged from reality and more personal. Crying was usually thrown in for good measure. That scared most men who didn't understand how to deal with a woman's feelings. They would feel embarrassed by their ineptitude and would do just about anything to make the irrational woman go away.

Brigitte felt somewhat guilty when she manipulated men. It was the 50's and people around the civilized world were just starting to realize the need for equality in the workplace and at home. Using emotion and flirting as a journalistic tool seemed to be contributing to the problem of inequality. But the movement for equality was still in its infancy and would take decades to achieve. Brigitte lived in the real world, where men still ruled the roost. She was forced to play by their rules no matter how stupid they seemed. Like most professional women, she was a feminist at heart but a realist in practice.

She was pleased that the sergeant had accepted her request for help without the need of manipulation. It gave her hope. He dropped her off at the public docks where private boats were moored. She had no idea what she was looking for. She knew she needed to get out to the French fleet and talk her way on board an aircraft carrier where she could hopefully hitch a ride to Cyprus. It was a long shot.

Most of the boats in the harbor were Egyptian. It was unlikely that she would be able to convince any of their captains to go anywhere near the French warships. The French were their enemy and could easily blow their vessel out of the water for getting too close. Even the fishing fleet steered clear of the Anglo-French area of operation.

There was one boat that caught Brigitte's eye. It was an eighty foot yacht-style vessel flying a Greek flag. She approached the stern of the boat tied to dock. There was a crewman oiling the teak deck with a rag. "Do you speak English?" asked Brigitte.

The crew man looked up from his work. He clearly did not understand her. He looked like deer caught in headlights.

"Est-ce que tu parles Français?" she said.

The crewman looked even more lost. He jumped and ran into the cabin. "Wait," said Brigitte on seeing him retreat.

After a few moments the captain of the vessel emerged from the cabin. "Can I help you?" he said in English.

"You are the captain?" said Brigitte.

"Yes. Philo Gabris."

"I am Brigitte Friang."

"Your accent… you are not English."

"No. I am French."

"I see. A little early, aren't you? The invasion is not for a few more days, I think."

"I was with the Israelis."

"You are Jewish?"

"No. I am a journalist. A war correspondent. I was embedded with the Israelis."

"Ah, I see. Brave woman."

"Thanks. What is a Greek vessel doing in an Egyptain port that is about to be invaded?"

"I ask myself the same. We were taking the boat's

owner and his family on a cruise to Alexandria when we had engine trouble. Then the war broke out. The owner and his family flew home to Athens on a private plane. We stayed to repair the engine. It is fixed now, but we are trapped."

"But you fly a Greek flag?"

"I do not think the British and the French are discriminating too well right now. They shoot first and ask questions later."

"Dangerous times."

"Dangerous place."

"Perhaps I could help you."

"How is that?"

"I have business aboard the French aircraft carrier *Arromanches*. You could take me to it then head home from there."

"Their destroyers and frigates will blow us out of the water before we get close."

"Not if they know you have a French citizen on board."

"Perhaps."

"You have a radio?"

"Of course."

"I will radio their ships as we get close."

"So they take you and sink us."

"No. They will know you are Greek and no threat once they board your vessel to retrieve me."

"That is a dangerous gamble."

"More dangerous that waiting in a port you know is going to be invaded? The first thing the French and British will do is shell the port. Your ship could be hit."

"I have considered that."

"You will be safer taking me out to the fleet."

Gabris considered for a moment. "Alright. I suppose you have as much risk as us. We shall gamble together, yes?"

Brigitte smiled and climbed onboard.

The Greek yacht topped off her fuel tanks, pushed away from the fueling dock, and headed out of the harbor. There were two Israeli patrol boats at the mouth of the harbor. Both crews watched the yacht flying a Greek flag but neither made any effort to stop the vessel. The Israelis didn't need to add Greece to their long list of enemies. They let the yacht pass unmolested.

Brigitte and Gabris had no real idea as to the location of the French fleet. They knew it was somewhere Northwest of Port Said about fifty miles offshore. The Mediterranean was vast. Even a flotilla of warships could be missed. Gabris and Brigitte had agreed that if they failed to contact the French fleet, Gabris would attempt to drop Brigitte off on Cyprus on his way back to Greece. She would pay for the fuel which she was fairly sure Gabris would pocket.

Thirty-six miles off shore, Brigitte and Gabris were startled to hear the wobbling blare of a ship's horn. They turned to see a destroyer heading straight for the yacht at top speed. Gabris got on the radio and attempted to contact the vessel in Greek, then English. There was no response. Brigitte was next, calling in French. Still no response. The destroyer pulled up behind the yacht. A lieutenant on a bullhorn ordered the yacht to cut its engines, heave to and prepare to be boarded. He spoke with an English accent.

As the destroyer pulled alongside the yacht, Brigitte and Gabris saw the problem. It wasn't a French destroyer, but British. The warship's main gun turrets swung around and aimed all their barrels at the yacht. They only needed to land one shell in the hull to send the yacht to the bottom of the Mediterranean.

A rubber raft powered by an outboard motor was lowered from the destroyer. A squad of armed seamen, led by a lieutenant, climbed into the craft. It zipped across the water. The seamen and officer boarded the Greek yacht.

They rounded up Gabris and Brigitte along with the crew and moved them to the rear of the yacht. Then they searched the boat. They found nothing. "Why were you approaching our fleet?" said the lieutenant.

"I assure you we meant no harm. We were on our way to our home port of Athens. We did not know the British fleet was out here," said Gabris.

"That's a lie. Everyone knows the British fleet is out here."

"That is true, but we did not know exactly where you were located. The Mediterranean is quite large. It was happenstance that we found you. I mean… you found us."

"Lieutenant, I am Brigitte Friang. A French citizen and journalist. I am trying to reach Cyprus," said Brigitte.

"Cyprus is off limits."

"I am aware of the military units stationed on Cyprus. I am trying to contact a commander of the French paratroopers, Colonel Marcel Bigeard. I have embedded with them before and hope to do so again. I assure you, I will be welcomed."

"Why is that?"

"I write the truth, and in the case of the French paratroopers that can at times be quite flattering."

"This operation is blacked out from the press."

"Not to me. I have permission from my government to cover the invasion."

"You have evidence of this?"

"No. My government preferred not to put anything in writing because of the nature of the operation."

"What do you mean by 'the nature of the operation'?"

"I think you know what I mean. Look, I have been imbedded with the Israeli armed forces this last week and…"

"So you are a Jewish spy?"

"No. As I said… I am a French journalist. We are your allies, in case you've forgotten."

"So what were you doing with the Israelis?"

29

"I was given special permission to cover the invasion from their side."

"And who gave you permission?"

"Ben Gurion, the Prime Minister of Israel."

"Why would the Prime Minister of Israel give a French journalist permission to report on their secret invasion?"

Brigitte knew she had said too much and decided to change tactics. "Lieutenant, I know you are busy fighting a war. Do you really feel threatened by a woman half your size and the civilian crew of a Greek yacht?"

The lieutenant considered for a moment and said, "You cannot proceed through our area of operation. You will turn your vessel around and head back to shore."

Gabris was about to agree when Brigitte said, "No."

"Excuse me?"

"I said no. We will not turn around. We are civilians. You have no right to prevent us from continuing our journey."

"You see those cannons pointed at your vessel? They give us the right to do whatever the hell we want."

"Very well. Shoot," said Brigitte.

"No. No. Don't shoot," said Gabris. "We will turn around and go back the way we came."

"I won't," said Brigitte. "I need to go to Cyprus. If the Greeks won't go then you're just going to have to give me a ride, Lieutenant."

"You're bonkers. You know that, ma'am," said the lieutenant.

"I've been told as much, Lieutenant. Now, rather than causing an international incident, for which you will surely take the blame, wouldn't it be easier to escort us around your fleet and send us on our way?"

"We will do nothing of the sort. You will turn around or we will open fire and sink your vessel."

"Very well. Have it your way," said Brigitte. Walking to the side of the yacht, she hopped over the guard rail and plunged into the water near the raft. "Jesus, Mary and

Joseph," said the lieutenant as he looked over the side in shock.

Brigitte was treading water. The seas were rough. She knew she wouldn't last long and hoped she hadn't made a big mistake. The seaman manning the boat looked up at the lieutenant for instructions. "Well, fish her out, man," said the lieutenant.

"I guess she is your prisoner," said Gabris. "Good luck with that, Lieutenant."

"Wait. You can't leave her with us."

"She's in international waters. She is no longer my problem, Lieutenant. My crew and I are heading back to Egypt as you ordered. She clearly doesn't want to go. I'm sure the British Navy can handle her."

The seaman pulled Brigitte on board the raft. "Lieutenant, I forgot my rucksack," said Brigitte calling up to the yacht. "Would you mind terribly bringing it with you?"

Gabris walked into the wheelhouse, retrieved her rucksack and handed it to the lieutenant. The lieutenant was thinking about how he was going to explain what had just happened to his captain.

The crew in the raft took their new prisoner back to the destroyer. Gabris, thankful to still be alive after having met Brigitte Friang, steered his boat back to shore.

TWO

London, England

The television was on in the sitting room at 10 Downing Street, the Prime Minister's residence and office. There were several bottles of prescription drugs sitting on top of the television and on the coffee table in front of the sofa. Sir Anthony Eden, British prime minister sat in his smoking jacket as he watched the BBC News. This was unusual. Both Eden and his wife, Clarissa, the niece of Sir Winston Churchill, generally thought that time watching the television was better spent reading a book or the newspaper.

Eden watched Aneurin Bevan, a senior member in the Labour Party, giving a speech in Trafalgar Square, surrounded by thousands of protestors. His black and white image was grainy but his message was clear, "Therefore I say to Anthony, I say to the British government, there is no count at all upon which they can be defended. They have besmirched the name of Britain. They have made us ashamed of the things of which formerly we were proud. They have offended against every principle of decency and there is only one way in which they can even begin to restore their tarnished reputation and that is to get out! Get out! Get out!"

Clarissa entered, carrying a tea tray. She set it down, walked over to the television and turned it off without asking her husband. He rolled his eyes in mock indignation. She served the tea and said, "Honestly, Anthony, I don't understand how you can watch such rubbish. You know what the doctors said about your blood pressure. I doubt you will get much rest while listening to Bevan."

"The man has no sense of history," said Eden. "All he talks about are hypotheticals. How can so many side with such an uneducated conman?"

"It's not as many as you think," she said.

"What do you mean?"

"I went down there today."

"To the rally?"

"Yes. I wanted to see for myself what all the fuss was about."

"I hope you brought security?"

"I cannot have security around me when I am undercover. It defeats the purpose."

"You can't go undercover, Clarissa. You are too well know."

"I didn't think so, but as it turns out you are correct. I was standing on the fringe of crowd listening to that blowhard Bevan when a woman recognized me. She told me she approved of your policies and that you should get on with it. There were others too. Anthony, the British people are reserved. The silent majority doesn't go about waving signs and chanting slogans. It's why they made you prime minister. You are their voice."

"Perhaps."

"No. Not perhaps. They support you. You must stand for what is right. You must protect Britain. You cannot give Bevan the last word. You must take your argument directly to the people.

"A strong statement on the BBC perhaps?"

"Yes. Television. The people can see the truth in your eyes and hear the determination in your voice."

"Why do you suppose Winston has not weighed in? All

those years serving as his Foreign Secretary and remaining loyal when others did not. I'm not saying that he owes me, but if ever I needed his help it is now."

"Anthony, my uncle believes in you. He has told me so on many occasions. But he also believes it is better that he stays out of the limelight for your sake. He does not want people to think you are his puppet. Trust me. He likes you and backs your policies."

"I suppose as prime minister one must carry one's own water at times."

"Yes. One must. You might also take care not to harm any Egyptian civilians if possible."

"Winston suggested that?"

"Not in so many words."

"I see. It's a war, Clarissa. There is bound to be collateral damage. It cannot be helped. Besides, the Egyptian people need a reason to rise up against Nasser. He brought this upon them. The bombings in Cairo remind them of that."

"I understand that but you do not want the international community accusing you of being a baby-killer, now do you?"

"Of course not," said Eden.

Clarissa knew when to stop talking and let Eden ruminate on what she had said. They finished their tea in silence.

Washington D.C., USA

Eisenhower used a magnifying glass to examine U2 aerial reconnaissance photographs showing bomb damage inflicted on Egyptian airfields. Having no designated reconnaissance room in the White House the photos were spread out on the coffee table in the Oval Office. To Eisenhower, who orchestrated Operation Overload – the invasion of Nazi occupied Europe in 1944 – the Oval

Office seemed a luxurious setting for clandestine analysis. He had grown used to the damp basements of London, where most of the Intelligence and planning leading up to D-Day had been held. The Oval Office was secure and he didn't want anyone outside a select group of cabinet and military officials to know the reconnaissance capabilities of America's U2 spy plane program, the development of which he had personally requested and approved. The photos he was examining were very clear, considering they were taken at forty thousand feet.

Eisenhower was grateful that American military forces were not involved in the fiasco that Britain and France were in the process of creating and he wanted to keep it that way. *They're making the mess. They can clean it up* was how he looked at the situation. Unfortunately, those two nations were also his strongest allies in NATO and he needed them as counterbalances against Soviet aggression. As much as he wanted to, he could not just stand idly by and watch things unfold.

He was deeply concerned with how the conflict in the Middle East was progressing. It was an embarrassment. Worse, it would probably push the Arab nations away from Western influence and into the Soviet's lap. He still could not understand why Sir Anthony Eden, Britain's prime minister, could not see the consequences of what he was doing. They seemed so clear, and Eden, while at times rash, was a veteran statesman and an intelligent man.

Britain and France had entered the conflict between Israel and Egypt as peacemakers, but their bombs were being dropped on Egyptian airfields and infrastructure, not on the Israeli forces that had invaded and still occupied the Egyptian's Sinai Peninsula. They were clearly one-sided in their aggression. Eisenhower knew that if he could see the collusion behind their actions, the rest of the world, including the Arab leaders, could see it too.

France's intentions were easier to understand than Britain's. While both nations had financial, economic and security interests in keeping the Suez Canal open, France had a side beef with Egypt. Nasser had been supporting the FLN rebels in their fight for the independence of Algeria. Algeria was considered part of France, an extension of the motherland across the Mediterranean Sea. Over one million French citizens lived in Algeria and were now targets of the FLN. Egypt was giving the FLN leaders sanctuary to raise funds, stockpile weapons, and plan their raids. Nasser was even allowing them to use Radio Cairo to broadcast their propaganda to the world. Guy Mollet, France's Prime Minister, believed that the FLN would have been defeated by now if it wasn't for Egypt's continuing support. There was no getting around it – French lives were being lost because of Nasser.

Britain on the other hand had purchased Egypt's interest in the Suez Canal almost a century ago when Egypt's National Bank was on the verge of collapse from bad monetary policies. The British, along with the original French investors, had been the operators and benefactors of the Suez Canal until it was nationalized by Nasser early in the year. Britain relied on cheap Middle Eastern oil to fuel its factories and rebuild its economy after so many years of war with Nazi Germany. Now, the very foundation of Britain's livelihood was in the hands of an 'opportunistic madman' – as Eden like to call Nasser.

Britain and France were outraged as was the rest of Europe over the nationalization of the Suez Canal. But to go to war? thought Eisenhower. Having been a soldier most of his life, he saw the need for each nation to defend itself and its interests. In a strange way the ability to make war and the formation of alliances created an equilibrium. No sane leader wanted war, especially Eisenhower. He saw diplomacy as the only true path to peace. The Allies had completely decimated Germany in World War I only to see it rise again in World War II. War was a never ending cycle that did not provide permanent solutions. The causes behind war needed to be dealt with to extinguish the flames of conflict forever. That could only be achieved through diplomacy. It was the whole concept behind the United Nations. While diplomacy offered the only lasting solutions to the world's problems, it did not always succeed. If diplomacy failed, there was no leader more capable of advancing war than Eisenhower. He was not afraid to use the big stick if there was no other way. He just didn't have much hope for the long-term results.

Eisenhower's biggest concern was the Soviets. He saw the expansion of Communism as the only real threat to the United States. The iron grip that communist leaders had on their satellite nations meant that as Communism grew the USSR's ability to propagate war grew stronger. There was a tipping point at which the communist nations would be more powerful than the free world. Once that was reached, Eisenhower was sure America and its allies would be attacked and World War III would begin. Right now, the scale was heading in the wrong direction and this conflict in Egypt wasn't helping matters. "Jesus. They really gave the Egyptians a shellacking," said Eisenhower studying the photos. "You say these are eighteen hours old?"

"Yes, Mr. President," said Allen Dulles sitting beside his brother Foster Dulles, waiting for Eisenhower to finish his analysis.

"Is British Intelligence still sending you updates?"

"Yes. They are. It's surprising when you consider the state of relations."

"Why? The Intelligence wonks know we are not their enemy. Not yet anyway. Besides, I am sure they still want our shared Intelligence."

"You still think that's wise... sharing Intelligence?" said Foster Dulles.

"For now. We're not showing them much they don't already know. Our photos are just less fuzzy," said Eisenhower. "We need to tamp down the animosity, not stoke it up. Britain and France are still our allies. Let's not forget that there is a greater threat out there and it's looking for cracks in the alliance that it can exploit. We keep sharing current intel with our allies as long as they do the same."

"Yes, Mr. President," said Allen Dulles.

"Does that mean we are taking military interdiction off the table?" said Foster Dulles.

"Nothing's off the table," said Eisenhower. "But for God's sake, this is Britain and France we are talking about."

"…and Israel," said Allen Dulles.

"The Israelis can take care of themselves. They just proved it. How long did it take them to overrun almost the entire Sinai? Forty-eight hours?" said Eisenhower. "They're single-minded in their mission and resolve. Britain and France don't have that luxury. They are part of a much bigger picture with a lot more balls in the air."

"Still, the Israelis will need to be part of the solution," said Foster Dulles.

"Eventually, yes. But right now our biggest concern is how to keep Britain and France from destroying Egypt and taking over the Suez Canal," said Eisenhower. "What's your estimate of current Egyptian air capability?"

"The British bombing campaigns have been less effective than they had hoped, but even so… the damage to the Egyptian airfields and aircraft has been extensive." Allen Dulles pulled some Intelligence reports from a folder. "Our latest estimates show Nasser's air force has been reduced to below 25% operational capacity. Most of his MiG, Meteor, and Vampire fighters are completely destroyed or out of action for the duration of the war. The majority of his Il-28 bombers and a few squadrons of MiGs escaped to Saudi Arabia and Syria before the British and French could get at them. They too are expected to sit out the war although they could be used against the Israelis should the Syrians and Jordanians decide to side with Egypt and attack Israel. Whatever is left of Nasser's airpower is pretty much useless. The British and French have destroyed most of the fuel storage facilities at the airfields and cratered the runways. The Egyptians may be able to get a few aircraft into the air when needed, but I doubt they will have much effect."

"That didn't take long," said Eisenhower. "We've got to find a way to prevent the British and French from invading. It's going to be a bloodbath that the Arabs will never forget. We could lose the entire Middle East for decades."

Israeli Field Hospital, Sinai

Coyle was asleep when a young doctor walked in and picked up the clipboard hanging at the foot of his bed. He read through the notes and returned the clipboard to its holder. He leaned over and lifted Coyle's wrist as if taking his pulse. The doctor squeezed hard until Coyle woke. "Hey, that's a little rough, Doc. What happened to bedside manners?" said Coyle weakly, his lips cracked and bleeding.

"Sorry. There isn't much time," said the doctor in a hushed voice.

"Time for what?"

"I need to ask you some questions."

"Okay."

"You were with Colonel Sharon and the Israelis paratroopers?

"Yeah. I was dropping off supplies and a couple of jeeps."

"Did you hear them say anything about the timetable for the British or French airborne or seaborne invasions?"

"Who are you?" said Coyle eyeing the young doctor.

"You're American. Do you still believe in your country?"

"Of course. What does that have to do with anything?"

"You worked for the Central Intelligence Agency in Vietnam when they were helping the French fight the communists."

"I'm not saying a damn thing until I know who you are. Are you Mossad?"

"No. U.S. Naval Intelligence. I'm with the Sixth Fleet."

"Do you have some identification?"

"Don't be stupid. I'm undercover. If I get caught with Naval Intelligence documents, they might just shoot me as a spy," said the doctor looking around to ensure that nobody was listening. "You're country needs you. Now answer the damn question."

Coyle considered for a moment and said, "No. I didn't hear anything from Sharon or the Israelis."

The doctor considered Coyle's answer and said, "But you did hear something from somebody else?"

Coyle did not reply. "Your girlfriend... the French reporter?" said the doctor.

"Leave her out of this."

"We will... if you answer the question and stop playing games."

Coyle took a long moment to think. He didn't know if he should trust the doctor but he had a feeling he was telling the truth about working for Naval Intelligence. Coyle had gotten to know some of the agents working for the CIA in Indochina and this guy seemed the same type. He didn't want to put Brigitte in a compromising situation but he also wanted to stay loyal to his country. "Two, maybe three days."

"That fast?"

"I think so. Yeah."

"Is there an airborne element or just seaborne?"

"Paratroopers. I think."

"Did she say how she knew?"

"No."

"Nothing about a secret meeting in Sèvres?"

"No. Nothing. She doesn't talk about the details of her

work with me."

"She doesn't trust you?"

"I told you what you wanted to know," said Coyle sharply. "Do with it what you want but I'm done answering questions."

"Alright. But keep your eyes and ears open. The Fleet is just off the coast. You can send a message through any embassy by using the code word 'Blue Deep' if you find something critical."

"Look. I love my country but I'm not spying for you."

"Really? You already have," said the doctor with a knowing smile and walked out of the tent.

"Shit," said Coyle to himself.

HMS Tyne, Mediterranean Sea

The *HMS Tyne* cruised the Mediterranean heading toward her final position fifty miles off the coast of Egypt with the rest of the fleet. The lookouts kept close watch for Egyptian aircraft and warships on the horizon. The Tyne was a bit strange-looking for a destroyer. Her main gun turrets were only located forward unlike most destroyers which had at least one main gun turret on the aft of the ship. Instead, her aft was filled with anti-aircraft guns and torpedo tubes. She was the task force flag ship and command HQ.

Seamen jumped out of the way and saluted as French General André Beaufre made his way up the ship's interior passageway. As usual he was in a hurry. He was full of energy; a man of action. He was second in command of the landing task force. There were many officers that would have preferred Beaufre as the commander of the task force instead of British Lieutenant General Sir Hugh Stockwell. Beaufre had a reputation as an aggressive commander willing to change plans to take advantage of a developing situation on the battlefield, while Stockwell preferred to stick to the original plan everyone had been briefed on and his staff was prepared to execute. Stockwell felt it essential that everyone under his command was on the same page. That way, there was less chance of a friendly-fire incident, and logistics during the operation would run smoothly if everyone knew their mission. To Stockwell meticulous planning and logistics were the way to win a war. To Beaufre it was all about tactics and taking advantage of opportunities. They were both experienced veterans of several wars and made an interesting team.

Beaufre entered a wardroom setup at the Task Force Command Center. Stockwell was in conference with several unit commanders. "When you have a moment, General Stockwell, I have something that needs immediate attention," said Beaufre.

"Of course, General Beaufre. Now is a good time. We were just finishing," said Stockwell.

The subordinate commanders took their cue and filed out the room leaving the two generals alone. Beaufre pulled out several photos from an envelope and set them on the table for Stockwell to examine. The pictures were aerial photos of a tank and an armored personnel carrier rolling across a bridge. "It's as I said, Sir Hugh," said Beaufre. "The Egyptians are in full retreat. More and more armored units are crossing over to the Western side of the Suez at all different points. They're highly disorganized and clustering their vehicles together."

"Just as we planned," said Stockwell. "It will take them days to get organized again. We should make sure air command targets those vehicle clusters. The more tanks and artillery we can destroy now, the fewer we'll have face at zero hour."

"About zero hour…"

"We've been through this before. I'm not moving it, André."

"Sir Hugh, this is a huge opportunity to invade with

little to no resistance. You said yourself, it will take them days to get organized enough to redeploy their forces."

"We would be increasing the risk by changing the plan this late in the game."

"We just came up with the final plan for the invasion three days ago," said the Frenchman.

"And we all signed off on it. Everyone knows what they need to do. Besides, half the troops are still en route to the rendezvous point. Even if we wanted to attack now, we don't have the men or the ships."

"We have the paratroopers. They're already on Cyprus."

"You want to send in paratroopers without knowing when we will be able relieve them?"

"We won't need to relieve them if the Egyptian army retreats to Cairo, which I am sure they will do if pushed."

"This operation is not going to become another Market Garden! We lost eight thousand paratroopers there because we were sure we could take a bridge and the enemy had a different idea!"

Beaufre waited a moment while Stockwell regained his composure. "Sir Hugh, this isn't the German SS we are facing. It's poorly trained and poorly led Egyptian troops."

"Who are fighting for their homeland."

"That's true. We must expect a fight. Perhaps even a hard fight. But our men can take them. They will take them. I know it."

"I know they will too, but according to the schedule and plan we have already put into motion."

"By attacking while the Egyptian forces are unorganized we will save the lives of hundreds perhaps even a thousand British and French soldiers. Isn't that a possibility worth considering?"

Stockwell sighed. Beaufre was like a dog with a bone and wasn't going to give in. He may retreat if ordered, but he would just be back with a new idea from a different angle. He was a general like himself and a damn good one.

Stockwell would be a fool not to at least hear him out. "What do you have in mind?"

Beaufre walked over to the map on the wall and pointed to an airfield to the west of the city of Port Said. "We take El Gamil airfield and airlift our forces and equipment into Egypt."

"Do we even have that kind of airlift capacity?"

"Not yet, but we can get it."

"Once the paratroopers land they'll be at the mercy of Egyptian armor and artillery."

"Not necessarily. Nasser knows we have air superiority. That's why he ordered his army to retreat back across the Suez. If we hit his armor hard enough with our naval guns and air forces, I think he will retreat again and pull them back to Cairo where he will make his final stand. He cannot afford to lose his armor if he ever hopes to stop us or if the Israelis should choose to continue their attack. If we hit him, he'll run."

Stockwell thought for a moment and said, "It's a bold plan, Andre. But even if I was to accept it, I seriously doubt you will get it past Knightly."

"I can try, can't I?"

"Perhaps. I'll need to approve it first. When would you want to go?"

"The fifth I think. I need to check the weather."

"All right draw up your plan in detail and I'll have another look."

"This evening after supper?"

"Of course."

Beaufre gathered his photos and left.

"Humph. The French," said Stockwell with mock indignation.

Washington D.C., USA

Allen Dulles entered the Oval Office where Eisenhower

and Foster Dulles were having a discussion. "Sorry to interrupt but I think this needs to be heard," said the CIA Director.

"What's that?" said Eisenhower.

"Navy Intelligence has developed a contact with the Israelis and the French. He gave us information that the French and British will invade Egypt in the next seventy-two hours."

Eisenhower and Foster Dulles exchanged a concerned look. Most presidents didn't question the sources of Intelligence but Eisenhower was no ordinary Commander-in-Chief. As an experienced commander he knew the reliability of the Intelligence source was just as important as the Intelligence itself. "How reliable is this contact?" he said.

"Apparently he has been flying for the French military for the last couple of years. He was sent into the Sinai to drop off parts and two jeeps to Colonel Sharon when he was shot down and crashed in the Sinai."

"That is an interesting contact. Why is he cooperating with out Naval Intelligence?"

"That's the best part. He's former CIA. He flew for the French as part of General Chennault's Civil Air Transport group during the Indochina war."

"He's an American?" said Eisenhower.

"He is. And he's with the Israeli army as we speak."

"Talk about being at the right place at the right time…" said Foster Dulles. "What else does he know?"

"I don't know but I sure as hell am going to find out."

"Didn't I ask you not to interfere and let me handle Admiral Burke?

"You did, Mr. President. And I didn't contact Naval Intelligence."

"Then how am I am hearing about this from my CIA Director and not from Admiral Burke?"

"External sources, sir."

"What the hell is that supposed to mean?"

"Mr. President… there are some things you are just better off not knowing."

"That is not a comforting thought, Allen."

"No, Mr. President. But it is true."

Eisenhower considered whether he should push the issue and decided now was not the time. He knew Allen Dulles was a true patriot and only had the best intentions in mind, even if he methods were shady at times. It went with the territory. "Keep me informed what happens with this contact. Does he have a code name?" said Eisenhower.

"Blue Deep, Mr. President."

British Paratrooper Camp, Cyprus

The 3rd Battalion of the British Parachute Regiment were nicknamed the "Red Devils" for good reason. They were created when Winston Churchill demanded the British army develop an airborne capacity during World War II. The Paras were considered to be on the same level as the infamous commandos – the tip of the British spear.

Private Ross sat with the other members of his platoon cleaning their weapons as Staff Sergeant Brooks strolled around the group offering an instructional rebuke when things did not look right.

The platoon was under the command of Lieutenant Howard, a twenty-one-year-old graduate of the Royal Military Academy Sandhurst. But it was Sergeant Brooks's platoon. Until the lieutenant gained actual combat experience, the members of the platoon would look to their sergeant to call the shots.

Howard wasn't stupid. In fact, just the opposite. He knew that Brooks would do everything he could to keep his lieutenant alive and for that he was grateful. He rarely questioned the sergeant's advice, especially when it came to deploying the platoon in combat. Howard was a fast learner but there was a lot to learn if he wanted to keep the men under his command safe. When he issued orders he always glanced at the sergeant to ensure it was the right move. Brooks would give him a discrete nod.

Brooks was not like most other sergeants. He was more of a stern father figure than a junkyard dog. He rarely raised his voice. He didn't believe yelling was necessary and that it often did more harm than good. When he did raise his voice his men knew it was for something serious and paid particular attention. The other sergeants and officers respected Brooks. He was an experienced veteran and the men under his command were well-trained. He believed in training. *Training is what saves us from panicking when the bullets start to fly,* he thought. *Do something enough times until it becomes second nature and you don't need to think. You just do it.*

Private Ross was new. He had shown great aptitude in basic training before he was asked to volunteer for the Red Devils. Brooks kept a close eye on him. He wanted more time to train the young man in the ways of the para before he was ready for action but that was not to be. The platoon would be deployed any day now. He would keep him close when the battle started. Brooks took great pride in keeping his men alive and Ross would be no exception. "Ross, you need to use more gun oil on your barrel. The salt air will play havoc with rust if you're not careful."

"Yes, Staff Sergeant," said Ross as Brooks looked over his shoulder. Unlike the other members of his section, who were armed with STEN submachine guns, Ross was cleaning his Lee Enfield .303 rifle with a special grenade-launcher attachment on the muzzle. He was his squad's grenadier. His rifle fired grenades using propellant bullets, and regular bullets when necessary. "Staff Sergeant, some of the men said you fought at Arnhem,"

"What of it?"

"So it's true?"

"I was a private like yourself. And like you, I didn't

47

know my arse from my elbow. Learned quick enough though. Had no choice," said Brooks, remembering with a chuckle. "Threw up my breakfast on my first combat jump. Men below me didn't care for that much."

"So, you faced tanks?"

"Not at first. It was easy pickings. Mostly Hitler Youth and old men just like Intelligence said. The Panzers came later, on the second day. SS. Mean bastards. Good fighters. Well trained. They took the west end of the city cutting us off from the bridge and 2nd Battalion. 2nd Battalion caught the worst of it. Tanks gave 'em a good pasting. We tried to get to them but the SS wouldn't budge. Chewed us up and spat us out like we was cow cud. Our regiment went in with over three thousand. We came out with less than five hundred. Not something you can easily put out of your mind watching your friends die like that. Hard to forget, especially at night."

"You think the Gypos are gonna have tanks waiting for us?"

"Oh, they'll have 'em. But havin' 'em and knowin' how to use 'em is two different things."

"Staff Sergeant, I know it's okay to be scared of dying an' all. But how do you deal with the fear of being a coward?"

"You don't need to worry yourself about that, son. When the fighting gets fierce, you'll have your mates on your right and on your left. Look at them and you'll find your courage. When you're in a fight for your life it ain't about honor or duty or even country. It's about the guy next to you. He's fighting to keep you alive and you're fighting to keep him alive. You just remember your training and keep your weapon clean. You'll do fine when the time comes."

The sergeant walked away trying once again to forget the bloody days of Arnhem and Operation Market Garden.

Suez Canal, Egypt

An Egyptian Army engineer pushed a blasting cap into a block of C-4. The explosive was part of a bundle wrapped around the steel support holding up the El Firdan bridge that stretched across the Suez Canal. There were more explosive bundles on the other supports. The blasting caps in each explosive bundle were connected to a wire harness that hung below the bridge and led to the Western bank. Another engineer waited by an electronic plunger. His job was to ensure that nobody endangered the other engineers as they finished placing the explosive charges.

Once the last of the engineers had left the bridge, the officer in charge gave the go ahead. The engineer with the plunger connected the wire leads from the harness. He pulled the plunger handle up, then with no fanfare pushed it down. Twelve C-4 bundles exploded at the same time, severing the bridge supports.

The bridge dropped into the Suez Canal and sank. The canal had already been blocked by the sinking of forty-seven blocking ships. Nasser wasn't taking any chances and had ordered the bridge to be demolished as an extra precaution. It was unnecessary. The Suez Canal would be void of ship traffic for the next eighteen months, cutting off Europe's Middle Eastern oil supply.

Moscow, Russia

Nikita Sergeyevich Khrushchev sat in his office in the Kremlin Senate in the heart of Moscow. He liked the coved ceiling, the wooden wall panels and marble floor covered by a thick handwoven rug to cut down on the echo and keep him warm during the Russian winters. It was a posh office, yet comfortable. It was nothing like the presidential palace with its abundance of gold fixtures, ornate tapestries and rare paintings, but the palace was for show. His office was where the real work got done and that was fine by him. He was the First Secretary of the Communist Party of the Soviet Union and that made him one of the most powerful men in the world. He was also a survivor.

He had survived the Russian Civil War in which eight million Russian citizens and soldiers had died in the struggle for justice. He had served his country with honor as a commissar for the Red Army and even met the great Lenin once.

He had survived Joseph Stalin and his Great Purge when most men in his position had perished. He had supported Stalin and was responsible for sending thousands of Russian citizens to their death.

During World War II, he survived the Eastern Front, where he again served as a commissar. He survived his failure in the attack on Kharkov, where a quarter of a million Soviet troops under his command were killed or captured by the Nazis because he was too stubborn to call off the attack, even when he knew it was a trap. Stalin threatened to execute him for his failure at Kharkov but instead sent him to Stalingrad where he could die with honor. He survived Stalingrad. Twenty-Seven million Russian citizens and soldiers died during the Great Patriotic War as World War II had come to be known.

Khrushchev had survived the execution of his son ordered by Stalin. He swore in his heart he would have vengeance against Stalin for the death of his son, but he waited until after Stalin's death when he became First Secretary. He became the founder of the De-Stalinization movement that erased much of Stalin's legacy and liberalized many of the Soviet Union's policies.

Khrushchev had waited patiently to take over the reins of the Soviet Union. He was finally in charge and making the most of it. The first few years were spent consolidating his grip on power by eliminating any of those that opposed him in the Party. He was more merciful than Stalin. He simply removed his enemies from their powerful positions and assigned them menial positions with little responsibility, outcasts within the Kremlin walls where he could keep an eye on them. There was no need for bloodshed. He had had enough of that as one of Stalin's henchmen.

Now that he had consolidated his power, Khrushchev had two problems. First, in order to continue the revolution as Marx and Lenin had imagined it, the Party needed to expand and bring more countries into the communist fold. The more countries that joined the revolution the more powerful it would become while its enemies became weaker.

The founders had envisioned that it would be the industrialized nations that first accepted Communism because of the disparity in wealth. In fact, it was the underdeveloped, mostly rural countries that were the first to accept Communism because of its promises of land reform. While he believed that all the nations of the world would eventually see the light and join the movement, converting the underdeveloped nations first had proved to be a problem. In most cases, the communist movement had to spend money and resources to help the people in the underdeveloped countries rather than the other way around.

The second problem that Khrushchev faced was hanging on to the countries that had already joined the Soviet Union. This turned out to be a much bigger problem than anyone imagined. The revolution required patience and perseverance. But under Stalin many of his followers grew tired of not seeing any real progress but were too frightened by his iron grip and terrifying purges. When he died, the dissenters seized their chance. It wasn't that they wanted to abandon the revolution, many wanted to try their own version of Communism rather than being dictated to by Moscow. It was the beginning of a revolution within the revolution.

Hungary was being particularly aggressive in their desire to leave the Soviet Union. There was a part of Khrushchev that felt that they should have a right to go their own way if that is what the Hungarian people wanted. But there was also a part of him that knew that if his reforms to the Soviet system were given enough time, the people of Hungary would realize that Communism was a success and would want to stay in the union. He was also concerned that if one nation abandoned the Soviet Union others might rise up and follow its example. Khrushchev had learnt that one can never predict the mind of the people. He could see the buffer zone the USSR had created between Russia and Europe breaking away. The fear of NATO tanks and warplanes on Russia's doorstep was too much. He could not let that happen.

The Suez Crisis could not have at a worse time for Khrushchev. He had worked hard to influence the Arab leaders. He didn't imagine that the Arabs would accept Communism right away. It would take time and friendly persuasion. It would take the failure of democracy and capitalism to relieve the Arabs' suffering before they would rise up. He was not prepared for Nasser's daring move of nationalizing the Suez Canal. In fact, he had warned Nasser against it. It was too early on the path to socialism and too risky. But Nasser had been emboldened by his new Soviet weapons and his fear of the Western nations had fallen away. As with Khrushchev, the British and French were in no mood for Nasser's impudence and were now threatening to invade Egypt. All that had been gained by the young leader would be lost, and with it his dream of Arab unity, an admirable goal in Khrushchev's eyes.

Khrushchev needed to focus on the problems in Hungary, not Egypt. His resources were stretched too thin. He couldn't possibly help Nasser militarily, not until the Hungarian problem had been dealt with. But there were other ways in which the Soviet Union might help Nasser. After all, international politics were just another arena of war and one that Khrushchev was quite good at.

Khrushchev did not want to pick a fight with NATO but he also knew that if he failed to back Egypt and failed to put down the demonstrations in Hungary, NATO members would see it as weakness. He knew that one day the USSR would need to destroy NATO if Communism was to become the dominate political system in the world. But today was not that day. He needed to prepare and organize his resources. He needed more nations with their armies under the USSR umbrella. He needed to sow discord among the Western nations and the countries that still hadn't chosen sides in the struggle between capitalism and Communism. He needed to develop the technologies that would give the Soviet Union the edge it needed against NATO. Most of all, he needed time.

Khrushchev was in a most difficult position. Like a cornered bear, his first instinct was to attack and demonstrate his power. It was to be a battlefield with two fronts; Hungary and Egypt. He needed to win them both to re-establish the Soviet Union's dominance. The decision was made. It was time to act. Khrushchev asked to speak at the Presidium the next day.

Standing in front of the Soviet Union's leaders, Khrushchev said, "We should take the initiative by re-establishing order in Hungary. If Hungary breaks away from the Soviet Union, it will give a boost to the Americans, the English and the French. The imperialists will be seen as successful in their feeble attempts to influence our satellite nations and bring down the USSR. The Western countries will interpret this as weakness on our part and will launch a major offensive against us. An offensive that we are not yet ready to repel. We cannot let that happen. We must show strength."

The members of the Presidium showed their support

by pounding their fists on their desks and cheering. Khrushchev knew that the leaders both respected and feared him. They didn't dare refuse his request. The vote that followed was unanimous, as usual.

Boston, USA

The air was brisk and most of the autumn leaves had fallen. The American election was only three days away. Hoping for a second term, President Eisenhower, bundled in his long coat, stood in the back of a limousine waving to the crowds gathered along the streets of downtown Boston. There was little doubt that he was going to beat his democrat opponent Adlai Stevenson but Eisenhower didn't like to take chances. Although he was considered a conservative, Americans knew that he was not a typical war hawk. The people had enough of war and wanted American soldiers to stay home. But there was also a growing fear of Communism. Eisenhower was a hardliner when it came to Communism and the Soviets. He wasn't keen on China either. He understood the threat of expansionism but felt it could be contained with constant pressure from the Western powers and NATO. He held the right combination of values for the time. A leader that would not rush into war unless it was absolutely necessary, but if he had to, he would fight to win.

Nuclear weapons weighed heavy on Eisenhower's mind. He knew their power and he had read the secret reports that talked about the potential for environmental devastation on a global scale. It was a new concept and the White House staff and advisors felt they had to keep the theories under wraps so the people would not panic. There was no need to worry America. It was just a theory, after all.

Foster Dulles rode with Eisenhower but kept a low profile. There were matters that needed to be discussed and the president's time was limited. Dulles liked getting out of the office even if the air blowing in his face was chilly. He could feel a cold coming on and that wasn't good for a man his age. He thought he might get out at the next stop and take the train back to Washington and have a car meet him at the station to take him to the White House. The train was faster than fiddling with the airport. Eisenhower could go on and press the flesh if needed, but Foster Dulles didn't see the point.

The last few days, as the crisis in the Middle East was heating up and the Soviets were putting down the revolt in Hungary, Eisenhower's opponent publicly questioned his policies. It would take its toll in the election booths but even so... Eisenhower was going to win. Foster Dulles felt time was better spent dealing with the British and French rather than the American public, who loved Ike and would surely re-elect him. "Do you think we should bring up sanctions against Israel at the U.N.? They are the aggressors in the whole mess," asked Dulles, shouting above the cheering crowd and the rumble of the car's engine.

"I think we need to be careful," said Eisenhower. "We cannot be seen as ganging up on the Israelis. Whatever we do to them we also need to do it to the British and the French."

"Are you worried about the Jewish vote?"

"No. I don't give a damn about the Jewish vote one way or the other. This is too important. I worry about the other nations that are sitting on the fence about this whole thing. I don't want to give them a reason to take a stand on the wrong side. We need the U.N. to stay strong and united in this affair if we want peace. We cannot allow world leaders to shrink from their responsibility. It's the only way forward in a nuclear age. The U.N. needs to grow up."

"Mr. President, there is some concern from our Intelligence group that the Soviets might use the airfields in Syria to land troops and equipment in support of Nasser."

"That would be unfortunate to say the least."

"Yes, well... I think we should consider the very real possibility that this war may expand into something much bigger. We need to decide what we are going to do if the Soviets attack British and French forces."

The president responded, "I've been giving that a great deal of thought. The Soviets are on the right side of this mess for once, but we cannot allow them to attack our allies without retribution. We need to make it clear that we will respond if they choose to attack Britain or France."

"Won't that send the wrong signal to Eden and Mollet?"

"Yes. But there is too much at stake. If anyone is going to attack our allies to stop this insanity it has to be us, not the Soviets."

"These are strange days, Mr. President."

"Indeed. Make sure our Ambassador in Moscow reminds Khrushchev that if he attacks any of our allies, America is prepared to throw the whole bucket at him."

"You think that's stop him?"

"God, I hope so."

Washington D.C., USA

Admiral Arleigh Burke, Chief of US Naval Operations, had been summoned by Foster Dulles. He sat alone in front of the Secretary of State's desk going over the possible scenarios that the Secretary might wish to discuss. Foster Dulles entered. Burke rose to greet him. "Thanks for coming, Admiral. I am sorry I'm running a little late. Things have been hectic to say the least," said Foster Dulles shaking his hand.

"Of course, Mr. Secretary," said Burke as Foster Dulles sat beside him instead of behind his desk. "How can I help?"

"The president asked me to inquire about our capability in the Mediterranean."

"The Sixth Fleet?"

"Yes. What is its current position?"

"About a hundred miles north of Port Said currently sailing West."

"And it's status?"

"All vessels are fully operational. Vice Admiral Brown and his men are ready and willing to achieve all objectives the president may wish ordered."

"What about the British and the French invasion task force?"

There was a long pause as Burke carefully chose his words. "Are you asking if the Sixth Fleet is capable of defeating the British and French fleets?"

"Hypothetically."

"Then yes. We can do it. The Sixth Fleet is armed with the latest technology and the men are well trained on how to use it. We would be able to defeat any navy in the region, including the French and British combined. In fact, we could also defeat the navies of the Israelis, the Egyptians, the Saudis and the Syrians. We could defeat them all at the same time if need be. Do you think it may come to that?"

"I hope not, but the president must know all options at this point. He is not one to bluff."

"No, he's not. But are you sure fighting our allies is the smartest move?"

"No. Not at all. But neither is letting them invade a Middle Eastern country without provocation."

"Without provocation?"

"Yeah, well... I suppose provocation is up for debate. Believe me, it's not an easy call."

"Have you considered all courses of action?"

"What do you mean?"

"Why don't we join them?"

"You mean the British and the French?"

"Eden may acting in an irrational manner but he's not wrong. Nasser will be holding the Sword of Damocles over the head of every international leader now that he controls the Suez Canal. If he doesn't like their politics, he'll cut off their access to the Canal and let them starve for oil. It's not the making of a stable situation for the region... or the world for that matter. Sooner or later we are going to need to deal with that situation, so why not sooner? Get it out of the way and get on with life. The British and the French are there ready to pounce. I say let 'em. In fact I say help 'em."

"That's not going to happen."

"Why not?"

"Because the president of the United States says so," said Foster Dulles in a firm voice.

"Alright," said Burke. "The United States Navy is at the president's command. Give us our orders and we will make it happen."

Foster Dulles calmed. He couldn't afford to have one of the president's commanders second guessing his decisions. "Arleigh, if we don't show our resolve against Britain and France solving their problem with Egypt by force, what is going to prevent other nations from doing the same next time they have a dispute? The whole point of the United Nations was to stop the madness. We live in a nuclear age. We both know that the next war will likely take far more lives than all previous wars combined. Nations can't keep fighting like they have been. If humanity is going to survive, we must find another way."

"It's a nice speech, Foster. But it's not based in reality. There has always been war and there will always be war. It's who we are. The only questions are who carries the big stick and who is willing to use it. I pray to God it's America."

"And I pray to God you're wrong."

Burke nodded. They were not going to agree. "Mr.

Secretary, unless there something else I can help you with... Please inform the president his Navy stands ready to serve."

"I will. Thank you, Admiral. I'll keep you advised as things progress and the president makes his decision," said Foster Dulles showing him to the door and shaking his hand. Even if they didn't agree, they respected each other and would do anything to defend their country.

Washington D.C., USA

Admiral Burke sat as his desk mulling over what Dulles and he had discussed. It all seemed so wishy-washy. The Americans needed to choose a side – and soon. The Soviets had already chosen to side with Egypt. He couldn't image America going against its oldest allies to side with the Soviets on anything. It felt twisted. Such were the days of the Cold War.

His secretary buzzed his phone and informed him that Vice Admiral Charles R. Brown was on the line. "Chuck, how's your tan coming along?" said Burke over the phone.

"Probably the same as yours," said Brown, commander of the Sixth Fleet USN. "Things have been a bit busy."

"I can imagine."

"Have you decided who we're fighting yet?"

"Everyone and no one. Boss hasn't made up his mind yet. We're in a holding pattern."

"It's getting kinda crowded out here. We got more aircraft flying over than a hornet's nest. Difficult to keep 'em all straight."

"What about the British and French fleets?"

"We're doing the dance. Trying not to run into each other."

"And the Egyptians?"

"The destroyers and frigates have moved to friendly ports and are out of the fight as far as we can tell. There

r

are still some smaller vessels puttering around but nothing we can't handle, should they decide they want to play rough."

"Good. You don't take any guff off anyone."

"Does that mean I can shoot 'em?"

"As much as I'm sure you would enjoy it, it's probably not a good idea until the president chooses a side. But you can harass 'em a bit if anyone gets snooty."

"Aye. Aye."

"Take care, Chuck."

"Always do."

Burke hung up the phone. He liked Brown. He was an excellent seaman and a good commander. Just talking to him made Burke feels better.

THREE

London, England

It was early morning. David Attenborough, the British Broadcasting Company's lead presenter, was asleep when the phone rang in his bedroom. On the line was William Clark, the prime minister's Public Relations Advisor. "Sir Anthony would like to speak to the nation tonight," said Clark.

"Tonight?" said Attenborough.

"Yes. He would like you to come to 10 Downing Street as soon as you are available to discuss the broadcast."

"Okay. I have a broadcast in the morning. I could be there early in the afternoon."

"That would be fine."

"Do you have any idea what it is about?"

"Yes. But it's best that the PM discusses it with you directly."

"William, what am I walking into here?"

There was a long pause before Clark responded. "I don't know. I haven't seen him like this before. He's not well. Quiet mad I think. I'll see you this afternoon, David."

Clark hung up. Attenborough lay in bed staring at the ceiling. The thought of sleep was far from his mind.

Pipeline Pumping Station #5, Syria

Two troop transports led by an armored car pulled up in front of an industrial building with a large pipeline entering and exiting the structure – Pipeline Pumping Station #5. A Syrian officer and a squad of sixteen men jumped out of the vehicles and stormed into the building.

Inside the building, foreign engineers and mechanics were rounded up and escorted out of the building. A Syrian engineer knelt by a large pump and placed a pack of C-4 high explosive with a timer at its base. He activated the timer, and the Syrian troops left the building.

The bomb exploded destroying the pump, severing the feeding pipelines, igniting the oil spilling out onto the floor and setting the entire building ablaze.

London, England

Harold Macmillan, Britain's Chancellor of the Exchequer, was sitting in his office at number 11 Downing Street, next door to the prime minister's residence when he received word by phone of the Syrian attacks on the pipeline. He froze for a moment like a computer with a bent punch card. His mind was performing calculations. He knew instinctively that Britain was in trouble, but he always liked to do the math before coming to any conclusion. He was, after all, nothing more than a glorified accountant as the head of Britain's Treasury. He finished his calculations. His instincts were correct.

The Syrians had destroyed three pipelines to show their support for Egypt. They had picked their targets well. One of the pipelines destroyed was Kirkuk to Tripoli. That pipeline alone was responsible for twenty per cent of Britain's oil supply. Combined with Nasser's blocking of the Suez with sunken ships, Britain had lost over fifty percent of its fuel supply.

Such a loss would wreak havoc on the British economy. Factories would have to close. Massive numbers of workers would be laid off. The welfare budgets would swell. Exports would drop, and with them Britain's revenue. Inflation would skyrocket. The British pound would drop in value.

The government would need to start rationing oil immediately if it was going to weather the storm. It was a disaster in the making and at that moment he was the only one who understood the true implications.

He decided he must tell Eden, but he didn't relish the prospect. Eden could be so prickly, especially when it came to things that he did not understand well, like national finance. Eden's solution was always to print more money. That would do little to solve the current problem. He picked up the phone and dialed Eden's office. He was informed that the PM's schedule was full up for the next five days. When he pushed, Eden's secretary said he would see what he could do to fit in the Chancellor at the beginning of next week. A shiver rippled down Macmillan's back. He had been chosen for the job as Chancellor because of steadfastness. However, at the moment he was fairly sure he would need to vomit within the next thirty seconds.

Cairo, Egypt

A lone British transport plane flew over the city of Cairo. There were no Egyptian fighters remaining to shoot it down. The back door opened. A crew member dumped box after box of leaflets out the door and into the wind.

Five hundred thousand leaflets fell from the sky like confetti from a passing parade. An Egyptian pedestrian picked up one of the leaflets and read the headlines –

ACCEPT THE ULTIMATUM

NASSER IS LYING.

He blew his nose into the leaflet before wadding it up and tossing it to the ground.

London, England

Attenborough was escorted into 10 Downing Street by Clark. They had been friends and they trusted one another. "Forget what I said earlier. The part about him being off his rocker," said Clark. "He's alright. I'm sure of it. He just needs rest… to clear his mind."

"Of course," said Attenborough, lying. *How can I forget the PM has gone bonkers?* he thought as he entered Eden's bedroom.

Eden was wearing his smoking jacket. He sat upright in his bed dictating his speech to a secretary sitting on the end of the bed with her typewriter clacking away. His advisors were gathered around the bed whispering among themselves. This was the most important speech of Eden's political career. It had to go well, and everyone had an opinion on what he should say.

Attenborough studied the room. It smelled a bit like chloroform. Rows of medicine and pill bottles lined the shelves of both nightstands. There were even pill bottles on the shelf above the bed's headrest. The lighting was dim and the curtains were drawn. He wondered if Sir Anthony's pupils were dilated and what that might mean. He knew of Sir Anthony's botched intestinal operation earlier in the year and the pain he had been suffering. It was no secret that the PM got very little sleep and could only doze off for a few hours if he was medicated heavily with both pain and sleeping drops. Eden preferred drops of medicine in water over pills so he could adjust his dosage to his current pain level. Besides, drops worked faster, and he hated pain. When he did sleep he would require a stimulant to snap back to full consciousness once he awoke. It was an endless cycle, that deeply concerned several on his staff.

Clarissa was always nearby to ensure that Sir Anthony was not overwhelmed by his throng of advisors. She understood all too well that this moment in time would determine Sir Anthony's legacy. His decisions had historic consequences and he needed to be clearheaded. A balance needed to be struck. He was the head of government but he was also human. She saw her job as the protector of her husband and his reputation.

She had faith in the family physician. It was clear to her that the older doctor had Sir Anthony's best interests in mind but also understood the stress of command that every PM faced. He monitored the PM closely as he wrote prescription after prescription to keep him functioning.

Attenborough was dismayed by what he saw in that bedroom. It was like watching a sports figure that should have retired long ago trying to stay one more day in the limelight. Seeing him, Sir Anthony stopped his dictation and called him over. "Thank you for coming, David."

"Of course, Sir Anthony."

"I am sure you are quite aware of the current situation in the Suez Canal Zone. We must force the two sides apart before they destroy the Canal. Britain depends on that canal as does Europe."

"I understand that Nasser has already blocked the Canal."

"Yes, proving me right all along. He's a madman that must be stopped. He cannot be entrusted with an international waterway so vital to the world's economy."

"I see. So, Britain and France will follow through with the invasion?"

"It's the only way to ensure our security, David."

"Naturally you will want to address the commonwealth."

"Yes. Tonight. Is that possible?"

"Of course."

"I have been preparing my remarks. I'd like your opinion."

"And you shall have it. But if I may recommend... You should seriously consider getting some rest before your broadcast. You will need your energy."

"If you think it is best."

"I do. I'll take a look at your speech and give you my suggestions. You can review them once you rest."

"Alright," said Eden turning to the others in the room. "If you all will excuse me. I think I shall rest for an hour."

Everyone filed out of the bedroom. Clarissa walked over to the nightstand, opened a medicine bottle and dropped two drops of a liquid into a glass of water. Eden drank it down, lay back, and closed his eyes. Clarissa would stay in the room while he slept to ensure he was not disturbed. Eden's slumber was fitful, like a dog dreaming of chasing a rabbit. It was the best he could muster.

Cairo, Egypt

A squadron of Canberra bombers flew over Cairo. Their target was a radio station that broadcast the Voice of Cairo throughout the Middle East. The pilots had attempted to knock out the radio station on a previous occasion. Much to their embarrassment, they had missed. They weren't taking any chances this time.

As they approached the target, the bombers went into a dive, one after the other. They swooped down from the sky and dropped their entire payload of bombs on the small building and radio antenna. Again, they completely missed the radio station's broadcast facility, creating over a dozen craters around the building. The last bomb dropped exploded at the base of the facilities antenna, toppling it like a freshly cut pine tree. Nobody on the ground was hurt but the station was out of action until the antenna could be replaced.

The squadron leader reported the news over his radio. The station was out of commission as ordered.

British Camp, Cyprus

A mobile antenna reached into the sky over the British camp on Cyprus. On hearing the news that the Egyptian station had been silenced, British Intelligence went to work. They hijacked the radio broadcast listened to by millions of Egyptian civilians and army personnel. Using the same frequency, British Intelligence broadcast counter programming calling on the army and civilians to overthrow Nasser before the allied invasion to prevent needless bloodshed and the entire country from being destroyed.

Unfortunately for the British, the hijacked broadcast had the opposite effect.

Cairo, Egypt

Ten of thousands of protestors stood in front of the British embassy waving placards and chanting. "Go to Hell", "Suez Belongs to Egypt", and "No More Foreign Intervention" were the most popular signs. Civilians threw rotten fruit and vegetables at the guards posted inside the iron gates.

A Maxim machine gun was set up and surrounded with sandbags at the end of the driveway leading into the embassy compound. The British gunner kept a steely watch on the gate with both his hands on the handle and his finger on the trigger. His orders were to shoot any non-British citizen that entered the compound without express permission from the ambassador. The gunner's expression was unmoving. He would obey his orders.

British Camp, Cyprus

A grenade training range had been set up far from the airfield between the sand dunes and the end of the British Camp. A plywood cutout of a tank and a halftrack had been set up downrange to give the new recruits something to shot at.

Private Ross loaded a clip of propellant rounds into his rifle's internal magazine. Next, he slipped an Energa anti-tank grenade on the end of his rifle. It was a practice grenade. A dummy. A real grenade would have had a shaped charge inside the steel casing which was designed to penetrate the armor of a tank or a concrete barrier such as a pillbox. It looked similar to a mortar round with fins at the bottom. Sergeant Brooks stood nearby coaching him, "They may have taught you how to use that thing in basic training but that don't make you an expert. You need to practice until it is like riding a bike. You should be able to do it blindfolded."

"Do we have enough time before kickoff?"

"You let me worry about that. You just focus on what you're doing. You will be the only one in your unit with a rifle capable of launching a grenade. Your mates will be depending on you to know your shit."

"Yes, Staff Sergeant."

"Your best angle is forty-five degrees. That will give you the longest range; about 300 meters. If your target is closer than that you must choose between a low trajectory shot and a high trajectory shot. If a tank is stopped and you feel confident you can hit it with your first shot then a high trajectory is best. The armor on the top and bottom of a tank is the thinnest. A high trajectory shot will bring the grenade straight down. It will penetrate the armor in and around the hatch and kill everyone inside. If a tank's moving side to side or coming straight at you go for a low trajectory. You'll stand a better chance of hitting it before the bastards run you over. But you've got to hit the chassis not the turret. The turret on a T-34 tank is too thick on the side and front, not to mention it's sloped to deflect the impact of a shell or grenade. Your grenade will make a nice dent but it won't stop it."

"But how do I know what angle to use?"

"Practice. It's like basketball. You shoot enough times at the hoop and its gonna go in every time."

"I can do that."

"One last thing… if a tank gets close and you take your shot, don't forget to duck or the back blast will take your head off. Remember, shoot and duck. You practice that too."

"Can I take a shot?"

"You can take a hundred."

Ross set the butt of the rifle on the ground using the edge of his boot as a backstop. He lowered the angle of the rifle until he thought it was forty-five degrees and swung the barrel to align with one of the tank cutouts in the distance. He pulled the trigger until a bullet fired. The gas from the bullet launched the grenade into the air. It arced across the range and landed short. Ross grunted his disappointment. He tried again; loading another grenade on the end of the rifle, checking his aim and angle, then firing. The grenade was again too short but closer. "Rome wasn't built in a day. Keep it up. I'll be back to check on you at lunch," said Brooks as he walked off. Ross continued.

Five hours later, Brooks returned to see Ross still practicing. His fingers were blistered and raw from loading the dummy grenades. He stopped when he saw the Staff Sergeant. "I brought you a sandwich from the mess. Figured you could use a breather. So, how did you do?" said Brooks.

Ross was dead serious. He loaded another clip of

blanks into the rifle, slapped a grenade on the end, placed the butt of the rifle against his boot, took quick aim and fired. The grenade sailed across the range and struck the tank cutout just below the turret. "Not bad," said Brooks.

Brooks looked around and spotted what he was looking for. He walked over to a fire bucket filled with sand and picked it up. He picked up a second, and a third. He walked out eighty yards and set one of the buckets down. Another ten yards and he set down the second. Next he walked to his left twenty yards and set down the third. He walked back and handed Ross his sandwich wrapped in a newspaper. "Sink one in all three straight in a row."

Brooks walked off. Ross took a bite of his sandwich and chewed while he lined up his first shot. He fired off the grenade and missed the first bucket by over ten yards. It would be a long day.

The sun was setting and Ross was still practicing. Brooks stood on a hillside in the distance and watched. He realized that if he didn't stop the kid he'd continue on into the night, which was against regulations. He went down to retrieve the young soldier. As he drew closer, Brooks saw that Ross was hitting his first shot every time but the second and third were misses. Ross was covered in sweat and dirt. His hands were bloody from open blisters. "Come on, Private," said Brooks. "We got one more day. You'll get it."

Ross nodded with confidence. He didn't need Brooks to tell him he would get it. He knew he would get it. Together they walked back to camp.

Cairo, Egypt

With the radio station out of commission Nasser was cut off from talking to his people. Few Egyptians owned televisions but every neighborhood tea house had a radio where the people would gather to listen to Nasser. That was gone now and Nasser felt hamstrung. It was the people that gave him power.

Nasser had ensured the military's support by promoting those loyal to him and eliminating the opposition. But in a country like Egypt that support could evaporate quickly if the old, respected generals felt the military or their position was being threatened. He himself had come to power after a military coup ousted the former King and later the president that tried to have him assassinated. Nasser knew he was in a precarious situation.

The armies of Britain and France were a big threat. There was a lot of boastful talk from the generals about crushing the invaders and driving them back into the sea. But nobody that truly understood the Egyptian army's capabilities believed it could win a war against a Western power with their advanced weapons. The British and French soldiers were too well armed, too well trained and most importantly too well led by experienced officers. The Egyptians would put up a good fight, an honorable fight, but in the end Britain and France would drive them into the desert where their bombers and fighters would grind them into powder. Nasser understood this. But all hope was not lost. Not while he had the people on his side.

The British and French could not hope to control ten million Egyptians. Nasser's plan was simple – never give up the fight and play for time. Eventually the international community would come to the rescue and force the British and French to leave. He just needed to ensure that he was still the leader of Egypt on that day.

Once the British and French landed and began to fight their way to Cairo, Nasser planned on dissolving his army. His soldiers would shed their uniforms and melt into the population where they could continue to fight as guerillas. He had ordered large stashes of weapons and ammunition to be hidden throughout Cairo and in the countryside. He had arranged for rendezvous points where the soldiers would go to receive their orders. Like the Vietnamese Viet Minh, the Palestinian Fedayeen and the Algerian mujahideen, the Egyptians would use the shroud of anonymity to protect them from the armies. They would hide in plain sight and make the British and French suffer as they had never suffered before. "We shall fight a People's War," said Nasser to General Amer, his childhood friend and the commander of the Egyptian military. "When the people fight for their homeland the British and French will slaughter them and the world will know their cruelty."

Nasser send trucks and cars with megaphones throughout the city and surrounding communities to announce that he would speak that night at al-Azhar Mosque, Cairo's oldest and most revered mosque. It would be the most important speech of his life. In fact, his life might very well depend of the outcome of that speech.

As the hour drew near, Nasser took an open limousine from the presidential palace to the mosque. He knew that tens of thousands of people would be lining the streets to cheer him on. He also knew that there could be an assassin with a rifle anywhere in the crowd. The British Secret Service had attempted to assassinate him eight times on Eden's orders. It was God's will that he had survived all of the attempts. He wondered if he was tempting fate as he stood in the back of the limousine and waved to the people with his enormous smile. It was a chance he had to take. The people needed to see that their leader was not afraid. He could hear the bombers overhead and bombs exploding in the distance as the British carried out another raid on the Egyptian Army barracks. There was no air force left to stop them. Nasser had saved what he could. The people chanted "We will fight! We will fight!" to drown out the bombing raid and bolster their courage.

Nasser attended evening prayers at the mosque. He prayed deeply for Allah to give him strength and power to convince the people of what they must do to save Egypt.

When prayers were finished, Nasser spoke to a crowd numbering in the hundreds of thousands. Loudspeakers were set up throughout the complex so everyone could hear his words of reassurance that even though there had been setbacks Egypt would win in the end. He explained to the people why he had withdrawn Egyptian forces from the Sinai. The British and the French had planned to drive the Egyptian army and its tanks into the sand where they would snatch out the heart of Egypt. Nasser would not let that happen.

He had ordered Egypt's army to ransack the store houses and bunkers the British had left behind as part of the evacuation agreement signed by both sides. Tens of thousands of tons of weapons, ammunition, vehicles and equipment were confiscated and rehidden throughout Cairo and the desert, supplies that would be used by the Egyptian people to drive a stake into the heart of the enemy when the time was right.

The crowd roared with enthusiasm.

"I shall fight with you against any invasion. We shall fight to the last drop of our blood. We will never surrender. Egypt has always been a graveyard of invaders and it will be once again," said Nasser as the crowd again broke into a chant of "We will fight! We will fight!"

In that moment, Nasser knew that the people were behind him and if the people were behind him, the military would have no choice but to follow. Fear left his heart and he took courage. He and his people were going to win this war.

London, England

Eden and Clarissa arrived at the BBC studios just ten

minutes before the scheduled broadcast. They were met by Attenborough who would introduce the live broadcast. Eden still looked somewhat sickly but Attenborough could tell that the rest had done him a world of good. He seemed lucid, almost energetic.

Eden and Clarissa were escorted into the studio. The room as hot. The lights had been burning for almost a half hour so they were sure not to flicker during the broadcast. Attenborough could see that Eden was starting to sweat. "Perhaps a little powder to knock down the shine off your forehead?" said Attenborough.

"Whatever you feel is best, David," said Eden.

Eden trusted Attenborough who was one of Britain's biggest celebrities as a BBC spokesman. The BBC was clearly on Churchill's side during World War II and Eden had no reason to feel that would change now that he was prime minister.

Attenborough saw himself and the BBC as an honest broker that was obliged to present all sides of a story, especially when it concerned war. He had already scheduled a presentation by opposition leader Hugh Gaitskell to be broadcast directly after Eden. Eden knew nothing about this. He would have been furious had he known Gaitskell was in the same building. Attenborough thought there was enough on Eden's mind and didn't want to upset him. He simply didn't tell him about the follow up broadcast.

A woman applied powder to Eden's forehead and chin. When she stepped away, Attenborough was standing next to Clarissa watching the television monitor. Clarissa gasped, "He looks like a ghost. You can't even see the prime minister's mustache."

"I'm sure it's just the camera lens. They will dial it down right before we go on air," said Attenborough trying to calm her.

Clarissa reached into her purse and pulled out a mascara brush. She stepped in front of the camera. "Lady

Eden we are on air in ten seconds," said Attenborough, panicking.

"We are on when the prime minister is ready," said Clarissa, undeterred as she used the mascara brush to darken his mustache.

The station manager counted down with Clarissa still in front of the camera pointed at the prime minister. There was nothing Attenborough could do except to introduce the segment as the broadcast went live. Just as the camera switched to Eden, Clarissa stepped out of the way. The Prime Minister looked better with the darkened mustache and Britain was none the wiser.

Eden began by recounting the recent events that let up to the British military action and his justification for invading Egypt. "Those that know me well, know that all my life I have been a man of peace," said Eden into the camera. "Working for peace. Striving for peace. Negotiating for peace. And I am still the same with the same conviction, the same devotion to peace. I couldn't be other even if I wished. But I am utterly convinced that the action we have taken is right. There are times for courage, times for action and this is one of them. Good night to you all."

Later that night, when Eden found out about Gaitskell's on air response to his speech, he felt betrayed by Attenborough and the BBC, which was, after all, supported by the government of which he was the head. Eden even considered retaliation by taking control of the news' editorial board but then thought better of it. *One war at a time*, he thought.

British Camp, Cyprus

The next morning, Ross went out to the grenade range before dawn. As the sun broke the horizon, Ross launched his first grenade. It was a miss but his second was better… closer. And so was the third.

Brooks, holding two cups of hot tea, walked up the hilltop and looked down at the practice range. Ross was sinking every shot. He walked down and handed the private a cup. "Showoff," said Brooks. "We'll see how you do when they're shooting back at ya."

Ross smiled. Brooks knew the boy would be okay. He was confident. That was the important thing. When the bullets started to fly, he would remember his training, fear would fall away and he would fight like a para.

London, England

In response to Eden's speech, the Labor Party organized a massive protest in Trafalgar Square. Over two thousand protestors marched carrying placards that read:

YOUTH WON'T DIE FOR EDEN
NO WAR OVER SUEZ
HANDS OFF EGYPTIAN PEOPLE.

The protestors chanted "Law not war. Law not war," as they strode down the narrow alleys and spilled onto the main street, blocking the traffic.

Police with clubs and heavy helmets took up positions around the square. They stayed in tight groups and moved as one to break up any trouble that started. Horse-mounted police with long hickory batons patrolled the fringe of the crowd and attempted to keep traffic moving by pushing the crowd out of the street. As soon as one or two cars made it through, the crowd swelled back into the street and once again blocked traffic. The police were frustrated and arrested several protestors who had become belligerent. They refused to obey the police commands and vacate the street. The mob was growing angrier by the minute.

Counter-protestors entered the square and attempted to shout down the anti-Eden protestors. It was an impossible task, as they were greatly outnumbered and the opposition protestors were determined to be heard. Pushing and shoving began and soon developed into a brawl with the counter-protestors getting the worst of it.

The police pushed their way through the protestors to protect the counter-protestors and escort them out of harm's way. That only incensed the protestors more as they saw that the police were playing favorites and protecting Eden's followers. Protestors threw tomatoes, eggs, and bags of flour at the police. When the police fought back, the protestors picked up rocks and pulled paving stones loose from the street. The brawl turned into a full-scale riot as the protesters hurled the rocks and stones at the police on foot.

The mounted police formed a line and charged into the protestors in an attempt to get to their fellow officers. They swung their batons, clubbing men, women, and students. Police on foot beat back the crowd and separated a group of university students from Oxford. Two of the students were picked up by their hands and feet and thrown over a wall. Behind the wall, out of the public eye, four policeman armed with clubs beat the two students severely. It was a warning to the other students that might consider joining the protests.

News crews had used film cameras to record the violence and broadcast the footage nationwide. That night, during the evening edition of the news, the people of Britain were stunned to see their police and protestors clashing so violently. Before that night, the British people trusted their police force to be benevolent and incapable of attacking their fellow citizens.

The whole of Britain's belief system was shattered by

the scenes of violence and terror on their television screens. For the first time, Britain realized that their government was capable of lying, cheating and committing unthinkable acts of aggression against its own people. The old days of unequivocal support for the prime minister and the party in power during time of war were gone. The people were furious they were being forced into a war that few wanted.

Attenborough watched the broadcast in the BBC control room and wondered if he wasn't partly responsible for the violence. It was his decision to allow the opposition party a platform to refute Eden. He couldn't help but feel that he had started the snowball rolling without knowing where it was heading or when it would stop.

Paris, France

Unlike their British counterparts, the people of France did little to protest the war. For over a year, they had been living with the Café Wars – terrorist attacks on the civilian population of Paris by the FLN. The bombings of cafes, bars and shops throughout the city had turned the people against the FLN and their movement for Algerian Independence. They demanded that their government do something to quell the violence. And their government listened.

The French people understood that the FLN was supported by Nasser. They saw the action their troops were taking in Egypt as a necessary step in achieving peace. If Nasser was overthrown, the FLN would lose his patronage. The FLN leaders would be forced to negotiate a truce. Parisians could once again enjoy their afternoon coffee and cigarette without worrying that the shopping bag under the table next to them might explode.

Allied Air Command, *HMS Tyne*

French General Brohan, commander of Armée de l'Air sat in a conference room with his British counterpart examining bomb assessment photos of the Egyptian airfield at Luxor. The bomb craters were North of the airfield in an empty field. The eighteen Il-28 bombers station at the airfield were untouched. "As you can see the eighteen bombers are still operational," said the colonel giving the presentation. "The problem is the restrictions placed on the bomber crews not to damage any of the ancient structures at Luxor. It's a difficult task to say the least with so many of the ancient ruins so close to the airfield. Our bombardiers are forced to aim wide and… well, you can see the results."

Brohan didn't comment during the presentation. He considered the information and pondered the problem as the meeting drew to a close. "Any thoughts from the French, general?" said a British Air Marshall.

"Not at the moment. It's a difficult situation. I need to think on it," said Brohan.

"You will get back to us?"

"Of course. Give me the day."

"As you wish."

Brohan walked through a hallway to his office in the aft of the ship. The French air force had been treated as a second class citizen by the Air Marshall. It was true that the British aircraft made up the majority fighting force, especially when it came to bombing. The French had no long-range bombers in the theatre. Their fighters were usually relegated to air cover for the British bomber squadrons. It was an important job but did little to boost the morale of French airmen.

Brohan was proud of his men and knew they could do much more than babysitting the British bombers. He picked up the phone and asked the operator to connect him with the French squadron commander in Lydda, Israel. Colonel Maurice Perdrizet answered. "Maurice, I have a mission for you and your men," said Brohan over the phone. "You've seen the bomb assessment photographs of Luxor?"

"Yes," said Perdrizet. "The Egyptians have left their aircraft in the open. Foolish."

"I was thinking we should give it a go with your squadron. No bombs. No rockets. There is too much risk of hitting something off limits."

"Brownings then?"

"That was my thinking. Your boys would need to get in close... real close."

"We can do that."

"Speed is important. We need to hit their bombers before their commanders decide to move them. When can you be ready?"

"The mission is straightforward. The boys are just returning from a mission. The ground crews will need to rearm the machine guns and refuel the jets. A few hours should be enough."

"Good. Let me know when it's done," said Brohan, then as an afterthought... "Oh, and Maurice... take photos."

"Yes, sir. It would be our pleasure," said Perdrizet.

Luxor, Egypt

A squadron of twenty French F-84F Thunderstreaks flew at thirty thousand feet over Sinai. The pilots were no longer concerned with the Egyptian fighters. They were all gone. But the pilots still worried about the occasional anti-aircraft battery in and around Egyptian military installations and with some of the armor columns still trying to make it across the Suez Canal.

The external tanks on each of the swept-wing jets gave the squadron the extra fuel needed to fly from Lydda, Israel to Luxor, Egypt and back again. Four .50 Cal M3 Browning machine guns were mounted inside each jet's nose with two additional M3s mounted in the wing roots. The jets carried no other armament, to save on weight and extend their time on target.

As the squadron approached Luxor, the lead plane saw a squadron of British Canberra bombers making another attempt at destroying the airfield and the Russian-built Il-28 bombers. The French squadron leader ordered his pilots to hold back until the British were finish. He didn't want the British pilots to confuse the French aircraft with Egyptain MiG-15 which had a strong resemblance to the Thunderstreak airframe.

The Canberras dropped their bombs and just as with their previous attempts the bombs landed to the north pocking the empty field with more craters. Not one structure or Il-28 bomber was damaged. The Canberras turned for home empty handed.

The Thunderstreaks were divided into two groups; one to provide air cover just in case an Egyptian fighter did appear and the other to attack the bombers on the ground. Once the first group had finished, they would switch places and the second group would take their turn at the bombers. The first group leader called out the targets for each of his aircraft. Each French fighter would go after one bomber. They would use all of the ammunition except for two hundred rounds held in reserve for defense or targets of opportunity on the trip home.

The first group of fighters dropped down to fifteen hundred feet before opening fire. At speeds approaching six hundred miles per hour, it didn't give the pilot much time on target, but the French were well practiced at the technique. Tracer rounds guided the pilots' aim. Orange streams of half inch diameter shells tore into each bombers' wings and fuselage. With less than five hundred feet to spare, the French pilots peeled off and pulled up at the last moment to avoid careening into the ground. Multiple bombers burst into flames when the tracer rounds ignited the remaining fuel in their wing tanks. It was an amazing feat of airborne marksmanship by the French pilots.

The gauntlet had been thrown down by the first group. They climbed up to take up defensive positions above the airfield and switched with the second group. The second group dove down just as the first had done. They targeted the remaining bombers, a cargo plane and a fuel truck. The airfield was undamaged as were the ancient runes of Luxor.

A French reconnaissance aircraft waited until the fighters were finished before making two passes over the airfield to snap photos of the damage.

Allied Air Command, *HMS Tyne*

General Brohan walked into the British Air Marshal's office and set a folder on his desk. "I promised to get back to you about your Il-28 problem. It has been solved courtesy of the Armée de l'Air. Good day, General," said Brohan and left without any further fanfare.

The confused Air Marshall opened the folder and examined the photographs inside. All eighteen of the Il-28s had been destroyed by the French fighter pilots. The evidence was irrefutable. The Air Marshall was dumbfounded. Brohan had made his point.

Port Said, Egypt

Six military trucks pulled up in front a mosque at Port Said. The Egyptian Staff Sergeant in charge had his men pull the first box out of the back of one of the trucks and set it on the ground. The people from the neighborhood gathered around. The Staff Sergeant opened the box. It was filled with antiquated Enfield rifles. He ordered a second box placed on the ground next to the first. He opened it. It was filled with five shell clips. He picked up a clip and loaded it into the rifle's magazine. The World War II Enfields used a .303 caliber bullet and kicked like a mule. Not the ideal weapon for inexperienced civilians. Many of the barrels and chambers were rusted and were of questionable use. "What are we supposed to do with those?" said a man.

"You hide on your second and third floor balconies and wait. When the British or French troops pass below you fire on them from above," said the Staff Sergeant.

"They will fire back."

"Yes. So don't miss."

"I've never even fired a gun."

"Our troops will instruct you. Everyone will be allowed to fire five rounds to practice before the invasion. We don't have enough rifles for everyone, so if your neighbor has a rifle and is killed, you will pick up his weapon and continue the fight."

The people formed a long line as the sergeant handed out rifles to each adult. Each rifle came with five rounds already loaded in the magazine. The army commanders did not think most of the civilians would last more than five rounds before they were killed by the more skilled British and French soldiers. Bullets were expensive and not to be wasted. More ammunition would be supplied later to the survivors.

The teenagers were not given rifles. Instead they were given Molotov cocktails - soda and seltzer bottles filled with gasoline and a rag stuffed in the opening. When British or French tanks, armored cars, or troop trucks passed below the balconies, the teenagers were instructed to light the rag and drop the fire bomb on top of the passing vehicle. The bottle would shatter and the fuel would ignite burning the vehicle and the soldiers inside. Again, the commanders figured more teenagers would set themselves on fire than actually destroy vehicles but Egypt had a lot of teenagers and the fire bombs were cheap.

Mediterranean Sea

Admiral Brown stood on the bridge of his flagship - the heavy cruiser *USS Salem*. He studied the position of various vessels marked on the navigational charts. No sooner would he calculate the distance between two ships, than the navigator would update the chart, changing the ships' positions. Brown grumbled. A communications officer approached, "Admiral, the commander of the French Aircraft Carrier *La Fayette* is asking us to reposition our ships farther to the west. He's concerned about flight safety for his aircraft landing and taking off."

"Humph. Tell 'em to fuck off," said Brown.

"Excuse me, sir?"

"You heard me. But do it politely."

"Yes, sir," said the officer and moved off.

"A little room won't hurt," said the commander of the *USS Salem*.

"We're in international waters. The U.S. Navy goes where it wants."

"Aye. Aye."

Within the hour the French cruiser *Georges Leygues* sailing in the opposite direction came within three hundred feet of an American frigate. Considered it took a ship the size of *Georges Leygues* over a mile to come to complete stop once it cut its engines, three hundred feet was terribly close.

When Brown heard the report of the incident, he chuckled, "Guess the French Commander didn't like my reply to his request."

Brown considered for a moment like a chess champion

calculating his next move. "Inform the commander of the *Coral Sea*, I want a flight of fully armed Banshees to do a close flyby of the *Georges Leygues*," said Brown.

"Aye. Aye," said the communications officer.

Four F2H Banshee jet fighters took off from the *U.S. Coral Sea* aircraft carrier.

The four fighters flew in a tight formation as they approached the *Georges Leygues* at over five hundred miles per hour. They flew just fifty feet above the ship's main mast, startling the French seaman onboard.

As the flight of jets swung around on the horizon, preparing for a second pass, four of the cruiser's 90 mm anti-aircraft guns swung around and targeted the aircraft. It would be a difficult shot taking down a jet traveling at high-speed, but not impossible.

Brown stood on the bridge watching with a pair of binoculars. "Admiral, the French cruiser is targeting the Banshee squadron. The air commander on the *Coral Sea* is asking permission to engage."

Brown took a moment to consider before answering. It was not in his nature to back down, especially from a force that he knew was inferior to his own. The crew on the bridge held their breath waiting for his answer. This could be the beginning of a war with France and possibly Britain. It was a war that the Americans were sure to win but not without heavy losses, the worst of which would be the dismantling of NATO and the loss of key allies. "Inform the air commander that his aircraft should not engage the French cruiser. The flight will return to the *Coral Sea* immediately," said Brown. "We've made our point. No need to start World War III."

"Shall we give the *La Fayette* some operating room?" said the flagship commander.

"Hell no. All vessels are to maintain their current headings," said Brown. "It's a big sea. Let them move."

DAVID LEE CORLEY

British Fleet, Mediterranean Sea

On board the British aircraft carrier *HMS Eagle*, ground crews prepared fighter jets for their missions. Everyone knew his job and worked fast to turn around the jets and get them back into the air. It was like a fine-oiled machine.

Crew members rolled a five hundred pound bomb under the wing of a Sea Venom fighter-bomber parked on the flight deck. Another five hundred pound bomb was already attacked to the hardpoints on the opposite wing. On the nose of the bombs were written the words "Love to Nasser" and "Nasser's Rock and Rolls" in chalk.

Cairo, Egypt

Camp Huckstep, the Egyptian Army's largest base, was located near Cairo International Airport. The camp was twelve square miles and included a one thousand bed hospital, armor repair facilities and barracks for over ten thousand soldiers.

On hearing the air raid siren, thousands of troops scrambled from their barracks and ran for the closest air raid shelter or stack of sandbags. A squadron of Sea Venom swooped down and unleashed their Hispano cannons on the fleeing soldiers. Soldiers unlucky enough to be caught in the stream of 20-mm bullets were blown apart. Bombs dropped onto the barracks. The explosions sent wooden shards flying through the air, killing and wounding dozens of soldiers. Egyptian anti-aircraft guns fired at the British jets as they streaked past at over four hundred miles an hour. The Egyptian gunners had been trained to fire at moving targets in the distance and at much lower speeds. With each attack, the Egyptians gained experience and their aim improved... if they survived.

86

When the British pilots returned to their aircraft carrier, they examined the bullet holes in their aircraft. The raids near Cairo and Port Said were getting tougher. The British were teaching the Egyptians how to fight by giving them experience.

The British pilots suggested to their commanders that a number of missions should be focused on taking out the anti-aircraft guns before the Anglo-French invasion. The allies owned the sky but that could change if the Egyptian anti-aircraft gunners' aim improved. Better to destroy them now while they were still somewhat helpless. The squadron commanders agreed and the targeting list was changed accordingly.

Port Said, Egypt

Just after sunset, four Hawker Sea Hawks flew low, hugging the waves at full speed toward the Egyptian coast. As the fighter-bombers approached the coastal batteries and anti-aircraft guns at Port Said they broke formation and flew in different directions. The Egyptians took the bait and opened fire. Tracer shells streaked across the night sky. It was easy to pinpoint the location of each of the gun emplacements.

A squadron of Sea Venoms followed the Sea Hawks into shore. The British fighter-bombers attacked the gun emplacements dropping bombs and strafing the gun crews with their cannons. The guns were soon silenced as the last of the tracer streams disappeared into the night. The British had reclaimed their air superiority.

November 4, 1956 – Budapest, Hungary

Twelve hundred miles northeast of Cairo, student

demonstrators in front of the Hungarian Parliament building watched as Soviet tanks rolled into the square and central park. Treads tore into the lawn as the tanks knocked over anything in their way including park benches, trashcans and even trees. It was an ominous display of an unstoppable force. The Soviets had had enough of the unrest in their satellite nation and had sent in two full divisions of troops and tanks to enforce their will.

Earlier in 1956, Khrushchev had done the unthinkable – in what was later known as the "Secret Speech" Khrushchev denounced Stalin. Hoping to usher in a less oppressive era, Khrushchev exposed the terrible atrocities that Stalin had committed during the purges and condemned his former mentor. Many saw it as revenge against Stalin for the execution of Khrushchev's son.

On hearing of the atrocities, several eastern bloc countries immediately revolted and demanded freedom from the Soviet Union. A worker's strike in Poland evolved into a riot that left fifty dead when Polish police cracked down on the disturbance. The Polish government made concessions to the workers to prevent more bloodshed. Khrushchev and the Soviets grumbled but did nothing to stop them.

Emboldened by the develops in Poland, the Hungarian opposition party decided it was time to take action against the communist government. Mass protests broke out in Budapest. Protestors tore out the hammer and sickle from the center of dozens of Hungarian flags and waved them like banners. Stalin's statue was toppled and hammered into pieces by striking metal workers. The billboard-sized Soviet red star was cut from the top of the communist party building and fell eight stories, crashing on the street.

To quell the revolt, the Hungarian party installed Imre Nagy, a reformist. Again, Khrushchev and the Soviets did nothing, deciding to give the new government time to get organized and establish order. Khrushchev assumed that if the Soviet Union showed restraint, the Hungarians would fall into line.

Inaction only encouraged the opposition who demanded Soviet troops leave Hungary. Soviet troops in the city were openly attacked by Hungarian protestors. The Soviet troops fired on the crowd and hundreds on both sides of the conflict were killed.

Khrushchev became convinced that Western agitators were behind the revolts in Hungary. He believed it was a secret plot to discredit the Soviet Union and wrestle away one of the USSR's allies in Eastern Europe.

At the same time that Hungary was exploding in revolt, the Suez Crisis was unfolding. Egypt was considered a new ally of the Soviet Union. Khrushchev believed that the British and French had instigated the invasion of the Suez Canal to embarrass the USSR and take advantage of events in Hungary. The Soviets could not hope to help the Egyptians while they were busy dealing with Hungary which was closer to the Soviet border and therefore a much bigger threat to stability. He believed the Suez Crisis was manufactured to further damage the Soviet's reputation in the Middle East. "The West believes we are weak and unable to control our allies," Khrushchev told his advisors. "We must show them the error in their thinking."

At that moment Khrushchev became determined to make a show of force that the world would not soon forget. He may not have been able to send troops to Nasser but he was able to project Soviet power. The USSR was a nuclear power with intercontinental ballistic missiles that could reach anywhere in the world, including Washington D.C. He would not be pushed around by the West. He would not be made a fool.

In Budapest, Nagy announced multi-party elections and declared that Hungary was leaving the Warsaw Pack. On hearing the news, Khrushchev sent Czechoslovakian,

Bulgarian, and Romanian tanks and troops into Budapest. The Hungarians would be made an example of to demonstrate the USSR's iron grip to its satellites. It was called Operation Whirlwind.

A group of Hungarian freedom fighters hid around the corner of a building. A tank occupied the square that they needed to cross to reach the parliament building. Their rifles and pistols were no match for Soviet armor. A woman whose husband had been killed that morning volunteered to attack the Soviet tank. She emptied her purse on the ground and placed a single grenade inside.

She walked around the corner and calmly walked across the street to enter the square. The Soviet tank commander standing in the turret hatch called out to her in Hungarian ordering her to go back. She kept walking toward the tank. The commander ordered his gunner to swing the turret around. The main gun and machineguns swung around and aimed at the woman. The commander continued to yell at the woman, cursing her and waving his arms. She kept closing the distance between her and the tank. The commander ordered his men to open fire. A disagreement broke out between the soldiers, questioning the order to kill an unarmed woman. She drew closer. The commander ducked down inside the tank and cursed his men for not following his order. Under threat of court martial, the soldier opened fire. The woman was torn to shreds and fell to the ground dead. But it was too late. She had thrown the grenade and it had landed in the open hatch and tumbled inside to the tank's floor. The grenade exploded, killing the crew. The woman became a Hungarian hero and a symbol of freedom.

Within the first week of the Soviet invasion, the Hungarian uprising was crushed. The Hungarians fought with whatever they could but the Soviet tanks were merciless. Over four thousand Hungarians were killed. Nagy was arrested and executed.

The world was outraged by the ferocity of the crackdown. For Khrushchev, the Suez Crisis became a welcome distraction, shifting the limelight away from the Soviets and Hungary. With things well in hand by the Soviet forces, Khrushchev was now free to deal with the West and their fabricated invasion of Egypt.

Washington D.C., USA

Foster Dulles stood outside the Oval Office door collecting his thoughts as he often did before talking with the president. He was the bearer of bad news. There had been so much bad news as of late Foster Dulles was trying to figure out how he might be able to present the news in a different light. He decided that was dishonest and the president needed to know the undiluted truth, even if it upset him. He entered the Oval Office. Eisenhower was not inside the office.

Foster Dulles walked out onto the veranda surrounding the Oval Office. Eisenhower was staring out at the Washington Memorial, smoking a cigarette. Foster Dulles could see that he was deep in thought and hated to disturb him. But the news couldn't wait. "Mr. President?" said Foster Dulles.

"Yes, Foster," said Eisenhower without turning around.

Foster Dulles smiled. "How did you know it was me?"

"You're the only man brave enough to interrupt me while I'm thinking."

"I've got news."

"That doesn't sound good."

"It's not."

"Well… let's have it."

"Soviet troops and tanks have entered Budapest and

opened fire on the protestors. They're fighting back but..."

"You don't have to explain, Foster. I know what happens when civilians go up against tanks."

"Yes, sir."

"Any estimates on casualties?"

"Not yet, Mr. President. But it's going to be high."

"I would imagine."

"I think we should put together some sort of response."

"Yes, of course. But tell me, Foster... How do we condemn Soviet tanks firing on civilians in Budapest when our allies are bombing civilians in Cairo?"

"I don't know, Mr. President. But we have to continue to fight the good fight."

"Yes... we do. Please draft something and I'll take a look at it. We should get it out as soon as possible."

"Yes, Mr. President," said Foster Dulles and left Eisenhower to finish his cigarette in peace.

FOUR

HMS Eagle, Mediterranean Sea

Brigitte sat in the galley of the *HMS Eagle* aircraft carrier nursing a cup of coffee. Sipping the coffee she understood why the British drank tea. The tepid dark liquid had a thin layer of oil floating on top and it tasted bitter. Her rucksack sat on the deck under the bench.

She had been dropped off from the British destroyer that picked her up from the sea. Three minutes after meeting her, the captain of the destroyer wanted nothing to do with the pushy French woman. He had elected to dump her on the *HMS Eagle* and make her the aircraft carrier's problem. The captain of the *HMS Eagle* felt the same way after only two minutes and ordered her held in the galley. She may have been a French citizen and technically an ally but she had no business onboard a British warship in a time of war. The fact that she was a reporter made matters even worse.

A seaman had been ordered to watch her and stood at the doorway. The phone on the wall rang and he picked it up. He listened and hung up the receiver. "Air commander wants to see you," he said to Brigitte.

She grabbed her rucksack and followed the seaman through the doorway and down the hallway. They entered the tactical center and approached the air commander. "You wanted to see the French reporter, commander," said the seaman.

The commander turned to Brigitte and said, "We've got a flight dropping off some reconnaissance film on Cyprus. It leaves in three minutes. Do you want to hitch a ride?"

"Yes, sir. That would be great," said Brigitte.

The commander turned to the seaman and said, "Take her down to the flight deck and find Lieutenant Lewis."

"Aye aye, sir," said the seaman, saluting.

Brigitte followed the seaman down to the flight deck where he asked for the lieutenant. Brigitte was handed over to a flight deck crew member and escorted to a two-seated Sea Venom being readied for takeoff. She was introduced to Lieutenant Lewis. "Have you ever flown in a fighter jet before?" asked Lewis.

"No, never," said Brigitte.

"Alright. The only thing you must remember is that when you puke aim away from me, Okay?" said Lewis handing her a barf bag.

"Got it."

They climbed up onto the inner wing and Lewis held her rucksack as she climbed into the cockpit. The seats were side by side. Brigitte sat in the left seat and put her rucksack behind her legs. Lewis handed her a flight helmet and she put it on. She strapped in tight. Lewis sat down next to her and went through his preflight procedure. The jet engine was started and the canopy closed.

The fighter taxied over to the steam-powered catapult where crew members guided the jet's nose gear over the shuttle slot in the deck and hooked up the tow bar. "Got your barf bag ready?" said Lewis.

"Yep," said Brigitte and gave him a thumbs up.

Lewis rolled his eyes, thinking, *This French woman has no idea what is about to happen.* He brought the engine to full throttle. The roar was deafening. The catapult was triggered. The jet accelerated down the runway hitting 160 mph in less than two seconds. Brigitte was thrown back into the seat and her eyes went wide from the g-forces. She couldn't breathe as the aircraft left the carrier flight deck and flew over the sea.

The g-forces lessened as the jet finished its takeoff acceleration. Brigitte gasped for air. "You, okay?" said Lewis.

"Hell yes. Can we do it again?" said Brigitte with a huge grin.

The Sea Venom lifted up into the sky, banked to one side and headed toward the island of Cyprus.

London, England

First Sea Lord Admiral Mountbatten waited patiently in the reception area outside Eden's office. He had been told that the prime minister was busy and didn't have room in his schedule at the moment. Mountbatten said he would wait in hopes that the PM's schedule would free up for a few moments to discuss an urgent matter. Mountbatten, the highest ranking officer in the Royal Navy, was not used to waiting.

Eden knew that Mountbatten was waiting outside his office. Mountbatten's opposition to the whole Suez affair was well known and Eden was not in the mood to hear from the Admiral. But with Mountbatten camped outside, he had little hope of slipping out unseen. He wished Mountbatten would just do as he was told and leave the politics to the politicians.

As the day waned, Eden decided to face Mountbatten and get it over with. His secretary called the Admiral into Eden's office. "Thank you for seeing me, Sir Anthony," said Mountbatten.

"Of course, Admiral," said Eden. "My door is always open to you."

"Good to know."

"You mentioned to my secretary that you had a matter

most urgent to discuss."

"Call off the invasion."

Eden was surprised by Mountbatten directness. "No," said Eden in response. "It's too late for that."

"It's never too late when men's lives are at stake."

"Save your platitudes, Admiral. I am well aware what is at stake. Nasser chose this path. We cannot let him dictate who will be allowed to use an international waterway and who will not."

"It is Egyptian soil."

"I don't care. We both know he will blackmail Britain the first time we disagree with one of his outlandish schemes. Nasser is not going to dictate policy for Britain or any other country. We cannot allow that to happen." Eden took a moment and changed his approach, "Admiral, we can have a war with Egypt now or we can have it later after it has done more damage to Britain's and Europe's economies."

"Then let's have it later. Things change. If we can avoid needless bloodshed, I say we wait."

"Fortunately that is not your call. We are there and we are ready. I say we go now."

"The world is turning against us. We will be seen as the aggressor in this affair."

"Perhaps. Or perhaps we will be seen as a savior and a peacemaker."

"I doubt that."

"I know you do. You have made your views very clear. One would almost believe that you are getting ready to retire and run for Parliament."

"That's not what this is about. Britain has already taken a big hit when Egypt forced our troops out of the Canal Zone and nationalized the Canal. Whatever influence we have left in the Middle East will vanish once we set foot on Egyptian soil."

"I think you underestimate the Arabs. They know Nasser is a madman. They don't want him to have any more power. They'll be grateful to see him fall."

"That's not what our Intelligence is telling us."

"But it is what my intelligence is telling me. The schedule for the invasion is set and you have your orders, Admiral. Can I count on your support?"

"You can count on me carrying out my orders, Sir Anthony."

"Thank you, Admiral. That will be all," said Eden turning back to the papers on his desk.

Mountbatten walked out. Eden took a moment to consider the situation and the Admiral's opposition to the invasion. It took him another thirty seconds to decide that he was right and the admiral was wrong.

Egyptian Coast, Mediterranean Sea

Captain Morcos said his afternoon prayers along with the rest of his men on the dock at Alexandria. It would be the last chance they would have to pray until their mission was completed. Morcos was a devout Muslim and commander of a squadron of four motor torpedo boats. He had been given orders to seek out and destroy French and British warships. It was a fool's errand. A suicide mission.

Morcos finished his prayers and stood up. He thought of his fiancé. They had met during a party at the naval academy. She was the daughter of one of the instructors – a veteran officer with high level connections and influence. They were due to be married at the beginning of November but all that had changed when war broke out. Like most good things, their nuptials would need to wait until the Westerners were once again driven from Egyptian soil. There would be time for the two of them when it was done. Her father would see to it.

Morcos gazed out at sea. It was getting rough with whitecaps forming on some of the waves. That was a good thing in his mind. Although rough seas made the torpedo boats less stable in the open ocean, they also decreased the odds of his boats being spotted by enemy vessels.

His boats were Italian-built with gasoline powered engines to give them speed. They were lightweight at fifteen tons and had no armor. The boats' only real defenses were speed and maneuverability. Individual boats were crewed by two officers and ten men. Each boat had an Oerlikon 20 mm autocannon and two heavy machineguns, but these would be of little use against a Western warship. Only the boat's torpedoes could severely damage – and with luck sink – one of the large British or French warships.

The two torpedo tubes were mounted on either side of the aft deck. To fire the torpedoes, his men would need to manually crank the tubes into place. The driver of the boat would use a sight to line up one tube on the target and give the order to fire. Once one torpedo was launched the driver was then free to seek another target or fire a second shot at the first target using the tube on the opposite side of his boat. It wasn't an elegant process. One torpedo could potentially sink a warship if it exploded in just the right spot. But it didn't happen often. In fact... almost never.

Modern naval radar systems could detect approaching surface vessels from as far away as twelve miles. The Egyptian torpedo boats had a top speed of thirty-five knots and needed to close within one mile of their target to have any hope of hitting it. That meant that it would take a torpedo boat over twenty minutes to reach a warship after the torpedo boat had been detected. One hit from a destroyer's or frigate's main guns would blow a torpedo boat out of the water. But radar had difficulty with rough seas especially if the top of the waves were higher than the boat they were trying to identify. Waves created a lot of electronic noise and for Morcos and his crews that meant they would probably be able to get a lot closer to their target before being spotted.

Morcos knew where the British and French fleets were located, about fifty miles due North off the coast. But he wasn't interested in the fleet. Hitting an aircraft carrier with a torpedo would make him and his men legends. But the aircraft carriers were well protected with a deadly ring of destroyers and frigates. His torpedo boats wouldn't stand a chance of getting close. Instead, he had something else in mind.

There were several troop ships sailing to rendezvous with the fleet. They too were escorted by warships, but not nearly as many. If he and his men could sink one enemy troop transport, they might delay the coming invasion. In fact, they might even cause the British and French politicians to give pause about the entire war when word arrived home about the massive loss of life. It was a long shot, but the command of torpedo boats was always considered a long shot post.

Morcos came from a good Egyptian family but they weren't rich and they couldn't afford the bribes required to get their son an officer's posting on one of Egypt's destroyers. He accepted his command and decided to do the best he could for his men and country. Today, that probably meant giving up his life unless he was very, very lucky or Allah needed him to live for some unforeseen reason. One never knew Allah's will.

Morcos and his men boarded their boats, secured the watertight hatches, and started their engines. Forming a H-shaped formation with two boats in front and two behind, they headed out to sea. Morcos and his navigator had studied the reports from Middle Eastern civilian fishing and cargo ships that radioed the coordinates of the British and French troops ships as they were spotted. It was like a huge spy network in plain sight and there was nothing the British or French could do about it. According to their calculations, three transport ships with escorts should be sixty miles to the north east of Alexandria. With luck, Morcos and his men would spot the escort ships before they themselves were spotted. It was a high seas game of cat and mouse.

They sailed at three quarter speed at just over twenty-five knots. Morcos wanted to ensure that his boats' engines were not overheated when they encountered the enemy. They would need a final burst of speed as they closed on their targets.

Two hours after leaving port, one of the lookouts on the bow spotted the convoy. Morcos signaled the other boats. As they drew closer, Morcos identified a frigate protecting the convoy. It was a Tacoma-class warship with three turret-mounted main guns; two forward and one aft. There was probably more than one warship, he thought, but this frigate was the closest to his squadron's position. Morcos had been taught to focus on the ship in your sights rather than the imaginary ones in your mind. As far as he could tell through his binoculars, none of the enemy ships had spotted his squadron. Luck was running with him that day.

Morcos decided to attempt a diversion. He ordered one of his four boats to attempt to draw the frigate off from the convoy. It would approach the frigate directly and open fire with its machine guns and autocannon. If the commander of the boat thought he had a chance of hitting the frigate he was authorized to launch his torpedoes. The other three torpedo boats would wait in the distance and see what happened. Hopefully, the frigate would act like a mad bull and charge after the attacker. With the frigate chasing the lone torpedo boat, the other three would attempt to slip through the defensive ring and attack the closest troop ship. With luck, they would sink her. All four boats would then rendezvous back at the port in Alexandria.

The lone torpedo boat sped off. Morcos kept the engines of the three boats idling while they waited. He knew it was a waste of fuel but he didn't want to risk one of the engines not starting when the time to attack arrived.

The lone torpedo boat approached the frigate and opened fire. The commander of the frigate radioed the other ships in the convoy that it was under attack. All of the frigate's 3-inch main guns turned and opened fire. The water around the torpedo boat exploded in geysers of white water. The crew of the Egyptian boat launched its port torpedo at the frigate. It missed but had the desired effect of pissing off the frigate captain who ordered his helmsman to give chase. The frigate broke the defensive ring around the convoy, exposing it just as Morcos had hoped.

Morcos waited until the frigate was well on its way to running down the pesky lone torpedo boat. He ordered his boats to attack the closest troop ship at full speed. They sped forward in a horizontal line like charging cavalry. Morcos felt the blood pumping through his heart. He and his men were going to achieve the impossible. They would save Egypt. He didn't notice the four Sea Hawks screaming towards his three boats just thirty feet above the waves.

The British convoy had spotted the torpedo boat squadron at about the same time Morcos spotted the frigate. The commander of the convoy radioed the fleet and the four Sea Hawks which had just taken off from the *HMS Bulwark* were rerouted toward the troop convoy. At five hundred and sixty miles per hour, the four aircraft reached the convoy within seven minutes. Each jet was armed with sixteen 127 mm rockets and four Hispano 20 mm autocannons. Their original mission had been an assault on coastal batteries. They were ideally armed to deal with the torpedo boats. On the first pass, the pilots fired their rockets. Two rockets hit one of the torpedo boats. The first explosion blew a gaping hole in the starboard side just above the water line. The second rocket hit the aft deck and ignited one of the boat's torpedoes. The resulting explosion tore off the entire main deck. Only a fiery hulk remained burning in the water. There were no survivors.

Morcos was shocked by the air attack. He could not hope to outrun the four enemy jets. He ordered his remaining two boats to continue their run toward the troop ship. The crews cranked the torpedo launch tubes into position. Morcos would launch all the torpedoes as soon as he thought a hit was possible. The gun crews on the torpedo boat did their best to return fire with their heavy machine guns and autocannon but the jets were moving too fast to target accurately.

In the distance, Morcos saw a huge fireball on the horizon. One of the frigate's main guns had scored a direct hit on the fleeing torpedo boat and blew a hole in the engine compartment. Hot shell fragments had pierced the gasoline fuel tank. The gas fumes at the top of the tank exploded, destroying the boat and killing all on board.

As the two remaining boats raced forward, the four jets banked and formed two lines of attack, one for each of the two boats. The pilots changed their weapon select switches to cannons. The first two jet approached the boats from directly behind and opened fire with their Hispano cannons.

The water behind the boats churned a double line of small white geysers as the stream of 20 mm shells raced toward the back of the boats. When the bullets finally reached the back decks of the boats, they tore into the aft decks and any crew members unlucky enough to get in the way. A stream of 20 mm shell took out both motors of one of the boats and ignited its fuel supply. The gas tank blew up. Again, one of the boat's torpedoes exploded, killing everyone on board.

The pilots in the jets had to be careful not to run into each other when they broke off.

There was one boat left and it was closing on the troop ship. It was Morcos'. Several of his crew members were already dead. The British escort ships were moving into position to block the remaining torpedo boat.

The second group of two jets swooped in and took aim at the remaining torpedo boat.

Morcos and his men had closed the distance and were close enough to take a shot at the troop ship with their torpedoes. His death and the death of his men would mean something. His family would be proud. His chest exploded in red when a stream of 20 mm shells hit him in the back. He tried to push out the words to fire the torpedo but it was useless. His lungs no longer existed. Besides, there were no crew left to execute his commands. Two minutes later the last torpedo boat exploded and sank. The squadron was finished. The invasion was happening. There was nothing the Egyptians could do to stop it. They would fight once the British and French troops arrived.

Washington D.C., USA

Vice President Richard Nixon sat on the couch across from Eisenhower. Nixon liked the Oval Office. He had a nice office in the West Wing of the White House but it didn't have the prestige of the president's office. A steward finished serving coffee and left as Eisenhower and Nixon chatted about their families before getting down to business. "So how is the campaign trail?" said Eisenhower.

"It's fine, Mr. President. The people are still enthusiastic about your presidency," said Nixon.

"It's our presidency, Dick."

"Of course, Mr. President. I'm getting a lot of questions about the current situation in Egypt."

"Oh?"

"Our supporters are wondering why we are siding with the Soviets on this one."

"I won't say we are siding with them. It's a matter of what is right, Dick."

"If I may be frank, Mr. President?"

103

"Of course."

"I think it is safe to say you and I agree that Communism is the main threat we face."

"It is."

"And the best way to deter that threat is with a united front. It's the whole reason behind NATO, isn't it?."

"Yes."

"So, why are we taking sides against Britain and France? They're our strongest allies for Christ's sake."

"I know how you feel, Dick. I ask myself the same thing multiple times a day. But they're flat out wrong on this one."

"And the Soviets are right?"

"Actually... they are."

"Dwight, we cannot expect to survive politically if we side with the Soviets. Our base will turn against us."

"I have considered that."

"This will be your last term, but it's not mine."

"True. And I appreciate your loyalty. But our highest calling is to protect America and that means her reputation too. America fought a war to free itself from colonialism. How can we possibly blame Egypt for doing the same?"

"Most Americans don't give a damn about Egypt. Hell, most of 'em don't even know where it is on a map. They do care a great deal about freedom and democracy. How can we possibly side with the communists?"

"Like I said, we're not siding with them."

"We can't look weak, Mr. President. Americans won't stand for it. They'll run us out of town on a rail. Hell, they might even impeach us."

"I doubt that."

"If the Soviets join the war which side will we be on?"

"We've got to make sure that doesn't happen."

"How do you propose to do that?" said Nixon in a huff.

"End the war before it's too late," said Eisenhower.

"Well, I hope to hell you've got more than a rabbit up

your sleeve, Mr. President."

"Well, Mr. Vice President…I assure you I'm working on it."

Syrian Coast, Mediterranean Sea

The British were concerned with the buildup of Il-28 Bombers flown to Syria by Egyptian pilots. It appeared that Nasser was saving his precious bombers and crews to fight another day rather than be slaughtered by the overwhelming number of British and French fighters and bombers. He had already lost most of his fighting capacity, he didn't want to lose his bombing capacity too. Although it was unlikely that the Syrians would allow Nasser to launch an attack against the British and French ships in the Mediterranean, the bombers were an unseen threat still out there.

There was an additional concern – Operation Beisan. Israeli Intelligence had informed the British and French about a potential joint operation between Syria, Jordan and Egypt against Israel. The plan developed by the Egyptians was for Syrian and Jordanian forces to strike through the middle of Israel cutting the country in half. The Israelis would be forced to fight a war on multiple fronts which would stretch their military resources to the limit. Egypt could then attack from the south and destroy the southern Israeli army while the Jordanians and Syrians kept the Israelis in the north busy. While Egypt was in no condition to attack at this point, the plan could easily be revised to draw Israeli forces back from the Sinai to defend their homeland. If that happened, the perceived motivation for the British and French invasion of the Suez Canal would simply disappear.

Eden wasn't taking any chances. He ordered the Air Ministry to fly reconnaissance over Syria to keep an eye on the Egyptian bombers. A squadron of Canberras designed for reconnaissance was assigned the mission.

The reconnaissance Canberras were outfitted with a high-resolution camera pod with seven cameras. The pod was mounted forward below the cockpit and triggered by the pilot as the jet overflew the target site. The seven different camera angles could then be combined to give a full picture the target area. Fortunately, the RAF had a photo processing lab on Cyprus, making the entire process fast and seamless.

All was going well on the initial fly-by until a lone Syrian Meteor intercepted the squadron. The squadron broke formation as was protocol. The Syrian pilot took his pick as the bombers scattered and headed for the clouds. He opened fire with the aircraft's four 20 mm Hispano cannons. They tore into the cockpit of one of the Canberras killing the navigator and wounding the pilot and another crew member. The survivors were forced to bail out as the bomber caught fire and plummeted from the sky. The bomber crashed in a ball of fire.

Once they reached the ground, the survivors were captured by the Syrians and taken to Beirut Military Hospital where they were detained until the end of the war.

French Paratrooper Base, Cyprus

Bruno led his entire battalion of paratroopers on an afternoon jog to the beach. He figured the exercise and a quick dip in the Mediterranean would keep their minds off tomorrow's mission and help them sleep that evening. They would need all the rest they could get before the planned jump.

General Massu had volunteered Bruno's battalion for what the Anglo-French generals believed was the toughest part the entire airborne invasion – the capture of Port Fuad and the two bridges that provided access to Port

Said. The commander of the British para units had flinched at the idea of dropping an entire battalion on such a small landing zone surrounded by water. He believed that many of his men might get tangled in their parachute cords and drown in the water if they missed the drop zone. Massu said his paratroopers were experienced at hitting small landing zones and volunteered to take the bridges and port.

Bruno knew that his men had had more practice than the British whose last battalion-sized drop was Operation Market Garden in 1944. Bruno's battalion of paratroopers, on the other hand, had fought in both Vietnam and Algeria since World War II.

The way the French parachuted into a landing zone was different too. The French jumped with access to their weapons, while the British could only access their weapons after they landed. This meant that French paratroopers could fire from the air as they dropped if the landing zone proved to be hot. This gave them a much better survival rate and chance of success. The two bridges were vital to the mission. Without control of the bridges the Egyptian army units could counterattack Port Said from across the Suez.

Completing their run, Bruno and his men crossed the last hill leading to the French Paratrooper camp next to the airfield. In the distance, Bruno could see a lone figure moving toward him. The sun was low on the horizon making it difficult to see but there was something vaguely familiar about the silhouette of the person. It was Brigitte with her rucksack over his shoulder. Bruno ordered his men to complete their run as he stopped to talk with Brigitte. "Little Bruno, I'm so glad I found you," said Brigitte with a smile and a kiss on both of Bruno's cheeks.

"Brigitte, what in hell are you doing here?" said Bruno.

"It's a long and boring story I will tell you over supper. But it's not important right now. When do you jump?"

"Sunrise tomorrow morning. Why?"

"I going to need a parachute."

"You're not going."

"Of course I am."

"Brigitte, this operation is not like the others. There are going to be casualties."

"There's always casualties, Bruno. I know the risks."

"Not this time, Brigitte. You are not going. Not with us."

"Okay. Fine. I will jump with the British and I'll tell their story rather than yours."

"You do that."

"But it will be your fault if I get hurt."

"What do you mean my fault?"

"We both know I would be safer with you. We've jumped four times together. You know me. You know how to keep me safe."

"That's ludicrous."

"But it's the truth."

"God damn it, Brigitte. Why won't you listen to reason?"

"Bruno, it's my job to ignore reason."

Bruno sighed. He knew she was right. She would be safer jumping with the French than the British. He also knew that Brigitte would be fair in her coverage of the paratroopers. Her articles had made him and his men national heroes after the defeat at Dien Bien Phu. "Okay. You can go. But you must obey my commands once we are in the field."

"Great. I snuck in a bottle of wine in my rucksack."

"You are going to get me drunk the night before a jump?"

"Just a little. It'll help you sleep."

Bruno sighed again. Again, she was right. He always had difficulty sleeping the night before a jump. The wine would help. He put his arm around her and they walked back toward the camp. "It's good to see you, Brigitte," he said with a smile.

"You smell like a goat," she said pushing his arm off her shoulder and moving an arm's length away. "A shower before supper please."

"Yes. Yes," said Bruno. "Anything else, princess?"

"Some bread and cheese would be nice with the wine."

"I'll see what I can do."

Brigitte had always been a force to be reckoned with. That's why Bruno liked her so much. They were cut from the same cloth. They understood each other like no one else.

El Gamil Airfield, Egypt

General Salahedin Moguy was the commander of the Egyptian forces in and around Port Said. As a teenager Moguy always dreamed of being a professional cricket player. He practiced every day and had a talent for the game. His family was wealthy and connected. They had other ideas for his future and insisted that he attend the Egyptian military academy.

He was a good student. In fact, he was good at just about everything he did. He believed he could rise through the ranks of the military on his own merits. But that wasn't the way things worked in Egypt and he soon found that his family connections and money were behind his quick rise in the army's hierarchy. He felt somewhat ashamed but didn't refuse when the promotions were offered. He had fought in several wars and distinguished himself. He was an excellent strategist and knew how to motivate those under his command. Now, he was a general facing the biggest challenge of his career. He was about to take on not one, but two Western powers.

Deep inside, he knew the odds were against the Egyptians. He kept those thoughts buried and projected confidence in front of his officers and troops. It was yet another lie but one he could live with to protect his country and his men. He knew his soldiers and the civilian militia would follow his lead. After all, he was a general and knew things that they didn't. They were sure he had a plan to defeat the British and French forces. He did nothing to dispel that wishful thinking. He needed those under his command confident and motivated.

He stood at El Gamil airfield as his troops made last minute preparations for the invasion they knew was coming. A half dozen machine gun nests lined with sandbags had been created around the perimeter of the airfield at strategic points. On the southern side of the airfield, facing the coastline, bulldozers pushed up long berms of sand and dirt to give cover to the hundreds of civilian militia that would fight with their Enfield rifles. The civilians at the airfield were given extra ammunition and instructions on how to track and kill the paratroopers as they descended from the sky. The bullets they were given were tracer rounds that would help them gauge their shots.

Civilians filled hundreds of empty oil barrels with sand and rocks. They rolled the barrels onto the airfield and placed them upright in and around the runway to prevent allied planes from landing. A transport aircraft's wings were high enough off the ground to pass over the barrels but a collision with the landing gear or props could be fatal to the aircraft and crew.

Moguy and his staff had studied the paratroopers tactics and surmised that they would make their assault at night or early in the morning to improve their odds. Floodlights were set up around the airfield to illuminate the British and French troops as they landed.

Gathered around Moguy were the unit commanders of the Egyptain Army and the civilian militia. "This is where it will start," he said. "The French and British will attempt to take the airfield to form an air bridgehead. If they succeed, they will fly in plane after plane of equipment, supplies and reinforcements. There will be no stopping them. The airfield must not fall. There will be no retreat. We hold our positions and fight these foreign invaders to the death."

His officers cheered and praised Allah for the victory they knew would come.

Moguy also knew that the Anglo-French forces must capture the two bridges that connected Port Said and Port Fuad. The bridges were a vital link to the Egyptian forces still position in the Sinai. If they failed to capture and hold the two bridges, Moguy would be able to counterattack when his forces still in the Sinai consolidated. The Egyptians would retake Port Said and drive the Anglo-French forces into the sea like all invaders that had dared to attack Egypt in the past. He had sent his best units to protect the bridges, including tanks and armored cars with machine guns. Moguy knew that the key to victory was to make the Anglo-French pay dearly for every foot of Egyptian soil. Time was on the side of the Egyptians. They just had to hang on until world opinion forced the British and French from their shores.

London, England

Eden was facing a critical cabinet meeting. On the eve of the invasion, the Israelis had faltered. Ben Gurion was worried that the Israelis had been seen as the aggressor in the Suez Crisis and were losing the sympathies of their allies. Israel's ambassador to the United Nations had suggested that Israel might accept the U.N. ceasefire.

The entire premise of the British and French invasion was based on the need to separate the two warring nations and protect the Canal. If the Israelis stopped fighting and accepted the ceasefire, the Egyptians might agree to the same. Nasser believed that in time the U.N. would side with Egypt and force the Israelis to withdraw.

The faces of Eden and his cabinet were long from

worry. Everything that had been achieved would be undone. The British and French would look foolish to the international community for having overreacted to the crisis. "Bloody Israelis. I knew we couldn't trust them," said a cabinet member.

"It was a French plan. They should be responsible for keeping the Israelis in line… if that is even possible," said another member.

"There will plenty of time to deal out blame should our mission fail. Right now we need to decide whether we will go ahead with the invasion with or without the ceasefire," said Eden.

"I don't see how we can proceed if the ceasefire takes effect," said a member.

"I am not sure that's true," said Eden. "We could claim that it is our belief that no matter what the Israelis say, they will not withdraw unless British and French troops are in the country."

"And what about the Egyptians?" said another member.

"They must withdraw from the Canal Zone as we stated in the ultimatum. If not, we will be forced to remove them," said Eden.

"I don't know. It will look very one-sided if we attack the Egyptians for simply exercising the right to protect their country's most valuable asset," said a third member.

"Isn't that what we were planning on doing anyway?" said Eden.

"Yes, but to protect the Canal from the Israelis and the Egyptians. If both sides accept the ceasefire there is little justification for continuing our operation," said the first member.

"The French may not see it that way," said Eden grasping at straws.

"Fine. Then let the French invade without us. Let them take the blame," said another member.

"Well, then… I think we should put it to a vote. Do we

invade if the ceasefire takes effect?" said Eden.

Another cabinet member entered the room. "I have news from New York," he said. "The Israelis have not accepted the terms of the ceasefire."

Everyone in the room cheered, including Eden. "Can I assume that we are unanimous in our decision to carry on with the invasion tomorrow morning?" said Eden.

There was no dissension. The invasion was on.

November 5, 1956 – French Paratrooper Base, Cyprus

Brigitte woke to the sound of dozens of jet engines starting with their high-pitched whine. *The bombers are taking off,* she thought. *The invasion is beginning.*

It would still be many hours before the paratroopers would take off and her with them. It would be her seventh combat jump in her fourth war. So much had happened since she first joined the French resistance in World War II. Back then she dreamed of a different life with a husband and children. Now there was nothing else she would rather do than write about the heroic deeds of the French paratroopers serving their country.

She tried to sleep more but only lay awake staring into the darkness of her tent. She wondered what the day would bring. Would it be her last? She knew there was little she could do to determine if she lived or died once the shooting started. She wasn't afraid. She had survived the siege at Dien Bien Phu. That was terrifying, especially at the end when the French ran out of ammunition and tens of thousands of Viet Minh charged the garrison's trenches.

The ground trembled as the first bomber took off. She smiled to herself almost laughing from the tingle running up her spine. War was like that; both terrifying and exciting.

British Canberra and Valiant bombers formed into squadrons before heading toward Egypt. They would be joined by French fighters providing air cover before they crossed over the mainland.

Mediterranean Sea

It was dark and the seas were frothy. Fifty miles off the coast of Egypt the British aircraft carriers *Eagle*, *Bulwark* and *Albion* and the French aircraft carrier *Arromanches* turned into the wind. Plane after plane took off and formed up into squadrons. Some squadrons would rendezvous with the British bombers passing overhead and act as escorts. Other fighter-bomber squadrons would seek out designated targets and targets of opportunity on their own. The air armada headed inland toward the Egyptian coast. It was the largest aerial assault since the end of World War II.

French and British cruisers, destroyers and frigates moved closer to shore. All guns swung around toward Port Said and Port Fuad. The gunnery crews were excited. Most were too young to have fought in World War II and had never fired their guns at a live target. The idea that people were about to die by their hand was an abstract concept. They were too far offshore to see the actual damage they would cause. Only the rising smoke plumes from the aftermath. Their main targets would be any coastal guns or anti-aircraft batteries that had survived the aerial bombardments. Ships trying to escape the port and any mechanized units were considered targets of opportunity. The battle plan was simple... unleash hell.

The six-inch guns on the cruisers fired first. There was no mistaking the deep roar of the big guns as the start of something ominous. The destroyers and frigates followed with their three and a half inch guns. The broadsides were about mass and shock.

Port Said and Port Fuad, Egypt

Naval shells rained down on the two ports. Coastal guns and anti-aircraft batteries were pounded into oblivion, killing the Egyptian gunnery crews brave enough to man them. The thick clay walls of houses and buildings exploded outward killing the occupants and people running for cover in the streets. Heavy tiled roofs collapsed killing any survivors. Fires broke out everywhere and burned entire neighborhoods. Shells exploded in the city cemetery crushing stone mausoleums and blowing open gravesites.

Israeli Field Hospital, Sinai

Coyle was awake. He had been sleeping for several days, only waking for brief periods. Extreme dehydration had made him feel exhausted and nauseated. He had not been able to eat or drink anything beyond a few sips of chicken soup and some crackers. The doctors had been pumping saline and electrolytes through two intravenous lines in each of his arms. He was finally feeling better and could at least think clearly. His stomach grumbled and he thought about real food for the first time. He considered calling for an orderly but it seemed like too much work. His limbs felt heavy and stiff from lack of movement.

He saw flashes of light through the tent screen window followed by deep rumbles. It sounded like lightning and thunder but there was a popping sound before each rumble and the strikes were too consistent. He knew instinctively it was a bombardment of some sort. He mustered his strength and slide his legs over the edge of the cot. His gown was wet with sweat and stuck to his body. He supposed that sweat was a good sign that his body had been rehydrated. He stood up slowly, wobbling a bit, then steadied himself. He was careful not to tangle the tubes in his arms from the two IV bottles as moved over to the window and looked out.

He could see the coastline and the Mediterranean Sea. The bombardment was far to the West. *Probably Port Said*, he thought. *Must be the start of the invasion Brigitte had been talking about. Brigitte. Where is Brigitte?* He struggled to remember their last conversation. She was going to find Bruno on Cyprus. That meant she was going to jump with his battalion of paratroopers. She was going to jump into that, he thought staring at the bright flashes in the distance. He felt helpless. *At least she will be with Bruno,* thought Coyle. *He'll keep her safe… if possible.*

He had grown to like Bruno over the years, working with him as a transport pilot. He trusted Bruno with his life but didn't trust him with Brigitte. Coyle knew that Bruno, who was Brigitte's former lover, still had feeling for her and would steal her away from Coyle if he got the chance. The funny thing was that Bruno wouldn't even recognize that it was wrong. He would laugh it off like he laughed off anything that went against the grain.

There was nothing Coyle could do about that now. Even if he wanted to find Bruno and Brigitte, he had crashed his C-119 in the desert. He was grounded. He felt nauseated and tired. Even that little walk to the window had depleted his energy. He climbed back into bed, laid his head on the pillow and stared out the window at the rhythmic flashes of light. It was like counting sheep. He dozed off.

Port Said and Port Fuad, Egypt

As the naval bombardment died down, people emerged from their hiding places and tried to help their neighbors, many of whom were trapped beneath collapsed structures. As they dug out the survivors, the civilians heard the deep whine of jet engines approaching. At first many didn't know what it was because there were so many jets and they had never heard such a thing. They discovered the source when they heard the whistle of bombs falling and the terrible explosions that followed. Again, everyone ran for cover, leaving the trapped survivors to fend for themselves.

Unlike the navel shells which seemed to hit randomly around the city, the bombs fells in groups. Explosions walked down the city streets tearing up everything in their wake. Entire streets were engulfed in dust and smoke from dozens of houses and buildings in flames. There wasn't enough water to put out all the fires. People resorted to bucket lines brought in the from the water's edge. Children wailed from fear, coughing from the thick clouds of dust in the air. Fathers and mothers wept at the loss of their spouses and children.

French fighters combed the coastline firing rockets and machine guns at anything that moved. When one of the pilots spotted an Egyptian tank platoon near one of the bridges, the prop-driven fighters swooped in like vultures, their radial engines straining for more speed.

The Egyptain crews abandoned their vehicles and ran for cover. It was a wise choice as multiple rockets tore into the armored cars and tanks. Everything burned. Ammunition inside the burning vehicles cooked off, adding to the rocket explosions. The platoon was obliterated.

The rest of the Egyptain army was busy organizing and preparing. They knew what was coming after the bombardment. The British and French troops would be landing soon, and it was their job to drive them back into the sea. Last minute prayers were said to ensure that God was on their side.

The townspeople that were given weapons retrieved

them from their closets and from under their beds. The frightened civilians struggled to remember their brief training and their hands trembled. They positioned themselves in second and third story windows and balconies as they had been instructed. They would meet the Anglo-French soldiers and the people would have their revenge.

French Camp, Cyprus

It was early morning and still dark. With her rucksack slung over one shoulder Brigitte approached the battalion command tent glowing from the lanterns burning inside. She could hear Bruno giving last minute instructions to his unit commanders. She slipped inside the tent and waited quietly in the back of the group.

Bruno saw Brigitte but was too busy to acknowledge her beyond a slight nod. "Do we have an updated weather report?" he said.

"Mostly clear skies with a five knot wind out of the North," said one of the Intelligence officers.

"Five knots. That's good. We can live with that. Make sure your men know the direction and speed of the wind. It's a tight drop zone with the Canal nearby. We don't need anybody going into the drink. It's water not whiskey."

The officers chuckled. "Okay. Let's get up and get at 'em. Viva La France."

"Viva Le France," repeated the officers snapping to attention and saluting.

Bruno returned the salute and the meeting broke up. Bruno walked over to Brigitte and said, "Once more unto the breach, eh?"

"Once more unto the breach," said Brigitte.

"I thought you might want to sleep in after you finished the bottle last night."

"And miss all the fun?"

"Are you sure you want to go this time?"

"What are you talking about? Of course I want to go. Who else would you have tell your story?"

"I could give you a full report when we return."

"It's not that same as being there, Bruno. You know that. This is my thing. I jump with the para."

"Yes. Yes. And we are glad to have you."

"Is there something you are not telling me?"

"No. No. Everything is fine."

"Really?"

Bruno considered how much to tell her, then said, "The Intelligence is mostly from the British. I don't trust it. It seems overly optimistic. Lacking in detail."

"Are you worried?"

"I am a battalion commander. It is my job to worry. Alright. You will be joining us in our little adventure," said Bruno picking up a parachute pack and handing it to her. "I had the quartermaster ratchet the straps down to the shortest length. It should fit."

"Thank you."

"You'll be jumping with Charlie Company. Find Major Dubois for which aircraft."

"I'm not jumping with you?"

"Not this time."

"You always said it was safer to go first before the enemy got organized."

"Yes. But they know we must take the two bridges connecting the ports. They'll be waiting. It's safer if you jump with Major Dubois."

"Bruno, you don't need to coddle me like a child. I can handle myself."

"Brigitte, can you just do as I say for once? I have to stay focused and I don't have the time for an argument."

"Alright, Bruno. I'll see you on the ground."

"Good luck and don't forget to duck when the shooting starts."

119

"You too, Little Bruno," she said giving him a kiss on both cheeks. She moved off to find the major. Bruno watched after her for a moment like there was something he had forgotten to say. It was too late. She was gone.

With her rucksack over one shoulder and her parachute over the other, Brigitte approached the Nord Noratlas transport plane to which she had been assigned and got in line with the paratroopers climbing through the open doorway. The French-built Noratlas was similar to the American-made C-119 that Coyle flew, but smaller and not as powerful. It held thirty-five paratroopers and one war correspondent in addition to the five-member crew. Like the C-119 Boxcar, it had twin tail booms and two air-cooled radial engines.

Brigitte had flown with Coyle many times in his boxcar and missed him. She had been unable to contact him from Cyprus as communications with Egypt were prohibited. She knew that Bruno, although he would never admit it, missed Coyle too. They had flown dozens of missions together in Algeria, chasing down the Mujahideen.

Even though Coyle's aircraft was just one of many that Bruno commanded, Bruno could always count on Coyle to be where he was needed at the critical moment of an operation. It was just one less moving piece that Bruno needed to worry about. This was the first time in almost two years Bruno was making an airborne assault without Coyle. It felt strange, like a forgotten lucky charm.

With the French paratroopers loaded, the Noratlas started it engines and taxied into its position next to the runway, along with eleven other transport aircraft waiting for the order to takeoff. Four hundred elite paratroopers, the crème of the French Army, would make the jump in Egypt. Not all would return.

FIVE

El Gamil Airfield, Egypt

British Major Ronald Norman and thirty-four airborne troops from Charlie Company rode in a Hastings C-2 transport plane as they approached the Egyptian coastline. Charlie Company was part of the 3rd Battalion of the British Parachute Regiment that had been designated to capture El Gamil Airfield. In all, six hundred and sixty eight British paratroopers would jump that morning.

Norman's beret was tucked into his belt. Once the landing site was secured, he would swap his helmet for the beret. The beret was a symbol of the Parachute Regiment esprit de corps. It wasn't nearly as safe as his helmet but he looked good in it and wore it every chance he got. He felt that a unit commander needed to portray an aura of confidence to the men under his command. Wearing a beret instead of helmet demonstrated his bravado and not his stupidity. In truth, it demonstrated both.

Norman was a veteran from World War II and had seen a great deal of action as part of operation Market Garden and the battle for the bridge at Arnhem. His battalion had almost been wiped out before it was finally forced to retreat back across the river. As one of the few survivors he was a bit of a legend to his men.

While the major basked in the glory of his past exploits, Sergeant Brooks sat at the back of the plane silently praying that he would never see another day like Arnhem. He wasn't a coward. Quite the opposite. He just hated seeing his friends die. He knew death was a part of the job of a soldier but he preferred to dish it out it rather than receive it. That's what made him such a good soldier. He had his priorities straight.

Brooks looked over at Ross sitting across from him next to the door. He looked a little sick. "You okay, Ross?" he said.

"Yeah. Just a little airsick, I think," said Ross.

"If your gonna puke try not get any on the soles of your boots. It makes 'em slippery."

"Okay, Staff Sergeant."

It was more than air sickness that was upsetting Ross. Brooks could hear the fear in Ross's voice. Ross was a member of a platoon about to enter battle. His fellow soldiers needed him to perform his assigned duty for his squad to function properly and survive.

"You're gonna do fine, Ross. Just remember your training and when the shooting starts put one foot in front of the other. That means you're heading in the right direction... forward."

Ross nodded. There was a loud crack like a board breaking outside the plane. Brooks looked out the open doorway. There were black puffs of smoke – anti-aircraft shells exploding around the plane. He could also see streams of tracer bullets streaking by on their way to the heavens. The Intelligence report had said that the British and French air forces had eliminated all of the anti-aircraft batteries along the coastline. Clearly they had missed a few. There was a loud bang on the side of the aircraft like someone had thrown a rock. A piece of shrapnel punched a penny sized hole through the skin of the aircraft. Fortunately it had entered high and nobody was hit. Brooks knew that there was nothing any of the men inside the aircraft could do to protect themselves, but he also didn't want to call attention to the danger. The men in his platoon were scared enough. Instead, he started to sing with his baritone voice, "Oh! I do like to be beside the seaside!

I do like to be beside the sea!

I do like to stroll along the Prom, Prom, Prom!

Where the brass bands play, Tiddely-om-pom-pom!"

The soldiers in the plane could not help but smile at the strange timing of their sergeant's outburst into song and quickly joined in. Even Major Norman sang along.

"So just let me be beside the seaside!

I'll be beside myself with glee

and there's lots of girls beside,

I should like to be beside, beside the seaside,

beside the sea!"

The mood lightened considerably as the men focused on remembering the words to the song rather than the danger they were facing. The red light on the jump indicator switched on, signaling it was time to prepare for their jump. "Stand up!" shouted the jumpmaster standing by the open doorway. The men stood up next to their leg bags but continued to sing. "Hook up!" The paratroopers hooked their parachute release straps to the static line running down the middle of the ceiling of the cargo area. "Move to the door!" The men picked up their leg bags and shuffled toward the doorway, forming a tight line. The singing died down. It was time to focus and for those that were religious to say a final prayer.

Ross was the first in the doorway and would be the first to jump. His leg bag with his rifle case were resting against his leg. He used both hands to hold onto the doorway to steady himself against the wind and keep from falling out. He would pick up the leg bag the moment before he jumped. While the other paratroopers had their weapons in protective cases tucked crossways in their harnesses, Ross had his rifle with its grenade adapter on the muzzle tucked into his leg bag where he thought it was better protected.

He looked out and saw the puffs of black smoke and tracer bullets against the pale predawn sky. It scared him but he was more afraid his mates would see his fear and call him a coward. He looked down into the blackness below. He could barely make out the coastline. He saw dozens of fires burning in Port Said. They were hundreds of houses and buildings that had caught fire during the bombardment. An oil tank beside the port had been hit and was burning sending a black cloud of smoke over the city.

Another fear hit him while standing in the doorway. What if he jumped too soon and landed in the ocean? He knew how to swim but doubted he would last long with all the gear strapped to him. He remembered he was wearing a Mae West life preserver over his harness. It reassured him until another thought filled his mind, *What if there are sharks? I'll be bobbing bait!*

Brooks was right behind him. Seeing the private's wide eyes, the sergeant leaned in and said, "Just do your duty. I'll be right behind you."

Ross nodded. The jump light changed to green and the jump master shouted, "Go!"

Ross didn't move. He wanted to jump but he couldn't move his legs and his hand wouldn't release from the doorframe. He was frozen with fear. Brooks cracked a wicked smile and gave Ross' leg bag a kick out the door. It fell and the strap attached to Ross' harness snapped tight pulling him out the door.

The parachute release strap attached to the static line inside the plane tightened. It pulled out the small pilot parachute and opened the main parachute's cover before it was released. The pilot parachute opened instantly in the one hundred and twenty mph wind and pulled the main parachute away from the back of the harness. The main chute popped open in a white billowing plume. Ross's risers tugged hard against his seat swing and leg straps as the chute snapped all the way open. He felt like someone had kicked him in the ass and he was being lifted up back toward the plane. It was only an illusion. His descent was slowed by the parachute. It wasn't his first jump so he knew what to expect. It was however his first combat jump and he could feel his heart pounding. He reminded himself that if the parachute was going to fail it would most likely be in the first few seconds after opening. He floated downward.

It was still a few minutes before sunrise, and strangely peaceful. He looked around at the hundreds of parachutes floating downward and the planes moving off in the distance. He felt a twinge of pride. He was part of it – the largest airborne operation since World War II. He tried to remember as much detail as possible so he would have a good story to tell those back home if he lived. It was all quite picturesque in the orange-pinkish light of predawn, like an artist's painting. A feeling of peace came over him.

He looked down and could see the crest of waves below his jump boots. He was still above the sea. He began to panic again. He looked out and saw the ghostly image of the white sand beach in front of him and beyond that El Gamil airfield. The wind was carrying him toward the shore at a good clip. He was pretty sure he was going to make it. *Thank God. I hate sharks,* he thought.

Another thought hit him. *What if the Egyptians had mined the beach in preparation for the amphibious landing?* He was going to be blown to bits when he landed and there was nothing he could do. His breathing was rapid and he thought he might hyperventilate. He needed to think about something else. Anything to keep him from panicking.

He thought about his last night in England before he shipped out. Some nurses had built a bonfire on the beach and invited him and a few of his friends in his platoon. The paratroopers brought beer and two bottles of whiskey. They wore their berets. The girls loved the berets and pretended to steal them for their own, especially from a lad they fancied.

One of the girls had stolen his beret and run off. He ran after her but waited until they were out of sight before catching her. They kissed. He unhooked her bra strap as his older brother had taught him. He groped. She moaned. Things were going great until the MPs showed up and hauled them back to base.

He snapped out of the daydream when heard a ZIT-ZIT-ZIT. He looked up at his parachute's canopy. There were three holes in the nylon panels. He could hardly believe it... someone was shooting at him. He looked around and saw hundreds of rifle flashes on the opposite side of the airfield. Bullets zipped past him on both sides. There was still nothing he could do. He would need to land before he could retrieve his weapon from its case and return fire. Like a marionette hanging from his master's strings, he was helpless.

He took another look down to gauge how long before he would land. It was the final one hundred feet. The sand of the beach disappeared. He was over grass, then concrete. He had reached the airfield, exactly where he was supposed to be. He smiled. He wasn't a total loser after all. The concrete looked hard and he knew it was gonna hurt when he landed. He remembered his training and bent his knees so he didn't break his legs. His leg bag landed first with a thump then his jump boots hit. He went limp and tumbled across the runway.

He heard more bullets ricocheting across the concrete and zipping past his head. He decided standing up was a bad idea. He rolled over on his side facing his parachute. The chute took a slight breath and then billowed across the hard ground like it wanted to go back up into the air where it was soft. He had to release his harness to rid himself of the parachute before he could unpack his rifle from its case. He reached up and found the fastener at the front of his chest and released it. He reached down and released the two fasteners on his leg straps. Then he gathered the parachute lines, as he had been instructed.

Parachutes were expensive and the army recycled them after every jump, even combat jumps. The parachute billowed again in the wind pulling the lines out of his hands and fluttered away across the runway. He thought about crawling after it until two more bullets ricocheted off the concrete. *Fuck it,* he thought. *They can take it out of my pay.*

Hundreds of his fellow paratroopers were landing on the airfield. Some had collapsed and were not moving. Most were working frantically to free their weapons and return fire on the hundreds of militia and regular soldiers firing from behind the berm. The Egyptian machine guns were blasting away at the paratroopers still falling from the sky. Many of the paratroopers on the airfield used the oil barrels filled with sand for cover and returned fire by peeking over the top of the barrels. Even a heavy machinegun's spray could not penetrate the sand inside the barrels. The Egyptians had unknowingly saved the lives of dozens of British soldiers.

There were slit trenches scattered all around the airfield with Egyptian soldiers waiting inside to ambush the paratroopers as they landed. As Sergeant Brooks came down, he saw an Egyptian emerge from a slit trench right below him. The quick-thinking sergeant grabbed the line holding his leg bag and swung it backward. The move was perfectly timed. The leg swung in an arc and came back. The heavy bag hit the Egyptain as he fired and knocked his rifle out of his hands.

Brooks landed next to the trench a moment later. His rifle was tucked away. He pulled his dagger from its sheath and lunged at the Egyptain reaching for his rifle. They fought hand to hand. The parachute tugged at Brooks preventing him from stabbing the Egyptain. The Egyptian picked up his rifle and used it as a club hitting Brooks in the side of the head. The Egyptain struggle to chamber another round into his rifle. The dazed paratrooper recovered and plunged his dagger into the Egyptian's chest, killing him.

After checking to ensure that the Egyptian soldier was really dead and no longer a threat, Brooks lay on his back and caught his breath. He found his harness releases and freed his parachute. He slipped down into the slip trench, said a quick prayer of thanks, pulled his leg bag to him and retrieved his weapon. He left the bag in the trench for retrieval later and went searching for his platoon. Unlike the officers, as a platoon sergeant Brooks was still expected to fight. But his highest responsibility was to gather his men scattered across the airfield and turn them into a coordinated fighting unit.

Ross lay flat on the ground, afraid to move. He was being shot at from multiple directions. Bullets were dotting the ground around him. He imagined what it was going to feel like when one of the bullets entered his body, cutting through skin, muscle and bone. The pain. He hated pain. The idea of extreme pain was overwhelming. *Am I a coward?* He thought. *Not if you keep moving.* He snapped out of it.

He recalled his sergeant's advice about putting one foot in front of the other and remembering his training. He saw his leg bag a few feet away, grabbed it and pulled it behind one of the barrels. He pulled out his rifle and removed the cover. He gave it a quick inspection to ensure it wasn't damaged. It wasn't. He had preloaded propellant shells into the magazine since he was the only soldier in his unit with a grenade adapter on the end of his muzzle and the only one who could launch grenades. He dug deeper into his leg bag and pulled out the ten grenades in cases that he had packed. He sorted through them pulling out the fragmentation grenades that he would use against infantry.

A soldier landed next to him. He was screaming. Ross looked over and discovered why. He had been hit in the face while descending. The left side of his jaw was torn from his face and hanging. Ross could barely make out what the soldier was saying, "Oh, God. My face. Is my face okay?"

Ross couldn't break his eyes away from the wounded soldier's face. He was terrified and frozen. "Fire your weapon, private," said a voice from behind him. "Take out that machine gun at two o'clock. It's tearing us to pieces."

Ross turned and saw Brooks kneeling beside him and firing his STEN submachine gun. "Medic," bellowed the sergeant.

"You'll be alright, son. Just stay down and keep quiet until the medic reaches you," said Brooks to the wounded soldier.

Ross looked down at his hands. They were shaking violently and he wondered how he would fire his rifle. "You fire that fucking weapon or I'm gonna shove it up your arse, soldier," said Brooks in the meanest voice he could muster.

Ross nodded and unpacked the first fragmentation grenade. He loaded the grenade on the muzzle adapter, looked in the direction of the enemy fire and picked his target – a machine gun laying down fire across the runway. He set the butt of his rifle on the ground, took aim and squeezed the trigger. Nothing happened. He panicked. Maybe his rifle had been damaged during the jump and was now useless. "Chamber a round, you idiot," said Brooks seeing the confusion in Ross's face.

Ross slid open the rifle's bolt, chambered a bullet into the breach and closed the bolt. Again, he took aim and squeezed the trigger. The rifle fired, sending the grenade into the air. Ross smiled. It was working. The grenade landed short and exploded on the runway near the machine gun. Ross frowned, disappointed. "Keeping going. You'll get it. One foot in front of the other," said Brooks, encouraging him.

Ross became more determined. He remembered his

training, loaded the next grenade and chambered another propellant round. He took aim and adjusted the angle of his rifle. He fired. The grenade landed short again but much closer. He loaded the third grenade, took aim and let it fly. The grenade exploded next to the gunner and loader, killing them both. The machine gun went silent. "At-a-boy," said Brooks. "Now target that line of riflemen behind the berm at the edge of the runway."

"I've only got two more frag grenades," said Ross.

"Then make 'em count."

Ross fired his remaining two fragmentation grenades. The last one was a direct hit behind the berm and killed three militiamen. Seeing their neighbors killed, a dozen of the militiamen around them broke and ran. "Up and at 'em," yelled Brooks to the platoon. The paratroopers jumped up and charged the berm. Out of fragmentation rounds, Ross reloaded his rifle with bullets so it would fire shells like a normal rifle. He jumped up and ran after the other paratroopers toward the berm.

The militia that had remained saw the British charging toward them and broke, joining the others fleeing. The paratroopers climbed over the berm and fired on the retreating militia. Brooks barked out orders breaking the paratroopers into three fire teams; one to pursue the militia and keep them on the run while the two other teams attacked in opposite directions along the berm. Their job was to roll up the flanks while the paratroopers still on the runway keeping the enemy occupied.

With the paratroopers now firing on the enemy from two directions it didn't take long before the entire line of militia behind the berm broke and ran for their lives. The few regular soldiers scattered among them fought on and tried to hold back the paratroopers to little avail. Outnumbered, they too broke and ran.

All enemy resistance was defeated in the first thirty minutes of the battle for El Gamil Airfield. The British were victorious but their losses were heavy. Over twenty paratroopers had been killed and dozens wounded during the drop and assault. Major Norman ordered the airfield secured and sent out reconnaissance patrols to identify the location of the nearest Egyptian forces.

Ross had been with the fire team that had chased after the fleeing militia. The paratroopers had kept up their assault until there were no more targets in sight. The militia had blended back into the civilian population and were hiding in houses and buildings. Ross and the other paratroopers returned to the airfield. He was exhausted and sat down to rest. It wasn't the physical exertion that got to him. He was a paratrooper and in tip-top condition. But he had never in his life had so many emotions pouring through his mind all at the same time. He wanted to cry and laugh but was afraid what his mates and Brooks might think. *That I am ready for the bleeding Loony bin*, he thought.

He walked back onto the runway and found the machinegun nest he had destroyed. There were two Egyptian soldiers lying dead, their bodies shattered from his grenade. He had taken his first human life, two in fact. He hadn't hesitated. He had done his duty. He thought how easy it had been, but how extreme the consequences of his actions. He wondered if they had families. He saw a postcard sticking out of one of the soldier's pockets. He removed it. The card showed a photo of the beach filled with people bathing in the sun and swimming in the sea. The writing on the back was in Arabic. It was already addressed and had an unused stamp. He didn't know to whom it would be sent, but he thought he should mail it. He tucked it in his pocket and moved off.

Ross walked past a paratrooper weeping for his fallen friend dead on the runway. His friend had been shot in the air and was still wearing his harness. His parachute took a breath and rose a few feet off the ground tugging at the lifeless body as if trying to wake its passenger.

Medics were busy tending to the wounded British soldiers. There were dozens; some worse than others. If they were able, the wounded would be patched up and go back to their units to fight on. In the paratroopers every man was needed until the battle was won. A flesh wound or missing finger was not an acceptable excuse.

At the edge of the airfield there was a line of bodies covered with blankets. Ross wasn't sure if they were British or Egyptian, or both. He wasn't sure how he was supposed to feel so he walked on; one foot in front of the other.

He found his leg bag and unused grenades. He realized that he was going to need more ammunition but probably wouldn't get any until the supply planes started landing. He needed to make do with what he had – four anti-tank rounds and one smoke grenade. It wasn't much, especially if they encountered armor.

"Everyone take a swig from your canteens. I don't want ya fainting from dehydration," bellowed Brooks. "This is just the warm up tune. We've got a whole symphony ahead of us." The men obeyed. Their sergeant had kept them alive this far and victorious to boot. They'd follow Brooks anywhere like mutts to their owner.

With Egyptian forces still active in the area in and around the airport's flight path, it was too dangerous for supply planes to land at El Gamil airfield. The supply planes slowed dramatically while landing and became easy targets for snipers and machineguns. Royal Navy helicopters ferried in a small amount of supplies to the British paratroopers.

Ross was able to resupply his anti-personnel grenades and stock up on ammunition for his rifle. Fresh water was also supplied to the British troops. It was the desert and fighting was strenuous. The soldier's uniforms were soaked with sweat after each battle. Dehydration was common. Each soldier needed several liters of water each day to remain functional.

Port Fuad, Egypt

Dozens of transport planes passed overhead with hundreds of parachutes dropping from the sky. Cracks from Egyptian rifle fire were drowned out by the French paratroopers firing back with their machine guns. Unlike the British paratroopers, the French were far from defenseless as they drifted downward and engaged the enemy below.

Bruno was floating down through the black smoke from the oil tank fire. He held his breath until he was clear of the toxic cloud. He looked down and saw one of the bridges he and his men had been ordered to capture intact. There were Egyptian soldiers on the bridge. They hadn't noticed him and his men approaching because of the smoke cloud. His jump boots were fifty feet above the top of its superstructure. He was grateful he wasn't lower or he would have slammed into it. He could see the stretch of riverfront land where he and his men were supposed to land. He could also see several Egyptian troops on the landing zone waiting to engage the paratroopers. They saw Bruno and opened fire. Several bullet zinged past him. Bruno did not have a machinegun or even an officer's pistol. He never carried a weapon into battle. There were two reasons for this strange behavior.

First, Bruno loved to fight. He was naturally aggressive and saw battle as a sporting event to be won, like wrestling or football. Once he became a battalion commander, he had realized that his responsibility was to command his men, not to fight the enemy directly. He had four hundred men jumping with him and their massed fire power was far more important than any damage he could do with his own machine gun or pistol. He needed to focus his attention on deploying his men correctly.

The second reason was morale. War was scary as hell. Bruno realized that his men looked up to him. He was a veteran fighter and a hero. When they saw their commander enter battle without a weapon, their fear diminished. They became more effective. They would follow him anywhere.

At the moment, Bruno was wondering if that was such a good idea. He was also known for being the first one out of the aircraft and that made him the first one to land... without a weapon. He saw there was a raised street that ran along the shoreline. If he could land on that it might buy him a few moments since the street was higher than the river bank and the soldiers would be unable to fire at him. He pulled the riser on one side of his parachute to steer himself toward the street.

A window on the second story of one of the houses on the street opened. A man holding a rifle poked his head out. He was surprised to see the French paratrooper floating past outside his window. He took aim and fired. The shell zinged past Bruno's head, missing him by only a few inches. The man loaded another round. Bruno was getting closer to the window and knew it was unlikely the man would miss again. The man aimed directly at Bruno's chest. Bruno had already been shot in the chest on two different occasions and had miraculously survived. He was not looking forward to the third time. He winced.

A submachine gun above Bruno and to his left fired a burst. The bullets stitched across the front of the house and drove the man with the rifle back inside to seek cover. It was Bruno's radio man, Corporal Charpentier that was firing. He had jumped directly behind Bruno from the plane carrying the battalion's staff. He was firing from his parachute as he floated down. It was tricky business firing accurately from a parachute because of the weapon's recoil and the pendulum effect that it caused. The paratrooper needed to constantly raise his muzzle to compensate for the reverse swing of the parachute. The French regularly practiced this method with live fire exercises. That practice saved Bruno's life.

Bruno landed and tumbled across the cobblestone street. Charpentier landed a few moments later. Bruno was the first out of his harness and ran to the corporal's side. "Corporal, your gun," said Bruno. Charpentier was still unhitching his harness and tossed Bruno his weapon. Bruno turned and opened fire as the first soldier from the shoreline appeared at the top of the stairs. Three bullets from the submachine gun hit him in the face and he fell dead back down the stairs. No more soldiers appeared. "Perhaps next time you will carry a weapon?" said Charpentier realizing how close Bruno was from being killed.

"Why? I have you," said Bruno tossing the weapon back to the corporal now out of his harness and able to fight freely.

The corporal provided covering fire as more and more of the French paratroopers landed near the bridge. Bruno rallied them together and formed a defensive perimeter.

Brigitte was in the last plane and the last to jump. The wind had picked up considerably the moment she jumped and carried her parachute farther down the canal and away from the landing zone where Bruno and his men were organized. She was experienced at steering her parachute but there was nowhere to land next to the Canal. She decided to go for the raised street that paralleled the Canal as Bruno had done. She pulled down on one of her risers and the parachute drifted toward the street.

Fifty feet above the ground, the wind that had been pushing her suddenly stopped and she came up short from reaching the raised street. She slammed into the stone floodwall and fell unconscious. Her parachute caught on a fence post at the top of the wall and kept her from falling into the water. She hung motionless.

Two militiamen from the opposite bank saw her hanging and opened fire. Fortunately, they were lousy shots but it would only be a matter of time until one of their bullet found her.

A bullet ricocheted just a few inches from Brigitte's face and the pinging sound woke her. She didn't know where was. Another bullet ricocheted off the wall. She realized someone was shooting at her and looked across the river to see the two militiamen taking aim with their rifles. She was a sitting duck as long as she hung from her parachute. She pulled and pushed at the release clasps on her legs and chest that held her in the harness but she wasn't strong enough to detach them while her full weight was pressed against them. She pulled out a pocketknife and went to work cutting her harness free starting with her legs. She always kept her pocketknife razor sharp and quickly cut free the two leg straps. She went to work on the chest strap as two more bullets ricocheted off the wall. The knife's blade sliced through the chest strap and she was free of the harness.

She fell down into the water below. She wasn't out of danger yet, but at least she was a moving target now. Bullets streaked through the water around her. She swam underwater as long as she could before coming up for air. It was of little use. The militiamen simply walked along the road keeping pace and taking potshots at her with their rifles. She saw a small boat landing and a set of stairs leading up the wall to the street. She swam toward it. The landing and stairs would offer her little cover but if she could reach the street, she could find a place to hide.

Machineguns fired from her side of the Canal. The militiamen on the opposite bank fled for cover. She couldn't see who was firing. She reached the landing and pulled herself out of the water. Bruno appeared at the top of the stairs with two of his men. "Are you alright?" he said.

"I'm alive. I'll settle for that," she said.

"We need to hurry."

"I just need to catch my breath."

Bruno ran down the stairs and hoisted her over his

shoulder. "You've got to be kidding me," she said as he ran back up the stairs carrying her. He plopped her down at the top of the stairs.

"Piece of pie."

"I think it's piece of cake."

"Yes, but I like pie better. Can you run?"

"Yes."

"Then let's go. We've got a bridge to capture."

Brigitte, Bruno and the two paratroopers ran back to the French defensive perimeter.

El Gamil Airfield, Egypt

The battle for Port Said raged in the distance. Two wounded British soldiers lay by the side of the airfield waiting, as a helicopter was unloaded. They were from the same home town and had known each other since childhood.

As teenagers they competed against each other on their secondary school football team. Both were talented centre forwards and for years, they vied for the spot, one winning one semester and the other taking it away the next.

When they came of age, they both join the army. It was the best way to leave their small town and see the world, not to mention that their uniforms attracted good looking girls. They fought over girls too, especially when they drank. They didn't see their competitiveness as bad. It made them try harder and kept them sharp.

Both had jumped on the airfield that morning and both had been shot; one in the chest and the other in the lower leg. The medics did what they could, but the war was clearly over for these two soldiers. They had done their duty and suffered the consequences.

The one with the chest wound found it hard to breathe. The bullet had pierced his lungs and they were filling with blood. The medic came by every thirty minutes and slid a long syringe into his chest to draw out the blood from his lungs. It made his breathing easier until they once again filled. The last time the medic became concerned when he took the soldier's blood pressure. He was losing a lot of blood and the pressure was dangerously low. He was in bad shape, but so were others. He would have to wait his turn to be evacuated.

His friend had been shot in the lower leg. The bullet had shattered the bone and cut the artery. The medic had to use a tourniquet to stop the bleeding. It hurt like hell. There was a tag on his shirt that read "Amputate." He knew his fate. "Hey, can I have your cigarettes? I don't think you'll be needing them anytime soon."

"Bugger off, ya vulture. They're mine," said the soldier with the chest wound. "I'll give 'em to my dad when I get home."

"When you get home? By then they'll be stale and no good."

"Ya gotta good point," said the soldier with the chest wound, gasping for breath. He opened his shirt pocket and handed his friend a pack of cigarettes. The soldier with the leg wound lit one. "Blow the smoke in my direction. It won't be same but at least I'll get something."

"Don't be an idiot. Ya can hardly breathe as it is."

"You're probably right."

"I'm completely snookered this time," said the soldier with the leg wound. "What girl's gonna want a one-legged man."

"Oh, I don't know. How about a one-legged girl?" said his friend.

"Get stuffed, ya bastard."

They laughed and fell silent for a few moments, then… "Ya think I'll be able to buy shoes at half the price? I'll only need the one."

"Don't be daft. They don't sell shoes that way. They come in pairs. You gotta find someone missing a leg on the opposite side."

"How am I supposed to do that?"

"You could try the personals in the newspaper."

"Yeah but what if we ain't got the same size feet?"

"I suppose one of you could stuff the toe with newspaper."

"That could work."

"Might wanna run a personal ad for that for the one-legged girl too."

"Push off, ya bloody prick."

Again they laughed. Two old friends in a world of hurt.

"Well," said his friend in between fits of coughing. "At least we'll be home for Christmas." He coughed heavily, trying to catch his breath. A few moments he stopped breathing and slumped over. His buddy called for the medic. There nothing he could do.

Port Fuad, Egypt

There were two companies of paratroopers with Bruno and two more at the other bridge farther down the Canal. The commander in charge of taking the second bridge radioed to Bruno that the Egyptians had badly damaged the bridge making it unusable. It would require extensive repair. That made Bruno's mission to capture the remaining bridge all the more critical. He asked the commander if he could use the bridge to access the opposite shore with his men. The commander replied that he could.

Two platoons of Bruno's most experienced paratroopers had parachuted onto a football field on the opposite side of the river. Bruno knew that the best way to take a bridge was from both sides. He ordered the commander of the second bridge assault force to join the two platoons already on the opposite side. They would coordinate simultaneous attacks on both sides of the bridge. With luck, the militia that made up a good part of the Egyptian force would flee once they realized they were being attacked from two sides and could be boxed in by the French.

Bruno and his company commanders surveyed the enemy positions on the bridge. Things had changed unexpectedly and they needed to come up with a new plan for the assault.

The Egyptian forces protecting the bridge had built up sandbag fortified positions with heavy machine guns on both sides of the bridge. There was no way around them. To take the bridge the French had to take out the machineguns. But the biggest challenge was the T-34 tank positioned in the middle of the bridge. It could fire in either direction to support the Egyptian infantry. The Egyptians must have moved it onto the bridge during the night; it hadn't shown up in the reconnaissance photos taken yesterday.

His battalion had several anti-tank guns. Bruno's men needed to be careful not to damage the bridge too severely. It was a truss bridge. A misplaced anti-tank shell could damage one of the beams and destabilize the bridge or even collapse it into the Canal. Because the tank was in the middle of the bridge, there was no way to sneak up on it. The bridge's truss superstructure over the bridge prevented British and French aircraft from destroying the tank. It would require a frontal assault by the lightly armed paratroopers. The losses would be heavy. Bruno was the most experienced soldier in the battalion but that never stopped him from accepting a better plan from his subordinates if it could save some of his men's lives and still achieve the objective. Bruno asked for suggestions. There were none.

Brigitte stood nearby taking notes on a pad of paper the radio operator had given her. Her notebook had been lost with her leg bag when she cut free her parachute harness over the river. She was hesitant to say anything, but she did have an idea that might work to take out the tank without putting too many men in harm's way. She was a journalist and supposed to be neutral. She was also patriotic and had previously jumped into battle with many of these men. She cared about them. Brigitte knew how to fight. She had been a member of the French underground during the Nazi occupation. She was experienced with homemade weapons and had participated in several attacks on German patrols, bridges and trains. "What about using Molotov cocktails?" she said.

"I don't think that is going to help, Brigitte. We still need to get close enough to throw them." said Bruno.

"Use the bridge's trusses. Your men can climb up and move across without exposing themselves to machinegun fire. That tank is a T-34. The firing angles on its main gun and machine guns are limited. Once your men reach a certain height they should be safe from enemy fire."

"That's not a bad idea," said one of the commanders. "And the fire wouldn't damage the bridge as long as it was small."

"I don't think Molotov cocktails are going to be enough to force them to abandon their tank," said Bruno. "They'll wait out the fire."

"You're probably right. But I bet they open the hatch to vent the smoke," said Brigitte. "You could drop grenades down from the top of the trusses."

Bruno and the commanders exchanged glances. *Why didn't we think of that?* "Alright. We will give it a shot. But I think we should also have a plan B just in case Brigitte's plan doesn't work," said Bruno.

"Oh ye of little faith, Little Bruno," she said.

"No, just pragmatic," said Bruno. "First things first. We need to secure both ends of the bridge before we can deal with the tank."

Bruno laid out a plan to take both ends of the bridge.

Avoiding the street that paralleled the Canal where they could be fired on from the enemy troops on the bridge,

Bruno and his paratroopers used the side streets and alleyways to maneuver their way in front of the bridge.

As the paratroopers moved through the side streets, militiamen armed with rifles appeared in the upper windows and balconies of houses and buildings as they had been instructed. Most militiamen only took one shot before ducking back inside. Those that were more persistent ended up being riddle with submachinegun fire or with a French grenade tossed through their window and killing everyone inside. The French leapfrogged from position to position as one squad protected the one advancing then vice versa.

When they reached the foot of the bridge, the French paratroopers entered the buildings on both sides of the street. Anyone that stood in their way was shot and killed.

As a general rule, the French paratroopers were few in number and usually fighting a well-armed force. Having no men to spare guarding prisoners, they did not take any, unless they wanted information. When it was safe to do so, they would disarm their captives and let them go, but for the most part they just shot them and moved on. The paratroopers gave no quarter and asked for none themselves. It was a brutal approach to modern warfare.

After the atrocities of combat committed during World War One, civilized nations had set up conventions to create rules that would govern war. The French had signed the international accord and for the most part obeyed the rules by having their armed forces take prisoners and treat them humanely. But the French and other nations turned a blind eye when it came to their paratroopers who were always outnumbered and lightly armed. There was no time or patience for rules. For a paratrooper warfare was about survival. Bruno knew this and accepted it.

The French set up firing positions in the windows and on the rooftops of the buildings around the entrance to the bridge. This gave them a downward firing angle on their enemy plus they could more easily identify their enemy's positions. It was an advantage they had learnt to exploit. Bruno wondered why the Egyptian commander had not placed better troops in the buildings. He guessed that the best troops were probably on the bridge or being held in reserve for a counterattack.

When the French opened fire from new positions, all hell broke loose as the two sides exchanged fire. The Egyptian soldiers seemed genuinely surprised that the French had set up fortified positions so close to the bridge.

A group of militia, led by a café owner, tried to retake one of the buildings from the French. Bruno had suspected this might happen. He had stationed two of his paratroopers to guard the bottom floor of the building. The militia had two grenades and a dozen men armed with rifles. Everyone attacked at the same time. The riflemen rushed in through the front and back doors while the two men with the grenades threw them through the windows before running inside.

The two French paratroopers saw the grenades and merely ducked behind the corners of the walls until the grenades exploded. The grenade fragments killed six of the militiamen already in the building. It was an amateur's mistake. The paratroopers pivoted back around the walls and opened fire with their submachineguns. It was a massacre as the French paratroopers mowed down the inexperienced civilians trying to return fire with their rifles. It took less than a minute and the skirmish to retake the building was over. There were no Egyptian survivors.

The Egyptian forces on the bridge used the metal beams of the bridge's trusses as cover. They also used the stairs and stone walls leading to the bridge. There was a guardhouse that was quickly taken out by a French grenade launcher with a lucky shot through a firing port.

The Egyptian soldiers stationed inside the sandbagged machinegun position fared better than most. It provided good cover from all sides. The French tried to mortar the machinegun crew several times but kept hitting a telephone pole next to the sandbags. The mortar shells would explode tearing wires from the pole and showering the troops below with sparks but doing little actual damage.

The tank in the middle of the bridge was shelling both sides, swinging its turret around, firing three or four shots, then swing back around the other direction and firing again. Its 85 mm gun had a muzzle velocity of 2,600 feet per second and could penetrate 3.6 inches of sloped steel. The high explosive shells it was using were punching holes in the building walls like they were made of cheese and taking its toll on the paratroopers inside.

Bruno was frustrated and cursing like a sailor. The assault was taking too long. The Egyptians could send reinforcements at any minute. If more tanks arrived, the paratroopers would be in trouble and forced to retreat back into the city. He needed to do something to break the stalemate. He ordered his men to ceasefire and reload their weapons. They would try a Big Push.

He ordered three of his best grenade throwers to load up their bandoleers with as many grenades as they could carry. Their orders were simple... when the shooting started again they would close their distance on the machine gun position and throw as many grenades as possible until the position was silenced. It was a sobering order and Bruno knew it.

When he had become a commander, he had promised himself to never order one of his men to do something that he himself would not do. He picked up a bandolier of grenades and said he would lead them. His men were horrified and tried to talk him out of it. Several officers volunteered to take his place but Bruno would not have it. In his mind, it was his time to put up or shut up. He also knew that the three men would stand a much better chance if he was beside them.

Brigitte pleaded with him, "Your men need you, Bruno. It's a suicide mission."

"Not if we win," said Bruno.

Bruno and his three grenadiers slipped outside the building and moved as far forward as they dared. They readied their first grenade in their throwing arms and their second grenade in the opposite hand. They had no other weapons so they could run faster. They were totally reliant on their fellow paratroopers to give them covering fire.

Brigitte watched from a second story window and held her breath. She could feel her heart pounding and fought back the tears. *This is who Bruno is*, she thought. *It's why you love him.* The realization surprised her.

Bruno waited until the tank fired three rounds and started turning its turret in the opposite direction. He signaled his men to open fire. It was a massive volley and forced the Egyptians to duck behind their cover.

Four paratroopers hurled smoke grenades from the rooftop. The canisters landed and spewed smoke, obscuring the French positions. Bruno ran toward the machinegun nest. His men followed. When he thought he was close enough he pulled the pin on the first grenade and threw it. The men with him did the same. All four grenades landed short and exploded. They ran closer. They threw their second grenades while on the run. One of the grenades landed by the side of the machinegun nest and exploded. It didn't do any damage but it meant they were in range.

Then came the hard part. They stopped running and took aim with their next set of grenades. They were in the open where even a child with a peashooter could have hit them. The paratroopers behind them poured on the covering fire.

An Egyptian with a rifle peaked above a wall and took aim. Bruno saw him from the corner of his eye and threw one of his grenades in the man's direction. The soldier ducked back down behind the wall until the grenade exploded. Bruno took his second grenade and heaved it with everything he had toward the machinegun nest. His grenade landed inside and exploded, killing the gun crew. Bruno waved his paratroopers still in the buildings forward. They filed out of the building and charged, firing their submachineguns as they ran.

The Egyptian soldiers at the mouth of the bridge broke and ran. The paratroopers took over the Egyptain firing positions but switched direction so they were pointing their weapons toward the bridge. The French had taken the entrance to the bridge. It didn't take long before the Egyptian troops on the opposite side of the bridge also fled from the coordinated attack.

The French had both sides of the bridge. Only the tank in the middle remained. It had stopped firing and was strangely silent. Bruno thought it might be running low on ammunition. When a squad of paratroopers attempted to advance on to the bridge the tank's machineguns opened fire, driving the Frenchmen back. The tank was still very dangerous and needed to be dealt with.

Two paratroopers carrying rucksacks on their backs climbed the bridge's support beams at a forty-five degree angle. When they reached the top beam they crawled on their bellies toward the center of the bridge. The metal beam served as cover from the tank's machineguns. That didn't keep the tank crew from trying to knock them down with several bursts. When the tank's machine gun could no longer fire at the paratroopers because of the angle, the tank commander popped out of the top hatch and used his rifle to take pot shots at the two paratroopers.

Bruno and his men saw what the tank commander was doing and opened fire driving him back inside the tank. He closed the hatch.

When the two paratroopers reached the center of the bridge, they opened their satchels and pulled out the Molotov cocktails. They lit the gas-soaked rags on three of the fire bombs and dropped them down on top of the tank. The glass bottles shattered, spreading gasoline all over the top of the tank and setting it on fire. The heat was intense and rose up to the paratroopers on the bridge trusses. The underside of the beams acted as heat shields offering their bodies protection but their hands holding on to the beams suffered second degree burns. They held their positions, roasting like chickens on a spit.

After a couple of minutes, the tank hatch opened and the commander again stuck his head out to get a breath of fresh air. Smoke from inside the tank poured out.

The two paratroopers fished out the grenades they had in their rucksacks. They synchronized their efforts knowing that once the tank commander realized what they were trying to do he would retreat back inside and close the hatch. They pulled the pins on the grenades at the same time and tossed them down toward the open hatch. One grenade hit the tank commander in the shoulder and bounced to the bridge deck. The other grenade hit the hatch and bounced onto the back of the tank. The tank commander dove back inside and closed the hatch before both grenades exploded harmlessly. The paratroopers had more grenades but they would be of little use against the outside of the tank.

Seeing the failed attempt Brigitte cursed. It was time for plan B. Bruno gave the two paratroopers a hand signal. They nodded agreement and went to work. Plan B was dangerous. One of the paratroopers opened the second rucksack they had carried to the top of the bridge. He pulled out a coil of rope and a satchel charge filled with almost nine pounds of TNT. The other paratrooper pulled out a box of baking soda and sprinkled it on the fire directly below them. The concern was that the fire could ignite the satchel charge before they were ready. The fire tapered off but didn't go completely out. A paratrooper let the rope down until it touched the deck of the tank beside the turret. He tied off the rope on the beam and pulled it up. Then he tied the satchel charge to the end of the rope. He turned to the other paratrooper to ensure he was ready. He nodded. The first paratrooper pulled the wire ignitor on the side of the satchel charge and lowered it down to dangle next to the tank. The fuse was only one minute. The two paratroopers stood up, walked to the edge of the truss and leaped off. They landed in the river, floated down with the current until they were at a safe distance and swam ashore.

The satchel charge exploded in a ball of flame and shook the bridge. When the smoke cleared, the French paratroopers cheered. The explosion had ripped the turret off the chassis. It lay on its side like a half opened can of peaches. No one could have survived the explosion. "Nice plan B," said Brigitte conceding to Bruno with a bit of a snarl.

"Piece of pie," said Bruno giving her a one-armed hug around the shoulders.

The French had their bridge.

Bruno supervised the rebuilding of the Egyptian defenses and added a few more of his own, including two more sandbag firing positions for the anti-tank guns on each side of the bridge. He also had his men reoccupy the buildings around both entrances to the bridge. With only one bridge to protect, the French were able to combine their forces and put together a strong but lightly armed defense. When the counterattack came, they would be ready.

The aircraft flying overhead would need to deal with any armored element the Egyptians might throw at the French. The French pilots were more experienced than their British counterparts because they had been fighting in both Indochina and Algeria. It was still a gamble when mixing ground troops with fighter-bombers. Accidents were common. At four hundred mile an hour it was hard for the pilots to tell which uniform was which since both were usually kaki. Armored units were a little easier because the Egyptians were mostly using Russian equipment and it had a very distinct look from the French and British vehicles.

With the defense for the bridge well on in hand, Bruno broke off one of the companies. There was still another objective that was considered vital to capturing the city – the waterworks. Port Said and Port Fuad were desert communities that had access to the waters of the Nile. The water was however polluted and needed to be purified before it was drinkable. The people living in the cities were dependent on the government water supply. The waterworks controlled the water. It was of vital importance that the waterworks not be destroyed during the invasion. Once the cities fell, the French and British would be responsible for the civilian population and that meant supplying them with water, not to mention food. It also meant that before the Egyptians surrendered, water was a weapon that could be used to break the will of the people. The militia and troops would not last long without water. The French were given the task of capturing the waterworks for Port Fuad while the British were responsible for Port Said.

Brigitte prepared to move with Bruno. "We are not going to be long. Maybe you should stay here. There could be a tank battle for you to cover," said Bruno.

"Maybe you should sit on a bayonet," said Brigitte.

"That doesn't sound pleasant. Suit yourself. We move out in five."

Bruno and the rest of his company advanced toward the waterworks next to the pipeline from the Nile. Brigitte stayed close to the radio operator. She could pick up bits of story when Bruno called in an artillery strike or airstrike or reported to Central Command on the *HMS Tyne*. There was so much going on during a battle it was difficult to keep up. The radio operator was also always close to the unit commander. He was the center of communication during any operation.

The resistance was light as they advanced. A few civilians opened their windows to take a potshot with their rifles but they were such lousy shots nobody in the French company really worried. The paratroopers would simply fire a burst of machinegun fire and the civilians would disappear back inside their houses rarely to reemerge like they had done their duty and had had enough.

The Egyptian commander had placed an entire company of soldiers to defend the waterworks compound. There were four light machine guns placed on each of the corners of the main building's roof. Below there were two more machinegun firing positions at the top of the front and back steps of the building. Infantry had dug slit trenches around the entire building like a castle's moat and had taken up firing positions inside them. There was also an anti-aircraft gun on the edge of the compound surrounded be a triple layer of sandbags. The weapon's 20 mm shells could easily rip through the paratrooper ranks and would be a high priority target when the assault began.

The simplest solution would have been for the French to call in an airstrike to take out the Egyptian positions. But that was out of the question. The French could not afford to damage the facility or the feeder pipelines. Like the bridge, the solution for the capture of the waterworks required finesse.

As with the assault on the bridge, the paratroopers captured and occupied the surrounding buildings. The buildings' rooftops would provide an equal firing platform against the machineguns on the rooftop of the waterworks building and allow the paratroopers to provide covering fire against the anti-aircraft gun.

Bruno placed his headquarters inside one of the buildings that his paratroopers had occupied. His radioman positioned himself and the radio behind a reception desk made of thick wood. Bruno also placed a machine gun in one of the front windows of the building. He asked Brigitte to stay inside when the shooting started.

It was safer, and she could still get a good view of events through the windows. When she objected, he said that he needed to stay focused during the battle and didn't want to worry about her. She reluctantly agreed.

The Egyptians opened fire as soon as they saw the French soldiers. The shooting only stopped when the Egyptians ran out of targets. Their ammunition was limited and they did not want to waste it. The French held their fire from the start. Most of the paratroopers were armed with submachine guns which only had an effective range of one hundred yards. While they might offer covering fire when one of their fire teams advanced, it really was a long shot that they would hit something until they were within range. The paratroopers did not like pointless activities. Everything they did had purpose. That's what made them so effective. When they moved to assault a position, it was a safe bet that they were going to find a way to take it... one way or another.

The French assault started on the Western side of the compound where the Russian-built ZPU-2 anti-aircraft gun was located. The twin gun barrels fired six hundred rounds per minute of 14.5 mm high velocity shells which made it a formidable weapon against both aircraft and ground assaults. The shells would rip through multiple walls of almost any building and could even collapse a building if it hit the supporting beams.

The motors that swung the heavy gun around on its platform were operated by battery power and their operation slowed as the batteries were depleted. The bulky ammunition magazines mounted below the barrels prevented the gunner from seeing troop movements on the horizon. The paratroopers were actually safer the closer they got to the gun which was designed for long-range targets.

Bruno had all of his machineguns, mortars and recoilless rifles focus their fire on the anti-aircraft gun. The throwing of three smoke grenades in the direction of the twin-barreled gun signaled the advance of the paratrooper fire teams assaulting the position. As the smoke engulfed the anti-aircraft gun the gunner fired wildly in whatever direction he thought the French might advance. The guns on the rooftop of the waterworks had a better viewing angle on the French assault and weren't hampered as much by the smoke.

Bruno ordered the machineguns, mortars and recoilless rifle teams to refocus their fire on the other threats shooting at the advancing paratroopers. He took a quick measurement of the wind coming off the sea and ordered his mortar crews to fire smoke grenades on to the rooftop of the waterworks building. It would obscure the Egyptian firing positions but also blind the Egyptians while the paratroopers made their assault. It was more important at the moment to take out the anti-aircraft gun than the Egyptian machineguns. The reason became obvious a few moments later...

A strong gust of wind cleared the smoke around the anti-aircraft gun. The gunner saw a burst of machinegun fire come from the window where Bruno's headquarters was stationed. The gunner swung his big gun around and opened fire.

The shells designed to take down an aircraft stitched their way across the front of the building taking baseball sized chunks out of the stucco masonry.

Inside the building, Brigitte watched in horror as the shells passed through the exterior wall like it was paper and killed the machinegun crew at the window. The furniture was torn to shreds but the bullets still didn't stop. They hit the back wall of the room and continued their journey. Brigitte saw the stream of bullets heading straight for her. There was no place to hide. She dove to the floor and lay as flat as possible. The bullets passed over, covering her with bits of plaster and paint from holes punched through the front wall. Her face was turned away from the wall. She opened her eyes for a moment to see the bullets stitching across the reception desk. She heard a grunt. The barrage stopped.

There was silence. The anti-aircraft gun had turned its fury at another target. Brigitte crawled over to the machine gun crew. They had been torn to shreds and were dead. She belly crawled back to the reception desk and peaked around the edge. The radio had a hole in the center of it and was sparking. It was destroyed. She looked over at the radio operator lying on the floor. His arm had been blown off and was bleeding badly. His shirt below the chest was soaked in blood. Brigitte knew the man had been gut shot by the large caliber bullet. It had passed all the way through him destroying his insides as it traveled. "Can't feel my legs," said the radio operator.

Brigitte realized that the bullet had probably snapped his spinal column as it exited his body. It was a strange blessing. His focus was on the lack of feeling in his legs not his arm or stomach wounds. There was a lot of blood around him on the floor. Brigitte crawled through the blood and cradled the operator's head in her arms. She had seen death many times when she worked in the field hospital at Dien Bien Phu before the garrison finally fell. Men died by the hundreds. She could see by his wounds and the amount of blood the radio operator had lost that he didn't have long. The operator looked over at the radio still sparking and said, "Radio's a goner. Bruno's gonna be pissed."

"He'll get it over it."

"Guessing I won't be dancing again," said the man looking down at the bullet wound in his belly.

"Do you like dancing?" said Brigitte trying to take his mind off his wounds.

"Yeah. In the summer. In the park. Girls wearing their best dresses. Band playing. Bar selling small glasses of wine and plates of cheese with bread."

"Sounds like heaven."

"It was," said the operator and he died.

Brigitte closed his eyelids and laid his head down gently. She shed a few tears and let herself feel the loss of all of the fallen. She cried for exactly one minute. That was all she would allow herself before getting back to work. She crawled back to the window and watched the battle.

The paratroopers had overrun the anti-aircraft gun position and killed the gun crew. Fire from the rooftop machineguns rained down on the paratroopers. Bruno ran up with a squad of reinforcements and surveyed the situation. His men wouldn't last long if he didn't do something. He pushed the dead anti-aircraft gunner out of the way and climbed into the operator's seat. He had no idea how to fire the weapon but figured he could learn through experimentation. He pushed the two pedals on one side of the gun mount and the gun pedestal swung from side to side using an electric motor. He whipped the guns around toward the waterworks building. He pressed the pedal on the opposite side of the gun and both barrels fired taking out a window on the second floor of the building. He turned the wheel on the left side of the gun mount and the two barrels moved up and down in unison. The wheel on the left side controlled the gun from right to left without swiveling it on the mount. The gun's sight was unusually large. He took aim at the light machine gun on the left side of the waterworks roof. He pushed the trigger pedal and the guns fired with a gut-wrenching thump-thump-thump. He stopped almost as soon as he started when he realized that his aim was too low. He adjusted the position of the guns to where he thought they should be and tried again.

The edge of the roof dissolved in a cloud of dust and flying debris. He fired a two-second burst which equaled about forty shells and released the trigger. He waited until the dust cleared. The entire corner of the roof was gone. There was no sign of the machinegun or its crew. His men cheered. He smiled. He liked the weapon. More machinegun fire rained down from the opposite side of the roof. Bruno whipped the gun around and took aim. He was getting the hang of it.

The Egyptian machinegun crew had seen what happened to the other crew and decided to flee their position before Bruno could fire. He was disappointed but fired the gun anyway to destroy the machinegun in case they changed their minds. His aim was dead on, and the edge of the building dissolved in a puff of dust.

The third machinegun at the front of the waterworks was a much trickier shot. It was located on the top of the stairs by the front door to the building. He was worried that the anti-aircraft gun's shells would penetrate the building and damage some of the machinery inside. His orders were to avoid any damage to the water system. He leveled the anti-aircraft gun barrels in hopes that the threat of being torn to shreds might be enough to scare the machinegun crew in fleeing. It wasn't. They held their ground and continued to fire on Bruno and his men. They would have to take out the machinegun the old fashioned way.

Bruno didn't want to leave the gun for the Egyptians to use in the future. He removed a grenade from his pocket and placed it near the weapon's trigger. He pulled the pin and watched the grenade's spoon flip away arming the grenade. He hopped off the anti-aircraft gun and ran for cover. The grenade exploded shearing off the trigger mechanism and rendering the weapon useless.

Bruno wasn't concerned about the machineguns or troops that were not in the fire line of his soldiers. They could be easily dealt with once his paratroopers occupied the building. But the machinegun at the front of the building was a big problem. It had a clear field of fire of the entire front of the compound. A frontal assault would cost the lives of a lot of paratroopers. He reassessed the situation and decided that the best way to take out the enemy machinegun position was to use the slit trenches around the building currently occupied by Egyptian soldiers and militia.

While basic slit trenches provide good cover for infantry forces, they were disastrous when the enemy advanced close enough to use grenades accurately. The grenade's shrapnel killed men on both sides of the explosion inside the confined area of the trench. There was no place to run for cover unless the soldiers left the trench and exposed themselves to enemy gunfire. Bruno only planned on occupying the trenches long enough to take out the machinegun position.

The second phase of the assault on the waterworks started with the French mortars firing smoke grenades to cover the paratroopers advance. The French belly-crawled toward the slit trenches on the Eastern side of the building and rolled grenades over the edges. Several Egyptians were killed by shrapnel and the rest retreated back down the trench to the back of the building. The paratroopers allowed them leave unmolested. They knew the Egyptian soldiers would be much easier to deal with once the building was captured and the paratroopers could use the windows and doors as protected firing positions.

With the position overrun, the French climbed into the trench and used it to advance closer to the machinegun position at the front of the building. Within grenade range it was a simple task of pitching multiple grenades over the sandbags until the weapon went silent. They charged forward to find the gun crew dead and the machinegun disabled. They swapped out the damaged machinegun with one of their own and reused the firing position to fend off the counterattack that they knew would come.

More grenades were pitched through the front door and windows. After waiting for the explosions, the French rushed into the building and took over the bottom floor. As planned, they attacked the machinegun position on the back steps by simply opening up the back door and opening fire with their submachineguns. The remaining

Egyptian soldiers on the outside of the building were driven from the trenches.

With the bottom floor of the building secured, the paratroopers fought their way up the stairs, clearing each of the three floors until they reached the roof access doorway. The Egyptians machine gunners and riflemen had turned their guns around and were waiting for the paratroopers to come through the doorway. More mortar smoke shells hit the rooftop, creating a thick cloud. Unable to see, the Egyptians opened fire on the doorway. The paratroopers waited inside, using the stairs for cover.

When the machinegun fell silent after using up all their ammunition, the French burst through the doorway and opened fire with their submachine guns killing the Egyptian soldiers. It was a one-sided battle with only two paratroopers getting wounded. The Egyptians lost over a dozen men with any wounded being quickly dispatched by the French.

French engineers did an inspection of the waterworks and determined that the water distribution system was intact. They then shut off the water to the city of Port Fuad.

Bruno returned to the building where Brigitte was hiding to report the successful capture of the waterworks to the command center on the *HMS Tyne*. When he saw Brigitte covered in blood he panicked, thinking she had been wounded. She told him about his radioman. Bruno was saddened by the loss. He inspected the radio and found it useless. Without the battalion radio set he could not communicate with his commander to report his status. But even worse, he could not call in artillery or airstrikes if the Egyptians counterattacked. "I've got to get back to the bridge," said Bruno. "They have a backup radio set."

"I'll go with you," said Brigitte.

"I'd argue, but I know it's useless."

"You're learning, Little Bruno. That's good."

157

Bruno gave instructions to the company captain to defend the waterworks at all costs. In addition to Brigitte, he took two paratroopers with him, armed with submachine guns.

SIX

Washington D.C., USA

Eisenhower was meeting Admiral Burke and Allen Dulles in the Oval Office. He was tired of the competition between the CIA and the Navy over Intelligence. He wanted them cooperating rather than competing. He knew it was a lost cause but decided to try anyway in the hopes that reason, coupled with patriotism, would outweigh personal interests.

There was a knock at the door. A naval messenger entered and handed a signal to Admiral Burke.

"In the spirit of Intelligence sharing... Naval intelligence picked up some radio traffic from a group of British pilots returning from a bombing run. They're reporting that a Russian MiG 15 strafed British paratroopers at El Gamil Airfield," said Burke after dismissing the messenger.

"How can they be sure it was Russian and not Egyptian?" said Eisenhower.

"Apparently the fighter had Russian decals."

"It's still possible it was Egyptian. We have reports that several of the MiG 15s have not been repainted since they were delivered," said Allen Dulles.

"I suppose that's possible," said Burke. "It could also be a Syrian pilot. We have reports that a Russian cargo ship unloaded one hundred and twenty-five MiG fighters, one hundred tanks and one hundred and twenty artillery guns at a Syrian port for eventual deliver to Egypt when things calm down."

"Jesus," said Allen Dulles. "Talk about pouring fuel on a fire. Where's this gonna stop?"

"An escalation by the Soviets would be unfortunate to say the least. But I think it is important that we don't overreact to rumors. Let's confirm what we think we know," said Eisenhower. "Gentlemen, now more than ever we need to be rowing in the same direction and sharing Intelligence so we don't duplicate our efforts. Do I make myself clear?"

"Yes, Mr. President," said Allen Dulles and Burke rising to leave the office.

In the hallway outside the Oval Office, Admiral Burke and Allen Dulles passed Foster Dulles on his way in to see the president. They exchanged pleasantries for a moment, then continued their separate ways. Before parting, Admiral Burke turned to Allen Dulles and quietly said, "Are we really going to share Intelligence?"

"Hell no," said Allen Dulles as he moved off toward his office.

Foster Dulles entered the Oval Office and said, "What was that all about?"

"An attempt at inter-agency cooperation," said Eisenhower.

"Sharing Intelligence? Go luck with that."

"Yeah, well… we fight the good fight."

"Of course, Mr. President."

"So what's so urgent?"

"We just received a letter from Khrushchev through the Russian embassy. I thought you should see it right away." Foster Dulles handed him a copy of the letter. "Khrushchev is asking America to join the Soviet Union in a bi-lateral military task force to kick the British, French and Israelis out of Egypt."

"He can't seriously think we would attack our own allies?" said Eisenhower reading the letter.

"No. I don't think that is the purpose of the letter."

"What is it then?"

"He's building a case with the international community that America is secretly conspiring with its allies to destroy Egypt."

"Shit."

"When you turn down his offer he will claim it is evidence of America's collusion."

"So, I won't respond."

"I doubt that will do much good. He'll claim your non-response is even more evidence you are secretly colluding."

"There is another possibility that we should consider..."

"Which is?"

"He could be preparing to attack our allies on his own and he's trying to put us between a rock and a hard place."

"Yes. But I don't think the Soviets are looking for a war beyond the Middle East."

"They won't need to. Not if they attack Britain and France within the theatre of war. Keep the conflict confined."

"You mean Cyprus?"

"Yes. The Soviets have medium range missiles that could reach Cyprus. If they were armed with conventional warheads, I would image they could do quite a bit of damage."

"And their ships in the Mediterranean?"

"High-altitude bombers would be my guess."

"And Israel?"

"All of the above."

"Do you think that would stop the invasion?"

"Maybe. But it would certainly require a response from us. Britain and France would demand it, not to mention the other NATO members."

"World War III without nukes?"

"I am afraid that would be like trying to close Pandora's Box," said Eisenhower, deeply concerned.

"So what do we do?"

"Keep the balls in the air until we find a solution."

"…And pray we don't drop one."

Port Fuad, Egypt

Bruno, Brigitte and their two paratrooper escorts moved through the streets of Port Fuad toward the bridge they had captured. They moved quickly at a slow run because Bruno thought it would be safer should a sniper take a potshot at them. Brigitte was in good shape for a civilian but nothing like the three paratroopers with her. She had to stop several times to catch her breath. When she did, Bruno and the two paratroopers took up defensive positions, just in case. Bruno wasn't of much use without a weapon unless the enemy came close. Then he needed nothing to be very deadly. They used the natural cover of an urban environment – doorways, parked cars and the corners of buildings and alleys. Resistance was surprisingly light. He speculated that word could have gotten out to the civilians about the aggressiveness of the paratroopers.

It was getting late in the day and the Egyptians had still not counterattacked. Bruno wondered if he was missing something. It didn't make sense. They may not have been well led, but the Egyptians weren't stupid. The bridge and waterworks were both key strategic points. Failing to retake those positions was paramount to surrendering both port cites and the mouth of the Suez Canal to the Allied Forces. While Bruno believed that would eventually happen, it was still too early in the conflict even for an inferior fighting force like the Egyptians to give up so easily.

As the group moved through a street intersection, Bruno discovered why the resistance had been so light; the civilians in the neighborhood had gathered into one large mob of about one hundred. They were about fifty yards away and didn't notice the French. They were all armed with rifles, knifes or homemade clubs. One man had a bow and arrow and another a leather sling with marbles. It was the mass that was intimidating. A woman in the group spotted the French. They shouted angrily and rushed forward. It wouldn't take long for them to overtake Bruno's little column. "I think it's time to go," said Brigitte watching the mob approach.

As Bruno and Brigitte moved back down the street in the direction they had come, the two paratroopers stood their ground and leveled their submachine guns. "No. Fall back," said Bruno pulling Brigitte down the street.

It was too late. Several riflemen in the mob fired at the paratroopers. The paratroopers fired back killing and wounding several civilians. The rage grew and the mob lunged forward. One of the paratroopers was hit with a bullet in the shoulder. Bruno saw his man go down and said, "Keep moving, Brigitte."

Bruno ran back toward the wounded soldier. The other paratrooper stepped forward to defend his comrade and fired into the closest civilians. Two more civilians went down, tumbling across the cobblestones. The paratrooper's submachine gun clicked empty. Bruno was still twenty yards away when the mob enveloped the two paratroopers. Knives, clubs and several rifle shots finished off the paratroopers within seconds. There was nothing Bruno could do.

Brigitte screamed. Bruno turned to see two men and a woman pulling Brigitte toward an open doorway. Bruno charged toward them like an angry bull. He had no weapon except for his knife. That was enough. He pulled it from his belt sheath and threw it, hitting one of the men in the side of the head. The blade pierced the man's skull and he fell dead. The other two pulled Brigitte into a building and slammed the door shut. Bruno reached the door. It was locked. He glanced back down the street and saw the mob approaching. He kicked three times with everything he had before the lock finally gave way and the door flew open. He ran back and retrieved his knife from the corpse.

Then he charged inside the building. The building had a courtyard with a fountain in the center. It looked like it was a school or religious center. Brigitte was nowhere in sight. He heard footfalls from a floor above. He couldn't see anyone but figured that must be them. He ran up a staircase and yelled, "Brigitte?"

"Third floor," yelled Brigitte followed by a yelp.

Bruno wasn't sure if the yelp was from Brigitte or one of her captives. He didn't wait to find out and sprinted up the stairs to the third floor. He ran out onto the interior veranda and saw an open door. He ran toward it and entered. "Watch out," said Brigitte on the far end of the room, her hands now tied with a rope.

Bruno turned to see a man with a baseball bat swinging at his head. Bruno ducked, then swung around and plunged his knife into the left side of the man's chest. Bruno knew every point on a human body that could kill or maim. His aim was true and the man fell dead. The woman holding Brigitte went wide-eyed and let go of Brigitte. She begged for her life in Arabic. Bruno waved for her to leave. She left. Bruno untied Brigitte and said, "Are you okay?"

"Am I okay? You almost had your head bashed in with a baseball bat," said Brigitte.

"He wasn't even close."

Brigitte hugged Bruno and said, "That was close, Bruno. All of it. Your men... are they..."

"Yeah. They're gone. They did their duty. Listen, we need to get out of here. The mob is outside..."

There was a crash below and many angry voices in Arabic.

"Make that inside the building," said Bruno. "Let's hope the roof connects to another rooftop. I've got to get back to the bridge one way or another."

"Go. I'll be right behind you."

Bruno retrieved his knife from the dead man's chest and they took off running toward the stairs.

The sun was setting over the city. Bruno and Brigitte ran across the rooftops. Fifty yards behind, twenty men from the mob pursued them, occasionally taking a shot with a rifle, causing them to duck for cover, slowing their progress. Below, the rest of the mob pursued them on the street, cutting off their escape.

Brigitte was clearly tired and sweating. Bruno did what he could to help her until she insisted that he stop helping and let her pull her own weight. They came to the edge of a building and looked down. It was a two-story jump down to the next rooftop. Brigitte looked concerned. "You can do this, Brigitte," said Bruno. "It looks worse than it is. Just relax and go limp like a parachute landing."

"Right," said Brigitte, unsure. "...like landing with a parachute. Tumble and roll."

"You got it," said Bruno. "You go first."

"No. You go. I want to see how you do it. As a reminder."

Bruno looked back at the approaching mob. There wasn't time to argue. "Alright," he said and jumped without warning.

He landed on the rooftop below and rolled unhurt. He jumped up and waved for Brigitte to jump down. She wanted to but she was frozen with fear. It was a long way down. Farther than she had ever jumped before. "Brigitte, jump. Do it now," said Bruno.

"I am," said Brigitte snapping back angrily. But still she didn't jump and the crowd was getting closer... much closer. They were within rifle range but they wanted to capture her and take their revenge by hand.

"Damn it, Brigitte. JUMP!"

A piece of roof tile flew by, inches from her head. She looked back and saw that the mob was almost on top of her. The thought of what they would do to her was more frightening than the distance between the two rooftops. She jumped.

Bruno instinctively wanted to catch her but knew he would probably do more harm than good. She landed and tumbled with a yelp. "Are you okay?" said Bruno.

"No. I'm not okay. I think I broke my ankle."

"It's probably just sprained."

"How the hell would you know?"

"It's doesn't matter. We've got to keep going," said Bruno helping her up.

The first members of the mob reached the edge of the building. They threw down pieces of roof tile and whatever they could find on the roof.

A chunk of tile hit Bruno on the wrist, cutting him. He grabbed Brigitte and lifted her over his shoulder in a fireman's carry. He ran to the next rooftop and then another putting distance between them and the mob. The mob was still on the higher rooftop arguing about who should be the first to jump down. At the end of the third rooftop Bruno came to a one-story drop in height to the next rooftop. He hesitated for a moment. "Don't even think about it, Bruno," said Brigitte realizing his intention to jump with her. "Seriously, you'll never be able to--"

Bruno jumped off the edge with Brigitte still on his back. In his mind, Brigitte was no heavier that a full military backpack. But a backpack didn't squirm and buck on the way down. Bruno landed and rolled. Brigitte went flying off his back and tumbled across the rooftop. "Are you okay?" said Bruno.

"Are you crazy?" said Brigitte, angry. "No I'm not okay."

"I'm sorry, Brigitte. I had no choice."

Brigitte felt her ankle and said, "Well if it wasn't broken

before, it sure as hell is now."

"We have to keep moving."

"Oh god. Do you ever stop?"

"Ah... no. Why would I do that?"

"Because... Oh, nevermind. Help me up."

Bruno helped her to her feet and said. "Piggyback this time, yes?"

"Yes," said Brigitte climbing onto Bruno's back.

They crossed several more rooftops at the same height until they reached a rooftop that was two-stories higher than the one on which he was standing. There was nothing to grab on to except for a rusty drainpipe near the corner. He doubted it could take the weight on one of them let alone two. It was just a sheer wall. He couldn't carry Brigitte on his back while climbing, without something significant to grab on to, and Brigitte wasn't strong enough to pull herself up without the use of one of her legs. They were trapped. Fortunately they were far enough away from the mob that they couldn't see their movements. Bruno and Brigitte looked out toward the canal. They could see the top of the bridge. "How far do you think it is?" said Bridgette.

"I don't know. Maybe ten or eleven blocks," said Bruno. "It's getting dark. I think we can make it."

"Of course we can make it," said Brigitte unsure.

Bruno carried Brigitte to the rooftop access door and opened it. It was dark. They went inside. He closed the door. There was no lock. "Damn it," he said.

"Put me down. I have an idea," said Brigitte.

Bruno set her down gently. She reached into her pocket and pulled out two coins. "Put all your weight against the door," said Brigitte.

Bruno didn't understand what she was doing but did as she asked and leaned hard against the door. With all of Bruno's weight against the door, Brigitte placed the two coins in the small gap between the doorframe and the door. The gap was too big. "We need more coins. Do you have any?" she said.

He reached into his shirt pocket and fished out three coins. "What are you doing?" he said.

"Jamming the door closed from the inside," she said.

"With coins?"

"Yes. Yes. They are better than a lock. They'll have to break the door down to get in."

"Really?"

"Yeah. When I was a senior at the university we would lock the freshmen inside a classroom as a practical joke. Their only way out was to crawl through a window."

She took four of the coins and wedged them into the gap so it was a tight fit. "Alright. You can let the door loose."

Bruno moved away releasing the pressure against the door. He checked the door and tried to open it. The door handle didn't budge. "I'll have to remember that one," he said.

"It's not going to last forever but it could buy us some time," said Brigitte.

"I don't want to turn on the lights and I will need both my hands to fight if we encounter anyone. Can you walk a little?"

"I can limp."

They walked – and hopped – down the stairs and entered the top floor of the building. The smell of leather and glue was strong. It was a shoe factory. The top floor was a large storage area. They found a small storage closet filled with spools of different colored threads and hid inside. Brigitte sat down. Bruno examined her ankle. She winced in pain. "Is it broken?" she said.

"I don't know. Maybe. I can't tell without taking off your boot."

"So take it off. It's killing me anyway."

"We can't. If I remove the boot your ankle will swell and we'll never get it back on. At least with the boot on your ankle has some support. You're just going to have to deal with the pain until we can get you to a medic."

"Bruno, you need to leave me and go get help."

"I'm not going to leave you, Brigitte. So forget it."

"Bruno, use your head. If you have to carry me that mob is going to catch us. Not even you can fight all of them off and carry me at the same time. The smart thing is to hide me as best we can and you make your way back to your men to get help."

"No. I am not leaving you."

"Why not? It's the smart move for both our sakes."

"I can't."

"Of course you can."

"No. I really can't do that. I can't leave you."

"You mean you won't."

"No. I mean I can't, Brigitte."

Brigitte looked into his eyes and saw the truth of the moment. Bruno was right. There was no way he could leave her. He would sacrifice his own life to save her. There was no question about it. She was moved deeply by the thought. Her eyes filled with tears. He loved her. And she knew that she still loved him. She reached up, pulled him close and kissed him deeply. He kissed her back like a man drinking water for the first time after being lost in the desert. He pulled her close. She yelped when her ankle moved. "Sorry," said Bruno. "I forget."

She smiled and pulled his lips back to hers. The moment was broken when they heard the sound of fists pounding on the rooftop access door. "We've got to go," said Bruno. "…together."

"Alright," said Brigitte knowing that arguing with him would be fruitless.

Bruno helped her up and said. "You want a piggyback ride, little girl?"

"Yes please, mister," she said with a smile.

Bruno hoisted her up on his back. She wrapped her arms around his neck and he held her legs. A normal man would not have lasted very long as he climbed down those three flights of stairs. But Bruno was no ordinary man.

The ground floor of the factory was dark and vacant. The workers had all joined the militia in defense of the city. Bruno and Brigitte moved to the front door and opened it a crack. There were a dozen civilians with weapons in front of the building. Bruno closed the door carefully so as not to alert the mob outside.

As Bruno and Brigitte moved back across the factory floor they heard a loud crack and footfalls inside the building. "They've broken through the roof doorway," said Bruno.

He carried her to the back door and opened it a crack to look out. It was an alley behind the building. At the end of the alley were two militiamen with rifles smoking cigarettes and talking. "Two armed civilians," said Bruno.

"Shit," she said. "Do you think you can reach them in time?"

"Maybe. But you're going to have to walk on your own. I don't think staying in the factory is the best idea."

"I agree. Do it, Bruno. Save us," said Brigitte giving a kiss on his lips and smiling. "You can do it. I know you can."

Bruno pulled out his knife and said, "You run in the opposite direction... just in case."

"No. I stay with you no matter what happens. We live or die together."

Bruno nodded and slipped out the door into the alley. Brigitte followed.

Bruno moved down the alley toward the two men still talking to each other. He stayed close to the alley wall so as not to draw their attention. He needed to close the distance between himself and his prey before they discovered him. They both had rifles. Even if they were lousy shots, Bruno was now too close for them both to miss. He kept moving, slowly, steadily, closing the distance a footfall at a time. He was twenty-five feet away when one of the two men noticed him. The man said something in

Arabic that Bruno didn't understand. It didn't matter. The two men leveled their rifles at Bruno.

Brigitte was thirty feet behind Bruno, deeper in the alley. She watched the two men take aim. She couldn't let that be the end of Bruno. She screamed a curse in Arabic and ran across the alley to the opposite wall. One of the men aimed at Brigitte and fired. The bullet ricocheted off the wall in front of Brigitte chipping a brick and cutting her face near her eye. She winced. It wasn't very deep but the brick's grit was painful like salt in a wound.

Brigitte's diversion was not what Bruno wanted. It was what he needed. With one of the rifles in need of reloading, Bruno focused on the man with the a round still in his gun's chamber. Bruno flipped his knife in the air, grabbed it by the blade and threw it in one graceful motion. It landed deep in the man's cheek with a crunch. He fell to his knees, dropped his rifle and tipped over dead. Bruno ran with everything he had. The second man attempted to chamber another round in his rifle but it was too late. Bruno had closed the distance and planted his boot in the man's throat crushing his windpipe. He fell to his knees gasping for air and dropped his rifle. Bruno picked up the weapon, chambered the round and fired into the man's chest putting him out of his misery.

The back door to the factory burst open and the mob ran into the alley. Brigitte shrieked as they came toward her. Bruno fired the rifle three times until it ran out of ammunition. All the shots found their mark killing three civilians. The mob was stunned at the French soldier's marksmanship and ran back into the building for cover.

Bruno dropped the empty rifle and picked up the other dead man's rifle that was still fully loaded. He searched both men's pockets for extra ammunition. There was none. He only had the five rounds in the weapon. He ran back down the alley and picked up Brigitte sliding her onto his back again. "That was really stupid what you did," said Bruno.

171

"You're welcome," said Brigitte as they disappeared around the corner at the end of the alley.

Sinai, Egypt

A C-119 with one engine smoking badly flew across the desert losing altitude.

In the cockpit sat, Coyle trying to gain control of the plane. His co-pilot was talking excitedly in Spanish which Coyle didn't understand. He turned to see his dead friend, Earthquake McGoon, sitting beside him in the co-pilot's seat. "McGoon?" said Coyle.

"Hola. Como estastas, Coyle?," said McGoon.

"English damn it!"

"Oh sorry. Don't know what that was about. I don't even speak Spanish."

"What are you doing here?"

"Feathering the left prop and cutting off the fuel. Beyond that... I have no idea."

"But you're dead?"

"You sure? I don't feel dead. Not yet anyway. I think that Egyptian bastard is coming around for another strafing run."

"He's not Egyptian. He's Israeli."

"Really?! That's not right. We're carrying a bunch of their wounded, aren't we?"

"I don't think he knows that."

"Well somebody sure as hell better tell him."

The plane shuddered. "Don't like the feel of that," said Coyle.

"She's just letting ya know how she feels."

"She ain't the Daisy Mae, McGoon."

"She ain't?"

"No. The Daisy Mae crashed in Dien Bien Phu. When you were..."

"When I was what?"

"Never mind."

"When I was what, Coyle?"

"When you were killed."

"Oh, man. Why'd ya have to tell me that?"

"You asked."

"A friend don't say things like that."

"You wanted me to lie?"

"Well, yeah. It's a white lie. No big deal. And I'd feel a hell of lot better. How'd I die?"

"Don't ask."

"Bad, huh?"

"It wasn't good."

"So what are you doing in the desert?"

"It's a long story."

"It's that dame, ain't it? What was her name?"

"Brigitte. And yeah, that's part of it."

"You said you'd find my girls, Coyle."

"How is it you remember me saying that, but you don't remember dying?"

"Selective memory."

An Israeli jet banked in front of them and lined up for a strafing run. "Ah, shit. Damn Jew's back," said McGoon. "Take her down to the floor, Coyle. It's our only shot."

"I'm on it," said Coyle pushing the plane down toward the desert then leveling it out with McGoon's help.

The Israeli jet opened fire with its Hispano 20 mm guns.

The huge shells shattered the front windshield on McGoon's side. "McGoon!" said Coyle.

Part of the cockpit tore away. The wind rushed in. McGoon looked down at three holes the size of baseballs in his chest. "That ain't good," said McGoon then slumped over with only his seat harness holding him up. Coyle was wide-eyed watching McGoon die… yet again. The plane disintegrated; pieces broke off one after another. Coyle was unable to control anything. He was going to crash…

"No," said Coyle as he sprung upright in bed. He was covered in sweat. He was shaking. It was a different dream each time but it always ended the same… with McGoon dying painfully.

It was dark in the Israeli field hospital. Some of the

other patients stirred for a moment, then went back to sleep. Coyle was safe. He remembered they were going to transfer him back to Paris in the morning. But it didn't feel right. Like there was unfinished business that he had to tend to. He knew in his heart the nightmares wouldn't stop until he returned to Vietnam, found McGoon's two whores and made sure they were safe. He owed it to his dead friend. He had promised.

New York, USA

The French and British had chosen to invade the day before the American presidential election. Eisenhower was doing some last minute campaigning. He rode with Allen Dulles through the streets of downtown Philadelphia waving at the crowd while standing in the back of a convertible limousine.

"Thank God the election is almost over," said Eisenhower. "It's hard to keep smiling with everything that is going on."

"The polls show you with a strong lead. That's got to feel good," said Allen Dulles.

"Frankly, Allen. I don't care about the election, not while the country is in peril," said Eisenhower. "I'm just here to reassure the people.

"You think it could come to war with the Soviets?"

"Don't you?"

"I suppose it's possible. But they have bluffed before."

"I don't think Khrushchev is bluffing. Look what he's doing to Hungary. He thinks we have taken advantage of the situation. He's angry. That makes the bear dangerous. Hard to say what he might do just to show his strength to the West."

"But Armageddon?"

"I don't think he thinks it will come to that. I hope to hell it doesn't. But events can be misinterpreted on both sides. That's what's so damn scary about nuclear weapons. There's so little time to think through things once a missile has been launched. You just have to react. Hell, it could just be that someone set their lunch pail on the wrong button."

"That's a scary thought."

"Yeah, well… it's all so absurd. We play the game because we have no choice. So, why'd you decide to tag along, Allen? I know you're busy."

"Mr. President, the British intercepted a message from the Kremlin to the Russian embassy in Cairo. The Soviets claim they will attack the British and French fleets in the next forty-eight hours if they do not withdraw from the Egyptian mainland."

"Humph. Do the Soviets suspect that we can intercept their diplomatic communications with the Egyptians?"

"Probably."

"Then who do you think was their intended audience?"

"The British and French?"

"Yep… and us."

"Then it's a bluff?"

"I didn't say that. It could be a warning."

"So what do we do?"

"Keep the Sixth Fleet on their guard. It'll be hard for the Soviet pilots to tell a British or French warship from an American warship at thirty-five thousand feet."

"Maybe you should move the Sixth Fleet out of harm's way?"

"I'd like to but our presence may be the only thing holding the Soviets from following through with their attack."

"And if they hit one of our ships?"

"We will have little choice but to retaliate. Then it's a whole new ballgame."

London, England

175

Eden sat his desk reading a letter of resignation from his Minister of State for Foreign Affairs. "Are you quite sure about this?" said Eden.

"I am saddened but resolved," said Sir Anthony Nutting sitting on the opposite side of the desk.

"You've been such a loyal member of our government, Sir Anthony. May I ask why you are choosing to resign at this time?"

"Of course. What we are doing now in Egypt seems to me to be contrary to everything I have stood for my entire political life."

"Perhaps you should be more concerned about Israel's threat to attack Jordan than its attack on Egypt which we all know has been antagonizing the Israelis for some time."

"In case you have forgotten, Sir Anthony. The perceived threat to Jordan was created by us to cover our tracks, not the Israelis."

Eden did not appreciate Nutting's aggressive comeback but did his best to hide his irritation especially since his statement was true. Eden had believed that while Parliament had its reservation about his actions, they would fall in line once the invasion had begun. It was the British way to support the government during time of war. But for the Suez Crisis the opposite had held true. Many members in the House of Commons were in open revolt. There were even accusations of British collusion with the Israelis and French. While he had expected a healthy dose of opposition to the invasion, Eden never expected his own cabinet to abandon him. Nutting was not the only member of his government threatening to resign and Eden was quite concerned at how it might look.

"Very well… if you are resolved, I accept your resignation," said Eden. "But perhaps we should keep it quick for the time being. The government does not need to demonstrate more chaos within its ranks during a time of war. Wouldn't you agree?"

"I can see the wisdom in delaying the announcement of my resignation until the conclusion of current events."

"We could explain your absence on a sudden illness."

"Asthma. It's plagued me my entire life."

"Asthma it is then," said Eden standing up and shaking Nutting's hand. "*Tout case sauf l'amitie.*"

"Everything breaks but friendship," said Nutting translating with a smile.

"I hope, in spite of all this, that we shall see something of each other again."

"The feeling is mutual," said Nutting.

The two men never saw each other again.

Port Said, Egypt

Using sticks as pretend rifles, three Egyptian boys kept low as they snuck into the city cemetery in hopes of watching the battle unfold with the British. The boys came upon two Egyptian soldiers crouched behind a mausoleum waiting in ambush. Seeing the young boys and fearful that they would give away their position, the soldiers waved them away. When the boys didn't move quickly enough, one of the soldier picked up a rock and threw at one of the boys, hitting him in the back. The boys got the message and ran off.

Sergeant Brooks and his men knew they were heading into an ambush as they advanced east toward the city of Port Said. They were the first to enter the city's cemetery which was surprisingly large, considering the population. A good portion of the hundred and twenty thousand construction workers that had died building the Suez Canal were buried in the Muslim cemetery.

The tens of thousands of headstones and mausoleums made perfect cover for the Egyptain army and militia. What made it worse was there was no way around the graveyard. It stretched for almost a half a mile between the airfield and the city. The narrow strip of land north by the shore was open and created a perfect killing field for the Egyptian machine gunners. The zone south of the cemetery was too far from the mouth of the Suez Canal, where the paratroopers were headed, and would require that they backtrack through the city streets. At least the cemetery was a two-edge sword and offered the British just as much cover as the Egyptians.

The bombardment by the Allied Navy and the Air Force had disinterred hundreds of corpses from their graves. The stench of death was almost unbearable and several of the paratroopers vomited as they moved through the gravesites. Rotting body parts were everywhere. The soldiers had to be careful where they stepped and took cover. More than one paratrooper ended up kneeling or lying on a dismembered cadaver that day. It was a memory that no one would cherished.

The platoon's point man could see the Egyptians changing positions from one headstone to the next as the British advanced. The Egyptian force was made up of militia and army troops. The regular army troops were better armed and trained than the militia. They were much more of a threat and the paratroopers always preferred to deal with them first. But the militiamen were more numerous and could pop up where they were least expected because they had no training to do otherwise. The rows of graves were a perilous labyrinth.

The paratroopers were leapfrogging, one group advancing, then covering the advance of the next group. The headstones made perfect cover. They were thick and made of stone that bullets could not pierce. Ricochets were unpredictable and wounded many on both sides. Grenades often became the weapon of choice as they could be tossed beside an enemy hiding behind a headstone or mausoleum.

No shots had been fired for almost an hour. The

Egyptians were waiting. Brooks knew they would pounce all at once and concentrate their fire. Their objective was to kill at many British troops as possible. He also knew that the enemy would fall back once they met stiff resistance. It was the way of the guerrilla fighter or soldier facing a superior force. The key for the paratroopers was aggression. If they could advance faster than the Egyptians could fall back, the enemy would have no time to set up a new ambush deeper in the cemetery.

It was Brooks that unknowingly started the battle. He rounded the corner of a mausoleum and came face to face with two Egyptian soldiers. They were startled and fired first. Both missed. Brook leveled his STEN machinegun and fired a burst. His aim was true and the two soldiers fell dead.

The Egyptians immediately opened fire in a massive volley. The paratroopers dove for cover and waited. By firing all at once, the Egyptians would need to reload at the same time. That was a mistake and the paratroopers took advantage of it. As the Egyptian fusillade entered a lull, the paratroopers returned fire killing a half dozen Egyptians, mostly militiamen that have forgotten to duck. The exchange of fire was so one-sided it shocked the Egyptians and several militiamen bolted from their positions leaving a gap in their firing line. The paratroopers advanced, filling the gap, turning to flank the enemy line. Even the regular Egyptian army troops were unprepared for the paratroopers quick reaction to the changing battlefield. It was frightening to face an enemy so well trained. The Egyptians pulled back and regrouped fifty yards deeper into the graveyard.

A .50-cal machinegun opened up on the paratroopers as they advanced. They took cover. Headstones cracked and broke apart from high-velocity shells. The paratroopers kept low and bunched up behind the mausoleums which had thick stone walls. Brooks snarled, "Spread out."

The men obeyed their sergeant and sought new firing positions. They knew he was right but the sound of a heavy machinegun so close was frightening to even the bravest, and they had forgotten their training. While the bulk of the platoon returned fire and kept the machine gunner busy, two fire teams moved to flank the machinegun position from both sides. When the machine gunner saw what they were doing, he swiveled his weapon to engage one of the fire teams. They dove for cover. The opposite fire team used the opportunity to close the distance between them and the enemy. Hiding behind headstones, they tossed grenades. The explosion shredded the machine gun crew and the weapon fell silent. Amazingly, none of the paras were killed, or even wounded. But it was a close call and everyone knew it. Again, the Egyptians pulled back and the paratroopers advanced.

The Egyptian commander knew that his men needed to stay engaged with the British. Any distance between them would allow the paratroopers to call in an airstrike or artillery barrage. He knew that many of his militiamen had an unwarranted fear of the allied warplanes. In fact, in close quarter fighting the enemy's warplanes were just as likely to hit the paratroopers as the Egyptians. But truth didn't quell their imaginations. He knew that many of his men would break and flee if the warplanes attacked. It was better to push his men to continue attacking the British, letting them fall back when the resistance mounted.

The Egyptians felt that time was on their side. As long as their resistance to the invasion continued, world leaders would put pressure on the Allies to withdraw. Even if the Egyptian forces lost territory, it was their job to make the Allies pay for every square foot. Even though the Egyptian forces were losing their battles, they believed they would win the war. They just had to hang on and keep fighting. Surrender would give the Allied forces a Fait Accompli and world leader resolve would falter. Nobody wanted to support the losing side of a conflict if it could be avoided.

Two British paratroopers advanced through the cemetery hopping from one headstone to the next, keeping low, searching for the enemy. They came upon a grove of trees surrounded by bushes. They approached cautiously. One of the bushes moved. They had been instructed by their sergeant that when in doubt they should fire first and ask questions later. They leveled their STEN guns and fired two burst into the bushes. The bushes were still. The paratroopers moved forward and pushed the bushes apart with the smoking barrels of their guns. Lying on the ground were the three boys that had snuck into the cemetery. They were dead, their bodies riddled with bullets. "Bloody hell! Look what we've done," said one of the paratroopers panicking.

"Don't be a puss. They would have grown up into filthy wogs. Better they die now and save the world the trouble," said the other paratrooper. They moved off leaving the boys' bodies where they lay.

London, England

It was night at 10 Downing Street and the office was quiet. There were still a few desk lamps on from overworked staff members attempting to stay awake while finishing the day's work.

Guy Millard, Eden's private secretary, sat at his desk reading the daily newspaper. It was the first chance he had had to relax. The Prime Minister was sleeping, yet there was still much to do between monitoring the phone and reading cables from overseas. He would catch a few hours of sleep while Eden was eating his breakfast. Millard had decided that he needed a quick break. It was important for him to keep up on the news. The phone and cables could wait.

Millard's assistant secretary entered the office and delivered a letter from the Russian Embassy. "I thought you should see this right away. It's addressed to Eden from the Premier of the Soviet Union, Nicholai Bulganian."

Millard opened it and read the contents. The look on his face showed that he was stunned.

"What is it?" said the Assistant Secretary.

"The Soviets are threatened to launch nuclear-armed ballistic missiles against London and Paris if allied troops do not withdraw immediately," said Millard absently.

"My God."

"Yes. My God."

"Are you going to wake the Prime Minister?"

"No, not immediately. He desperately needs to rest and he just fell asleep. I'll show it to him first thing in the morning, when he wakes."

"But it's a threat of nuclear war."

"Yes. But when you have been doing this as long as I have you come to realize there are very few things that cannot wait until morning… even nuclear war," said Millard then suddenly changed gears. "Besides, there is much to be done. We should inform MI5 to prepare a brief on the latest Intelligence on the Soviet's current ballistic missile and nuclear capability. The PM will be asking for it when he reads this and I want to have it ready. And send a discrete inquiry to the French embassy to see if they received a similar letter. Call the White House and ask to get on the President's schedule for a call from the Prime Minister early tomorrow morning our time. Eden will need to talk with Eisenhower. It is election day in America and we need to make sure the president is available."

Washington D.C., USA

The White House butler woke Eisenhower and said, "I'm sorry, Mr. President. Allen Dulles says there is an urgent matter he must discuss with you."

"Of course," said Eisenhower putting on his robe. "Tell him I'll be right out."

Eisenhower sat with Allen Dulles in the residence living room. Allen Dulles wasted no time and came right to point, "We've intercepted a letter from Bulgarian to Mollet and I think it is safe to assume that Eden received a similar letter."

"Okay. Out with it. What's it say?" said Eisenhower warily.

"The Soviets are saying they will attack London and Paris with nuclear missiles if the French and British do not withdraw immediately."

"Well, that was a quick escalation."

"Yes, Mr. President. So, do you believe him or is this another bluff?"

"I don't know, Allen. Khrushchev has been bragging that his weapons factories have been cranking out missiles like sausages. But somehow I doubt he would be saying that publicly if it were really true."

"But still... It's nuclear war we are talking about."

"War is war, nuclear or otherwise. We must analyze our enemy's capabilities objectively if we are going to effectively defend ourselves and our allies."

"You really think it may come to that... nuclear war?" said Allen Dulles with a slight tremble in his voice.

Eisenhower could see that Allen Dulles was disturbed by the prospect of nuclear missiles being unleashed. "Let's not get ahead of ourselves, Allen," said Eisenhower. "We need to de-escalate the crisis as swiftly as possible. To do that we need reliable Intelligence. Your roll is key. Focus on that."

"Yes, Mr. President."

"I'll let you show yourself out. Let's meet first thing in the morning. We both need our rest and there is nothing to be done until our allies call me."

"You're sure they will call?"

"I'd bet the house on it," said the president getting up.

"How can you possibly sleep after news like that?"

"Practice, Allen. Lots of practice," said Eisenhower moving off toward his bedroom.

In a strange way, the thought of the President sleeping on the eve of Armageddon was somewhat reassuring to Allen Dulles. *If there was ever a time the world needed a leader like Eisenhower... it was right now,* he thought as he left the residence.

SEVEN

Port Fuad, Egypt

It was early morning, but still dark. Bruno carried Brigitte on his back. They moved down a street staying close to the walls and ducked into doorways whenever possible. There were militia patrolling the streets. One or two militiamen didn't bother Bruno now that he was armed with a rifle but the sound of the shots would surely draw others. He avoided confrontation, for Brigitte's sake.

Several of the streets had been blocked off with barricades that prevented Bruno and Brigitte from passing. They were forced to move through alleys and side street that paralleled the Canal. They found themselves going more and more out of the way to get back to the bridge. Bruno was concerned that he had not been in contact with his men. The unit commanders he left in charge were experienced and intelligent but not knowing their status bothered him. He could hear the war raging around him, distant explosions and gunfire. He knew the Egyptians would need to counterattack both the bridge and the waterworks if they wanted to hold the city. It was just a matter of time.

As they came to another street corner, Brigitte asked to be let down. Her ankle was swollen badly and throbbing. Bruno set her down. She raised her foot and set it on an upside down bucket she found by a faucet. With her ankle elevated, she could feel the blood rush back into her leg. The swelling would go down and reduce the throbbing if only for a few moments.

Bruno moved to the corner of the building and took a peek around it. To his surprise, it was clear. "Brigitte, the street's clear. We should go now," said Bruno.

"Just a minute more. I'm just getting the feeling back in my leg," said Brigitte.

"Alright, but just a minute."

Bruno didn't waste any time. He calmly walked across the street and looked down the street from the opposite side. It was still clear. He walked back to Brigitte and said, "We've got to go now. We may not get another chance like this."

"Okay. Maybe I should try walking. At least it will get my blood flowing."

"Alright," he said helping her up and putting his arm around her slender waist.

They turned the corner and moved down the intersecting street toward the Canal, clinging to the shadows whenever possible. When they came to the end of the block, Bruno peeked around the corner. There was a small group of men at the end of the side street but the street directly in front of him that led back to the bridge was clear. Bruno decided to risk it. "Okay. There are six militia at the end of the side street armed with rifles. It's dark enough I don't think they will be able to see my uniform. We're going to walk across the street like we are civilians. Don't run."

"I think there is little chance of that. I can barely walk."

"If anything happens, I am going to pick you up and make a run for it."

"Okay."

"Try not to limp too much. It will draw attention."

"I'll do my best."

They walked across the street. Brigitte winced from the pain but did not limp.

One of the militiamen glanced in their direction but didn't pay much attention until...

Brigitte's ankle buckled and she fell to the ground. Bruno helped her up.

The militiamen called out to them in Arabic. Bruno waved back at them like they were okay, but said nothing. The militiamen advanced toward them at a walk.

"Oh, shit," said Bruno lifting Brigitte over his shoulder in a fireman's carry. He handed her the rifle and ran.

The militiamen called out again and picked up their pace. One took a shot with his rifle. The bullet shattered a corner window in a shop as Bruno and Brigitte ran past and disappeared around the corner. "I'm sorry, Bruno. I tried," she said.

"It's not your fault. We'll just have to make the best of it," said Bruno running as fast as he could while carrying Brigitte.

Bruno and Brigitte were almost at the end of the next block when the militiamen rounded the corner and opened fire with their rifles.

Bullets zinged past them. "They're shooting, Bruno. We need to find cover."

"It's too late for that. If we stop they'll just corner us."

"What are we going to do?"

"We're doing it."

"You can't run ten blocks with me on your back, Bruno."

"I can do it. Just hang on."

Bruno was in amazing shape, especially for a man that had been shot in the chest a few months ago. His tolerance for pain was high. He didn't ignore it. He embraced it. Pain was the great equalizer with most men that pushed their bodies to the limit. But it was different with Bruno. He saw pain as an opportunity to excel and move ahead of the pack. His ability to endure it was what made him different. It made him better.

Bullets flew past them and ricocheted off the walls of

buildings, houses and shops. Bruno kept running. His legs felt like they were on fire. His back ached like never before. Still he kept running. Their lives depended on it. Brigitte's life depended on it.

Brigitte counted the blocks out loud as they ran past so Bruno could gauge where they were in relation to the Canal. The sound of gunfire drew people to their windows and doorways. Some retrieved the rifles they had been given and took potshots at Bruno and Brigitte as they ran past. A man with a rifle appeared in a doorway. "Brigitte, rifle" said Bruno.

Brigitte swung the rifle up under Bruno's arm, took aim as best she could and fired. It was a miss, but it scared the man enough that he ducked back inside and shut his door. Bruno and Brigitte raced past the doorway. Brigitte looked back at the mob now chasing them. It was much bigger. Twenty-five to thirty people, some with rifles, others armed with knives and homemade clubs. One man carried a cricket bat. They were closing in on Bruno and Brigitte.

Bruno was exhausted and slowing down. Brigitte could see his chest heaving for oxygen. She could feel the hot sweat that drenched his shirt. Even Bruno had limits. "Bruno, you can do this. We're almost there."

"Yes. Yes. Almost… there…"

"Put me down, Bruno. I can run."

"No."

"Bruno, you can hold them off with the rifle. We still have a few shells left."

"No."

Brigitte knew it was useless. He would run with her on his back until he body was spend and he fell. The mob would catch them and rip them to pieces. She fired the remaining rounds in the rifle at the mob chasing them. She didn't hit anyone but it caused the mob to scatter for a moment and slowed their pursuit. Moments were the difference between life and death. The rifle was empty and heavy. She threw it to the ground to lighten Bruno's load.

"Three blocks to go, Bruno," said Brigitte encouraging him.

Bruno stumble but caught himself. He gave Brigitte a shove into the air and redistributed her weight. She grunted when she came down. "Sorry," said Bruno.

"Do whatever you need to do, Bruno. Just keep running for God's sake. Two blocks."

At the end of the next block, four men with rifles appeared from around the corner directly in Bruno's path. They were militia. They shouted something at him that he didn't understand but he imagined was something like "stop". He didn't. He kept running toward them. They leveled their guns and took aim, waiting for Brigitte and him to get close enough that they could not miss. Bruno knew it was over but refused to give up. He heard a man's voice shout in French. "Get down!"

Bruno let his body go limp. Brigitte and he tumbled to street. Machineguns fired. The four men in front of them went down, shot in their backs. As they fell, Bruno looked beyond them and saw four French paratroopers running toward them with their machineguns firing.

The paratroopers' bullets hit the mob. Six of the militia fell dead or wounded. The rest scattered, fleeing for their lives. "Vive la France, you sons of bitches!" shouted Brigitte with tears welling up in her eyes. "We're okay, Bruno. You made it."

Bruno was heaving, trying to catch his breath. Two of the paratroopers stepped over Brigitte and Bruno putting themselves between them and the mob. The other two lifted Brigitte and Bruno over their shoulders in a fireman's carry and ran back toward the Canal. The two paratroopers guarding them fell back, firing whenever a target presented itself. "We thought you were dead," said the paratrooper carrying Bruno.

"No. No. Just doing my morning run a little earlier than usual," said Bruno.

Brigitte laughed while crying tears of relief and said,

"That's my little Bruno."

Paris, France

It was very early in the morning when U.S. Ambassador Dillon was summoned by the French prime minister. It didn't matter. Dillon wasn't getting much sleep these days anyway. He sat in the reception hall of The Hotel Matignon. As with many things in France, the 18th century mansion was over-the-top picturesque with its gold-leafed ceilings, crystal chandeliers and antique furnishing that would make a king blush. The French could get away with being gaudy because they invented the term and knew how to pull it off with style.

Dillon thought it strange that a hotel was the official residence of France's prime minister. It was obviously a palace disguised as an office building. Rooms were not been rented to guests in over a century, yet the French insisted on calling it a hotel. *They are French and wonderfully peculiar*, he thought. *One must make allowances.*

Guy Mollet, the French prime minister entered and greeted Dillion. They sat off to one side of the great hall in chairs originally commissioned by Marie Antoinette. Dillon wondered if Benjamin Franklin or John Adams might have sat in these very chairs when they were ambassadors. It was all slightly intimidating, which was probably why Mollet chose to meet in this room – a sense of history – that France should be regarded as special. "Are you aware of the letter?" said Mollet, getting down to business.

Dillon thought about playing coy concerning the letter from the Kremlin threating to launch nuclear missiles at Paris, but decided this was no time to play games. He knew that Mollet was familiar with America's ability to intercept communications. It was also possible that the British had shown their letter to the Americans. "I am aware, Mister Prime Minister," said Dillon.

"And what do you think? Will they do it? Will they use nuclear missiles against a civilian population?"

"You've seen what the Soviets were willing to do against their own people in Hungary. I don't think it is much of a stretch for them to kill French, British, or even Americans to achieve their goals."

"But we are part of NATO. They know the other members would retaliate in response."

"Khrushchev believes he must one day face off with NATO. He believes it is inevitable and it's just a question of timing. With the invasion of Egypt, France and Britain have given him a reason to ask if that time is now."

"This is absurd. Would Khrushchev really go to war over a canal?"

"It's more than just a canal to Khrushchev. He believes you are challenging the Soviet Union's influence in the Middle East. He believes you are taking advantage of the events in Hungary."

"That is preposterous. We are doing no such thing. We did not start this war. We are peacekeepers."

"Really?"

"What is that supposed to mean?"

"It means... I don't think Khrushchev believes that is true. He believes France and Britain have ulterior motives."

"And what does Eisenhower believe?"

"He is withholding judgment. You are his allies. Until the Suez Crisis he has had little reason to doubt you."

"Your president and UN Ambassador Lodge are saying many bad things about France. You must ask them to stop."

"I believe they will stop on their own, once France withdraws from Egypt."

"Their rhetoric is making us question America's commitment to France. Will America keep its pledge to France and retaliate against the Soviets if they attack?"

"Of course. Why would you doubt our loyalty? We

have always been honest with one another, have we not?"

Mollet knew what Dillon was inferring and chose not to answer. "America must let the Soviets know in no uncertain terms that they will retaliate with nuclear missiles if France is attacked."

It was Dillon's turn at avoiding the request. "You know… you could end this escalation by simply calling for a ceasefire?"

"Eisenhower would have us backdown against Soviet aggression?"

"My president would have France and Britain listen to reason and do the right thing. It's not just America, world opinion is against you."

"The world is wrong. Nasser will use the Canal as leverage against any nation that disagrees with him."

"I don't doubt it. But there are other ways of dealing with Nasser."

"How can you deal with a madman?"

"We do it all the time. It's called diplomacy. Even a madman can be made to see reason if the right pressure is applied."

"We must agree to disagree."

"We do not have that luxury, Mister Prime Minister. Not this time. You must withdraw."

Mollet was frustrated and not in the mood to listen to another lecture. He rose, signaling the end of the meeting. "You will convey my warmest regards and concerns to your president?" said Mollet.

"Of course," said Dillon as he was escorted out by Mollet.

November 6, 1956 – Mediterranean Sea

At first light, thirty-two British Sea Venoms each carrying eight squash head rockets took off from their aircraft carriers, maneuvered into formation and headed inland towards Port Said. Their mission was to destroy the remaining Egyptian shore batteries to pave the way for the coming seaborne landing.

From distance the pilots could see that both Port Said and Port Faud were covered with heavy clouds and a layer of smoke from burning buildings and houses. This made identifying targets more difficult. The shore batteries were well camouflaged and protected inside concrete bunkers. Most of the anti-aircraft guns had been destroyed during earlier air assaults but those that remained were still dangerous even to the fast moving jets. The Sea Venoms dove through the cloud cover and unleashed their rockets.

The squash head rockets launched by the fighter jets were filled with plastic explosives and delayed-action base fuses. The plastic explosive was "squashed" against the surface of the target on impact and spread out to form a disc. The delayed-action fuse detonated the explosive milliseconds later, creating a shock wave that was transmitted through the concrete wall. The bunker's walls were shattered and chunks of broken concrete were launched by the shockwave into the interior. Technically it was the bunker itself that killed the occupants and destroyed the artillery. Only fifty percent of the rockets hit their targets but it was enough to silence the guns.

The airstrike was followed by a forty-five minute naval gun bombardment of the beaches and harbors. With world opinion turning against the Allies, Eden had ordered that the caliber of naval guns be limited to 4.5 inches to hold down the number of civilian casualties. The restriction did little to prevent the city from burning, as shells crashed into the poorly constructed buildings and houses.

The air turned an ugly dark brown from smoke mixing with the marine layer. Fires burning out of control illuminated the shoreline and harbor with a strange red glow. Civilians and soldiers alike choked and coughed, gasping for a clean breath of air. There was none. They covered their nose and mouths with wet clothes to filter out the noxious particles and cool the air as it entered their lungs.

At 4:30 in the morning, the British and French LSTs sailed as close as possible to Sierra Red and Sierra Green beaches. They slowly and opened their massive bow doors. Dozens of landing vehicles tracked - LVTs, each holding thirty soldiers and their equipment, emerged from the interiors of the transport ships. The LVTs churned their way toward shore at a slow but steady seven knots. Unlike the Navy's early World War II landing craft, the LSTs pulled right up onto the beach and lowered their ramps on sand. The soldiers ran out with dry boots and took up firing positions across the beachhead. It was a text book seaborne landing, but unnecessary. There was no resistance after the Allied air assault and naval bombardment. The surviving Egyptian soldiers had moved away from the shoreline and into the city, where they hoped to ambush the Allied troops.

Fourteen waterproofed Centurion tanks emerged from LCTs at the edge of the sea and drove up onto the beach. They were a welcome sight for the commandos as they prepared to push into the city. There had been multiple reports that the Egyptians had hidden many of their armored vehicles, including Soviet-built T-34 tanks and SU-100 tank destroyers, inside the city's factories and warehouses, where they were waiting to ambush the Allied commandos when they began their clearing operations. The British Centurion tanks and the French AMX-13 tanks that would land later leveled the playing field somewhat. The Allied tank crews were well trained and could out maneuver the Egyptian tanks. However, the Egyptian armored forces still outnumbered the Allied forces nearly three to one.

Once Nasser and his generals realized that there was no

way to stop the allied forces, their plans shifted to saving as much of their armed forces as possible while continuing to resist the invaders. The Egyptian military simply could not stand toe-to-toe with the Western military. The solution was obvious – turn the Egyptian army into a guerilla army. In preparation of fighting a guerilla war, the Egyptian soldiers were ordered to shed their uniforms and mix with the civilian population where they would be protected from the Western forces... or not. Either way, Nasser saw this as a win. The Allies would either resist attacking the civilians in which case the Egyptian soldiers would pick off the British and French troops until they were forced to retreat or the Allies would attack the civilians and the world would be outraged, forcing the Allies to abandon their invasion. The Allies chose the latter and no longer distinguished between regular military, militia or civilians. Any Egyptian became fair game.

It wasn't that the Allied forces went out of their way to kill civilians. If the civilians stayed inside their homes and cooperated fully when the Allies entered to check for weapons they were usually safe. But anyone showing even the slightest act of resistance was squashed like a rodent. Even running away was considered a hostile act and was chastened with a spray of machinegun fire. A sniper shot from any building or house meant all the occupants inside were complicit and they were killed by grenades, airstrike or artillery.

The commandos and paratroopers were both feared and hated. As the battle for Port Said and Port Fuad progressed, hatred outweighed fear and the Egyptians fought more aggressively, especially after a family member or friend was killed. It was urban warfare at its worst.

The primary responsibility of the Egyptian soldiers was to organize the civilians into small guerilla groups and distribute weapons and ammunition so they could defend their city. Egyptian snipers hid weapons around the city so that they could fire on the allied troops and abandon their weapons when the enemy troops overran their positions. If the ruse worked, they could simply pick up another weapon and once again attack the Allies from a new sniper position. This made it seem like there were a lot more resistance fighters than there actually were and caused the British and French to be more cautious when entering a neighborhood.

Egyptian fire teams of four soldiers in civilian clothes carried automatic weapons and grenade-filled satchels. Acting as the fighting core, they organized bands of militia with Enfield rifles to occupy the windows of the buildings lining the streets and the roadblocks at the end of each street. As the Allied soldiers approached the roadblocks at each street intersection, the civilians under the command of the soldiers would all appear at once, open fire with their rifles and toss grenades down from second-story windows, ambushing the Allied troops. The commandos and paratroopers took heavy casualties until the Centurion tanks started leading the way, spraying the windows and roadblocks with machinegun fire as they advanced. The roadblocks were easily breached with a shot from the main gun. The tanks easily pushed debris out of the way or climbed over it with their treads. Once the tank entered the intersection, it would open fire down both side streets to discourage any enemy militia or soldiers from emerging from their hiding places.

London, England

Dressed in his housecoat and sitting at the breakfast table, Eden had barely finished reading the letter from the Kremlin when Mollet called on the phone and asked to speak with him immediately. Eden considered refusing the call until he had time to think things through but decided he had better calm Mollet down before he did something rash. He took the call. There was no time for pleasantries and Mollet got right down to business. "You've read the letter?"

"Yes, of course. It's a bluff," said Eden trying to reassure Mollet. "Our Intelligence tells us that the Soviets don't have the capability to fire nuclear-armed missiles at London or Paris."

"You don't know that. Not for sure. Intelligence is often wrong."

"Not this time. Our sources are solid. I am telling you Khrushchev is bluffing."

"That is a very big bluff."

"He's Russian. It's in their culture to talk a big game. He is hoping we will run scared and call a ceasefire."

"Time is running out. We must focus our efforts on destroying Egypt's military rather than securing the Suez Canal. Nasser must fall."

"We cannot do that. The justification for our invasion was the protection of the Canal and separating the two warring parties. If we focus our efforts on Cairo and the military the world will know our true intentions."

"World leaders have already seen through our pretense. Everyone is turning against us."

"Not everyone. But I do agree we should move our time table up and capture the Canal as soon as possible."

"And what about Nasser?"

"I am afraid we have underestimated his resilience. The Egyptian people are still behind him."

"The people and his generals will not feel the same if he is dealt a military defeat."

"That will take time," said Eden.

"We don't have time. I am telling you the Americans are wavering. If we lose their support, there is nothing to keep the Soviets from attacking us. I did not get into this conflict to start World War III."

"The Soviets are not going to start a war with NATO.

"If NATO still exists."

"Don't exaggerate, Guy. Eisenhower may be angry, but

197

NATO is his baby. He's not going to abandon it over Egypt. America will stand by us if the Soviets attack."

"If the Soviets attack with nuclear weapons there will be nothing left to stand by."

Eden considered for a moment. Mollet was panicking. Eden needed to calm him. "Perhaps it would be prudent that we alert our own Air Forces of the potential Soviet attack. We could put our bombers in the air on standby as a warning to the Soviets."

"Yes, yes. A warning."

"But we must continue with the invasion in Egypt. We have come too far to give up now. Our people would never stand for our forces to leave emptyhanded. We must take control of the Canal."

"I agree. We must destroy Nasser. We will continue according to plan." And Mollet broke the connection.

Mediterranean Sea, Egypt

Four hundred and twenty-five soldiers of No 45 Commando knelt on the deck of the aircraft carrier *HMS Theseus* waiting to board the Twenty-two Whirlwind and Sycamore helicopters that would shuttle them to Port Said. It was the first British airborne assault using helicopters in history. The word "Experimental" had been dropped from the operation name to calm the already strained nerves of the commandos that would be flying in the small aircraft that morning. Everything not absolutely necessary had been stripped from the helicopters to allow them maximum lift. Each Whirlwind carried five soldier in the cargo area, while the Sycamores only carried three. It was possible to cram more soldiers in each type of helicopter but the engines were limited on how much weight they could handle.

There was no need for the aircraft carrier to sail into the wind as with jets and fixed-wing aircraft. The helicopters simply started their engines and the soldiers climbed in their assigned helicopter. All twenty-two helicopters took off, quickly flew into formation and headed inland. It would take the helicopter squadron ten trips to bring all of the commandos and their equipment to shore.

Port Said, Egypt

The helicopter assault squadron swept in low over the sea. All of the surviving Egyptian gun batteries on shore opened fire as the helicopters approached. There were not many anti-aircraft guns left but those that had survived were effective. The helicopters flew much slower than the jets and fixed-wing aircraft. They were easy targets.

One of the Whirlwinds took a direct hit from a Russian-built AZP S-60 autocannon. The 57 mm impact-fused fragmentation shell slammed into the airframe just below the cargo compartment. The explosion ripped the helicopter apart, killing all those on board. The fiery wreck crashed into the sea. The helicopter assault squadron continued inland. An airstrike was immediately called in. The gun was destroyed and gunnery crew killed by a well-placed five hundred pound bomb from a British F-84 Thunderstreak fighter-bomber jet.

Reconnaissance teams had inspected several potential landing zones for the helicopters. They finally settled on a landing zone near the harbor. It was flat and free of obstructions that might interfere with the helicopters' rotor blades. The only problem was its size. Only eight of the helicopters could land at a time.

Major Dixon, the commander of E Troop of No 45 Commando, rode in the back of a Whirlwind as it circled the landing zone. The engine and blades were loud, making it hard to communicate with the pilot. "This is ridiculous. At this rate we won't land for another ten minutes," yelled Dixon over the noise.

"More like twenty minutes, sir," said the co-pilot.

"It looks like there is little resistance. Land someplace else and we'll walk back to the landing zone."

"Can't, sir. If we hit telephone or power line it's goodbye, Charlie."

"What about there?" said Dixon pointing to the infield of a nearby stadium.

"It hasn't been properly scouted."

"It's flat and there ain't any telephone or power lines. What more do you want?"

"I know they considered it as a potential landing zone but it wasn't big enough."

"Well, it'll just gonna be us, so set us down and let us get on with it."

The co-pilot and the pilot had a quick discussion that Dixon could not hear. At the end of the discussion, the pilot nodded and flew the helicopter over the stadium.

The helicopter lowered until it touched down on the grass-covered infield. Dixon and the four commandos with him jumped out through the cargo compartment doorway. Once clear, he gave the pilots a thumbs up as he had been instructed during practice runs. The helicopter revved its engine and lifted off.

The commandos immediately looked for the fastest way out of the stadium. Rifle shots rang out and one of the commandos was hit in the upper leg. He went down. Dixon and the other commandos swarmed around the wounded man as they searched the stadium for the origin of the shots. "You okay, Peterson?" said Dixon kneeling next to the wounded commando.

"Just a flesh wound, sir," said the commando.

More shots zinged past the commandos. "There," said the wounded commando pointing to the stands on the East end of the stadium.

Three militia men were taking pot shots at the commandos then hiding behind the chairs as they reloaded.

The commandos returned fire with their STEN machineguns.

The militia men stopped firing and took cover as bullet chipped away at the wooden seats around them.

More shots rained down on the commandos and another soldier was hit in the ear. It bled badly but it didn't prevent him from returning fire.

The new shots were coming for seven militia men that had entered the stadium from one of the exit tunnels on the second level. They fired their rifles as they spread out and took cover.

"We're sitting ducks out here. Let's move," said Dixon, helping the wounded commando to his feet and putting his arm around his waist as the commando put his arm over the Major's shoulder.

The British commandos retreated towards a tunnel on the far end of the field firing their weapons as they advanced. As they approached the tunnel entrance, flashes of rifle fire lit up the darkness. A dozen militia men had joined the fight.

"Bloody hell," said Dixon looking for another way out. "There. The team box."

The commandos ran toward the home team box and jumped over the half-wall. The half-wall was wooden and didn't provide much cover from the bullets flying at them from every direction but it was better than fighting on a flat field with absolutely no cover.

In the sky above the stadium, the co-pilot of the helicopter took one last look down to check on the commandos' progress. He saw the fire fight. He tapped the pilot on the shoulder and pointed to the fighting below. The pilot again nodded. The helicopter swung around and descended into the stadium.

The commandos saw the helicopter approaching and cheered.

The militia saw the new target approaching and shifted their fire in hopes of hitting the British helicopter.

The commandos realized that the diversion of the helicopter landing should not be wasted. They jumped back over the half-wall, now pitted with bullet holes, and ran across the infield toward the helicopter.

The windshield on the helicopter cracked into spiderwebs in several places as the militia bullets found their mark. The pilot was hit in the right side of his chest and slumped over. "My stick," said the co-pilot took control of the aircraft and landed. The commandos piled back into the cargo compartment and the helicopter took off again. Bullets punched through the metal walls but nobody was hit.

When the helicopter cleared the stadium the firing from below ceased. "That was one hell of a brave thing you just did. Thanks," said Dixon to the co-pilot. "Is your pilot going to be okay?"

"I think so. He's still breathing," said the co-pilot checking on the wounded pilot.

"Is there anything we can do?"

"No. They stripped out the medical kit to make room for you guys. I just gotta get him back to the ship as soon as possible."

The co-pilot looked down at the original landing zone as the last of the helicopters from the first wave took off. "You still wanna land?" said the co-pilot.

"Will you take care of our wounded?" said Dixon.

"Absolutely."

"Then yes."

The co-pilot turned to the pilot and said, "You okay with that?"

The pilot nodded weakly. The co-pilot landed the helicopter. Dixon and the two unhurt commandos jumped out. Dixon gave the pilot a thumbs up and moved off to join the other commandos in the troop. The damaged helicopter lifted off with the three wounded soldiers and headed back out to sea.

Port Fuad, Egypt

Bruno refused to let the paratrooper continue to carry him once they were out of range from the mob. There was still danger all around them, but Bruno was not willing to die while being carried. He did not think it would sound good in his eulogy. He did however let the other paratrooper continue carrying Brigitte. His legs had had enough and he desperately needed to stretch them so they didn't cramp.

The paratroopers gave him a quick report on the war and what had happened on the bridge and the waterworks. There had been several counterattacks on each, but nothing the paratroopers couldn't handle, especially with the dedicated air support they had been given.

Bruno found it curious that the Egyptians had not been more persistent in their attacks. The paratroopers were lightly armed and most enemy commanders would have thrown armor at them. *Why no armor?* he thought. *Is it possible their forces were degraded more than we thought?* It was wishful thinking and Bruno drove it from his mind. His job was to be prepared for anything they may throw at him and his men.

The paratroopers continued their briefing, informing him that both French and British troops were landing troops and unloading their armored vehicles. Once the Allies had their armored vehicles operational it would be almost impossible to stop them from overrunning the city and taking the Canal by force.

When they arrived at the bridge, Bruno went to work inspecting his men and the defensive positions they had built. He made changes where he thought necessary. He was careful not to change too much. He didn't want to undermine the unit commander he left in charge and he didn't want to wear out his men, all of whom had been awake for over twenty-four hours. They would need their strength when the real counterattack came.

Brigitte was exhausted and decided sleep was her highest priority. Bruno insisted that she find a place to sleep in one of the buildings the paratroopers had occupied but she insisted on staying near the bridge… and Bruno. She felt safest when she was around him. Being surrounded by three hundred French paratroopers also helped. She decided on the anti-tank nest built from sandbags. It was protected on all sides by three layers of sandbags. She curled up in a corner and fell asleep a few seconds after she leaned her head against one of the sandbags.

Once Bruno was satisfied that everything on the bridge was in order, he radioed his commander, General Massu on the *HMS Tyne* and gave him a full report on the actions at both the bridge and the waterworks. He requested an increase in the air support around both positions and extended reconnaissance flights. He wanted to know well in advance what he would be facing before the Egyptians attacked. He also requested armored reinforcements to protect both the bridge and the waterworks. Both requests were granted.

As the temperature rose with the sun, exhaustion caught up with Bruno. He knew he was not the only one feeling fatigued. He ordered every third man to get three hours' sleep while the other two kept watch, then trade off. Three hours was enough to recharge a man's energy to about ninety per cent. He wanted to give them more sleep but he didn't dare risk it. His men had learnt to fight on little sleep, but even a paratrooper will eventually hit the wall of fatigue and become almost useless. They needed sleep. It was time.

He climbed into the anti-tank position where Brigitte was already sleeping and sat next to her. He ordered the company radio operator to stand watch next to him and wake him the moment he received any report on the enemy's movements. Laying his head against a sandbag, he fell into a deep sleep within a minute.

Brigitte opened her eyes for a moment and saw Bruno sleeping near her. She wanted to reach out and hug him for all he had done to keep her safe, but she knew he would not approve of any affection in front of his men. She settled for having him near, closed her eyes and fell back asleep.

Sinai Desert, Egypt

Coyle boarded a Douglas C-47 Skytrain with Israeli markings along with twenty-seven Israeli soldiers on their way to Tel Aviv. From Tel Aviv he could catch a connecting flight to Rome then Paris. He had considered trying to find Brigitte but thought better of it. She could take care of herself and he would just be in the way. His flight suit had been in tatters and smelled to high heaven after several days wandering around the Sinai. He asked that the Israeli medical staff burn it after they offered an Israeli uniform as temporary replacement.

Inside the transport plane he sat down on one of the two long benches that stretched from the front to the back of the cargo area. Israeli soldiers filled the benches on both sides. It was a full flight. The soldiers' gear was stowed in the middle of the cargo area and tied down by the crew. It was far from being comfortable but Coyle was grateful to be on his way back to Paris. The thought of sitting on the patio of a little café, sipping his morning coffee and munching a croissant seemed like heaven. It had been a rough couple of weeks and he felt he deserved it.

He felt tired and closed his eyes. Even walking seemed like an immense amount of effort. Sitting to his right, Corporal Yitzhak Bonnier turned to Coyle and spoke in Hebrew. "I'm sorry. I don't speak Hebrew," said Coyle thinking that would be the end of the conversation.

"You must be a new immigrant," said Bonnier not waiting for a response. "Me too. From Czechoslovakia. Fortunately, my father made me learn Hebrew growing up. So, where are you from?"

"America," said Coyle not bothering to explain that he was not an immigrant.

"Really? And you moved to Israel?"

Coyle was too tired to correct Bonnier. He didn't have the energy to explain what had happened and how he ended up in the Sinai with the Israelis. He hoped the guy would just shut up if he ignored him. He didn't.

"So, what unit were you with?" said Bonnier.

"I was with Sharon," said Coyle again hoping he could catch some shuteye. *Of all the seats on the plane and you had to sit next to a chatterbox. Smooth, Coyle. Real smooth,* thought Coyle.

"A paratrooper. Impressive. So, was the Mitla Pass as bad as they say?"

"I don't know. I left before all that."

"Smart man. So, where are you headed?"

"Tel Aviv. Same as you."

"No. I mean Syria or Jordan?"

Coyle thought for a moment. Up to this point in the conversation he had not lied to the Israeli corporal and therefore was not technically a spy. But now it was decision time for Coyle. He didn't want to spy for anyone but he felt like he owed it to America if it would help. There was no way to know if the information he might get was even of any interest to the American military. But there was really only one way to find out. "I don't know. I haven't received my orders yet," he said, playing along.

"You should hope for Jordan. I doubt it's gonna be much of a fight. Jordanians can't fight worth shit. I'm heading to Syria. I think it's gonna be a bloodbath. Ben Gurion wants to destroy the MiGs before the Syrians figure out how to fly 'em."

"The MiGs?"

"One hundred and twenty new ones just unloaded from a Russian freighter. And that's not counting the Egyptian MiGs that hightailed it to Syria before we could blow them out of the sky. Well... us and the British and French. Ben Gurion is determined that they never see the sky again."

"Why is that?"

"You think all this is gonna end anytime soon? Nasser is gonna attack Israel as soon as he gets his new toys up and running. You can bet on it. Better we just stay where we are in the Sinai and destroy his arms in Syria. That'll make him think twice."

"Any idea when they're gonna happen... the raids?"

"Soon. I think. Probably two or three days at most. General Dayan is not one to wait around. He loves the element of surprise."

Coyle was pretty sure US Intelligence would find interest in what he had just learnt. The war was about to widen to Syria and Jordan. That was big news. He would need to contact the Sixth Fleet Intelligence group and deliver the information without being detected. *It sure feels like being a spy*, he thought. Life just got a lot more complicated.

Tel Aviv, Israel

Coyle walked from the tarmac where his plane had parked and entered Tel Aviv Airport terminal. It was strange seeing so many Israeli soldiers mixing with civilians. The Israelis used many of their public spaces for both military and civilians. It was a country that was constantly on a war-footing and Israeli citizens understood they needed to do whatever was required to survive, including sharing their airports with the military. He checked on his flight to Rome. He only had two hours before its departure.

Coyle walked outside the terminal and hailed a taxi.

"The American Embassy," he said to the driver as the cab pulled away from the curb.

It took twenty-five minutes to reach the American Embassy. Coyle knew he would miss his flight if he didn't get back to the airport soon. There was a long line outside the embassy front gates. Coyle hated cutting in line but this was important. He jumped out of the cab and asked the driver to wait for him. He walked to the front gate where two Marine guards were controlling the flow of visitors allowed inside the embassy compound. "I need to speak with the Station Chief right away," said Coyle flashing his U.S. passport.

"We don't have a Station Chief," said the guard.

Coyle knew that the Marine guard had been instructed to deny any knowledge about the CIA station chief attached to the embassy. "Right," said Coyle. "Then tell your Ambassador Blue Deep is here to see him."

The guard studied Coyle for a moment and said, "Can I see your passport?"

Coyle handed the Marine his passport. The Marine opened it to the photo page and checked it against Coyle's face. "You're American. What are you doing in an Israeli uniform?"

"Oh, that. My flight suit got torn up. This uniform was the only thing available to wear."

"You're a pilot?"

"Yeah. I flew fighters in the Pacific War. Now I fly cargo."

"Alright. Please step inside, sir," said the Marine.

Coyle stepped through the gate and was escorted to the front desk where a Marine lieutenant was seated. The Marine guard saluted, then walked over, handed the lieutenant Coyle's passport and spoke to him in a whisper. "What did you say your name was?" said the Lieutenant to Coyle.

"Blue Deep. I don't have a lot of time. I have a flight in

just over an hour."

"Right," said the lieutenant unimpressed as he picked up the phone and made a call. "I have a visitor holding an American passport that says his name is Blue Deep, but his passport says Thomas Coyle."

The lieutenant listened for a moment, hung up the phone and turned to the Marine. "Please escort, Mr. Coyle to the director of farm aid."

"No. I need to the see the CIA Station Chief," said Coyle. "I don't have time for this run around.

"Do as ordered, Private," said the lieutenant.

The Marine saluted and escorted Coyle deep inside the embassy.

Coyle sat across from William Carter who was studying his passport. Carter's name and title - Director of Farm Aid - were engraved on a name plaque sitting on his desk. "Who sent you, Mr. Coyle?" said Carter.

"No one. I mean... there was a doctor... Actually, he wasn't a real doctor. He was posing as a doctor at the Israeli field hospital I was sent to."

"Sent to?"

"My plane crashed in the Sinai. Some Israeli soldiers found me and took me to their hospital."

"What were you doing flying around the Sinai?"

"I delivered a couple of jeeps and some spare parts to Colonel Sharon on his way to the Mitla Pass. Look, none of that matters. I need to speak with the CIA station chief right away. I was told I could get a message to the Sixth Fleet Naval Intelligence group through this embassy."

"So what's the message?"

"I'm only going to tell it to the CIA Station Chief."

"That sounds reasonable," said Carter leaning toward Coyle and looking him straight in the eye. "What's the message?"

Coyle understood that the man sitting before him was the CIA Station Chief, "Oh, I see... Okay. You can get the message to Naval Intelligence group?"

"I will make sure the information is passed along to those that need it."

"Alright. I guess that's okay. The Israelis are going to attack Syria and Jordan in two to three days. The Israelis plan to destroy the Egyptian MiG fighters before they can be sent back to Egypt. They also plan to destroy 125 new MiGs that were just unloaded from a Soviet freighter in Syria."

"Really?"

"Yes, really."

"And you know this how?"

"An Israeli corporal told me on my flight to Tel Aviv."

"And why would he do that?"

"He thought I was with the Israeli military. The uniform I guess… plus I may have mislead him a bit."

"How do you know he wasn't trying to deceive you?"

"To what end?"

"Passing on false information to deceive the Americans?"

"I suppose it's possible. But it doesn't really make sense for him to pass on that kind of information. It would only upset the American government and possibly get them to take action to prevent the invasion."

Carter grunted knowing that Coyle was right. "Look, I've got to get back to the airport or I am gonna miss my flight. I told you what I know. Do with what you want," said Coyle getting up.

"Alright. How can we contact you if we have follow up questions?"

"I'll leave my phone number and address in Paris."

Coyle had mixed feeling as he jumped into the cab and headed back to the airport. He felt like he had done his duty even if the intelligence service decided not to use the information he provided.

He also felt like he had somehow betrayed Brigitte and

Bruno… and maybe himself. He had wanted to leave the CIA behind him when he left Vietnam. He knew they played an important role in protecting America but he didn't care for the way they did business. He felt like he was generally an honest person and lying wasn't something he was comfortable doing. He wondered what he would say to Brigitte or if he should even tell her what he had done.

Gettysburg, USA

Eisenhower stood for a photo op outside the Gettysburg polling station his P.R. handlers had selected to cast his vote. He was used to this sort of public relations stunt and no longer argued with his handlers when it came to making appearances at historic military locations. Because of his well-known military career, he was part of America's history, even before he became president. Besides, he liked Gettysburg. It was a turning point. Something he was hoping for in the Suez Crisis.

Foster and Allen Dulles had accompanied him. It was important not to be far away from the president at this critical juncture. They stayed out of the limelight. This was Eisenhower's moment, not theirs. "Five bucks says 'Who'd you vote for?' is the first question," said Foster Dulles to his brother.

"I'll take that bet," said Allen Dulles.

"Is it true Khrushchev threatened to drop nuclear bombs on London and Paris?" said a reporter as Eisenhower emerged from a voting booth.

"How the hell did he find that out?" said Foster Dulles.

"Word travels fast in times of war," said Allen Dulles. "You owe me five bucks."

A Marine guard approached and handed Allen Dulles a cable. "Interesting…," said Allen Dulles reading the message.

"What's up?"

"The Israelis are getting antsy," said Allen Dulles handing the cable to his brother. "Ike's going to want to see this."

Allen Dulles waited until the president was back in his limousine before showing him the message. "Where's this come from? That Blue fellow?" said Eisenhower reading the cable.

"Blue Deep. Yes, Mr. President," said Allen Dulles.

"He's turning out to be quite a source."

"Yes, sir. He is."

"Do you believe him?"

"It seems to make sense. We know that the Soviets dropped the aircraft off in Syria. The Israelis will want to stop them from getting to Egypt."

"But will the Israelis expand the war into Syria and Jordan?" said Eisenhower.

"And God knows who else will jump into the fight," said Foster Dulles. "The Iraqis, maybe even the Saudis."

"The Soviets might see it as a further provocation," said Allen Dulles.

"Gentlemen, it's time to put an end to this madness," said Eisenhower. "It's gone far enough. I am done being patient with our Allies."

Washington D.C., USA

Eisenhower entered the White House like a man on a mission. George Magoffin Humphrey, the U.S. Secretary of the Treasury, was waiting for him in the Oval Office. "George, how is our little project on British bonds coming along?" said Eisenhower getting right to the point.

"Well, Mr. President, we've sold off about three percent of our British bonds and it is definitely putting downward pressure on Sterling. I think the British are getting the message," said Humphrey.

"Good. Now I want you to prepare to dump the rest of them."

"All of them?"

"Every last farthing. We are done sending messages. It's time to take real action."

"Sir, we will take a financial beating if we sell our British bonds that fast."

"Yes, and so will the British."

"I see."

"If I decide to pull the trigger on the bonds, you are just going to have to deal with it, George."

"Alright, Mr. President. I will handle it," said Humphrey. "Sir, there is one other matter concerning the IMF that I would like to discuss."

"What's that, George?"

"It's a request…from the British," said Humphrey with a somewhat innocent smile.

Eisenhower grinned broadly.

London, England

Macmillan waited outside of the Prime Minister's office. Eden was ignoring him. Good news was rare from Britain's Chancellor these days and Eden would just as soon avoid any conversation with Macmillan, if possible. But on this day, Macmillan would not be deterred. He waited.

He may have been a glorified accountant, but Macmillan was also a member of parliament. Like Eden he had been voted into the House of Commons. And like Eden, he had political aspirations. He saw the unfolding crisis as an opportunity. He would never wish ill-will on Britain, but he hadn't created the situation the people now faced. For him to benefit all he needed to do was ensure that blame for the financial mess rested squarely on the shoulders of he who caused it, namely – Eden. As the pound melted away and Middle Eastern oil sanctions hit British workers, Macmillan could see the spotlight turning onto him. Reporters by the dozens would be asking for an interview in hopes of finding the latest financial nugget of information that they could report on the economy. If he played it right, he could see himself being portrayed by the media as Britain's savior once the crisis had passed.

Diplomacy and public relations were not his forte but he had been watching Eden over the years and had learnt from the master. He felt this might be the one opportunity in his career to make a play for the top seat; to become prime minister. There were those in the Conservative party that liked Macmillan's pragmatic bearing and had nicknamed him "Supermac." *Prime Minister Supermac,* he thought. He liked the sound of it.

Eden finally emerged for a lunch meeting. "Harold, what are you doing out here waiting like a commoner?" said Eden, knowing full well the reason.

"I was hoping to have a conversation with you, Prime Minister," said Macmillan.

"You do realize that we are in middle of a military operation?"

"Yes, sir. I am quite aware. But the matter is urgent."

"But of course. Please make an appointment with my secretary for the soonest possible date."

"I am afraid it cannot wait, sir."

"Very well. I shall see you after lunch."

"Why don't I walk with you, Prime Minister? It really is quite urgent that we speak."

"Alright. If you must."

They walked down the hallways and stairs of 10 Downing Street. "So, what is so important that it can't wait until after lunch?" said Eden, perturbed.

"It's the Bank of England, sir. It's lost forty-five million pounds in the last four days."

"Forty-five million. Good lord."

"Yes, sir. My feelings exactly. The losses in oil shipments have been extensive."

"Well, I'm sure you will find a way to keep old Britannia afloat."

"That's just the thing, sir. I'm not sure I can."

Eden stopped and turn to Macmillan. "You're joking, right?"

"I'm afraid not. The financial situation is getting worse by the day. And now with the threat of oil sanctions, I fear we may be in very serious trouble. Britain cannot live without oil. Within a week, factories will start shuttering their doors and when that happens revenue will plummet and well... we sink."

"What in hell does 'we sink' mean?"

"We will run out of money, sir. We won't be able to pay for our food and material imports, let alone oil if it is available."

"Good God, why didn't you tell me sooner?"

"Scheduling, sir. Your secretary said there were no appointments available until next week."

"So, what are we to do?"

"I do have an idea, sir."

"Well... what is it?"

"The International Monetary Fund. We could secure a loan."

"Like a third world beggar?"

"Sir, we will be a third world beggar if this situation continues much longer. Without oil, Britain is doomed."

"Alright. Do what you must."

"I have already made inquiries, sir. And there is a problem?"

"A problem? A problem with what?"

"With the Americans. They sit on the board of the IMF and they are refusing consent for the loan."

"We also sit on the board, don't we?"

"Yes, sir, but the American's have veto power."

"They're vetoing us."

"I would appear so. I was hoping you could call President Eisenhower and see if there was something that could be done. We are in quite a desperate financial situation."

"You want me to call Eisenhower?"

"Yes, sir. Right away, please."

The thought of calling Eisenhower made Eden lose his appetite.

It was possible that Macmillan may have exaggerated the numbers a bit and made the financial crisis seem worse than it actually was, but who would know. It was he that oversaw the books and he answered to Eden. He had little fear that Eden would ask for an audit in the middle of a war. If Eden ever did figure it out it would be too late. Eden would be gone. It was a calculated risk. Time would tell if it was worth it.

Port Said, Egypt

Egyptian trucks and cars rigged with loudspeakers rolled through the streets of Port Said. The mobile PA systems broadcast Cairo's version of events to the Egyptian people resisting the Allied invasion. Prerecorded audio tapes falsely reported that the Egyptian Air Force and anti-aircraft guns had shot down one hundred and eight-five Allied aircraft. They encouraged the resistance, saying that reinforcements would soon arrive from the Soviet Union and that together with Egyptian forces the Allies would be driven into the sea. They said that both London and Paris had already been destroyed by nuclear missiles launched by the Soviets and that World War III had started. Armageddon was finally here as prophesied.

The Egyptian people believed that they were winning the war and that God had chosen Nasser to lead them to a final victory over the infidels. The reality of the battlefield was somewhat less optimistic. One only needed to look out the window to see the British and French warplanes flying over the city and the hundreds of Allied troops pressing forward as they occupied the city streets and key buildings. Even the kitchen faucets and neighborhood wells that had run dry told the story of who really controlled Port Said and Port Fuad. It wasn't Nasser.

Port Said, Egypt

Dixon and his commandos advanced into the city of Port Said. The air was sour and smelled of salt, smoke and blood. Their orders were to clear the houses and buildings in their sector of any resistance.

The commandos were aggressive like the paratroopers. The tip of the British spear. Accustomed to the most dangerous missions. Unit commanders were given a large amount of latitude on how they accomplished their mission. They expected no pity from their enemies and offered little in return.

When they entered a neighborhood, they staked out the four corners with light machinegun posts to protect the troop and prevent any combatants from escaping. Discerning the difference between a civilian and a combatant was left up to the individual soldiers. Anyone holding a weapon was not given a second chance and dispatched immediately. Male, female, young or old it didn't matter. Their job was to crush the will of the resistance, and if necessary, wipe it off the face of the earth.

If shots were fired from a window, the commandos would assault the building or house by tossing grenades into every room regardless of the occupants inside. It was a very effective method of reducing British casualties and accomplished their objective of clearing the area of militia. When the commandos mopped up one neighborhood, they would move to the next and the bloody process would start all over again.

Dixon was moving his troop when he realized that he had misread his map and they were moving into the wrong area. He halted his men and ordered them to backtrack to the previous neighborhood. They had walked two hundred yards when he heard the heavy thrum of an aircraft engine approaching from behind. He didn't think much of it since aircraft were constantly flying around the city on bombing and rocket raids against the enemy. He wasn't concerned about Egyptian warplanes since the Allies clearly owned the sky. He turned back to see an American-made Corsair F4U with British decals flying low over the city. It had already expended its rockets and was heading back out to the sea to refuel and reload. He found it strange when its wings began to sparkle. It took him a moment to realize that the warplane was firing on him and his men. "Down," he shouted.

The commandos didn't think when they heard their commander bellow his order. They just reacted and hit the ground. Dixon's fast reaction saved many lives as .50 Cal shells from the aircraft's six Browning M2 Machineguns churned up the street and surrounding buildings.

The pilot was young and this was his first war. Before his mission he had asked his commander how to tell the difference between Egyptians and Allied troops since both of their uniforms were khaki in color. His commander half joking replied, "Simple. The Allies will be heading inland." The young pilot took this as gospel. When he saw Dixon's commandos heading toward the shoreline, he mistakenly identified them as Egyptian troops and opened fire. It wasn't until he had finished his strafing run and passed over the carnage he had just unleashed that he realized he had just attacked his own men. Strangely calm, he continued straight out to sea.

Seventeen of Dixon's men were hit by the aircraft's large caliber bullets. Bones were shattered beyond repair and limbs were torn from their bodies. Surprisingly, all but one of the commandos survived. If the warplane had been any other British fighter it would have been armed with 20 mm Hispano Autocannons and there would have been few, if any, survivors.

Mediterranean Sea

The young pilot of the Corsair landed on his aircraft carrier and turned off his engine. His crew chief ran over, climbed onto the wing and opened his cockpit's canopy. He informed the young pilot that his commanding officer wanted to see him right away. Without a word, the young pilot stepped from his cockpit, climbed down off the wing and walked straight into the plane's still spinning propeller. Only his boots remained intact.

EIGHT

Port Fuad, Egypt

Two hours into his sleep, Bruno was awakened by his radio operator, "Boss, we got a problem."

Bruno snapped awake, "What is it?"

"A reconnaissance plane has spotted an Egyptian armored column heading our way. They're about one hour out to the southeast."

"How many vehicles?"

"Fifty. About half are Shermans and the rest are Soviet tank destroyers and armored cars."

"We need to alert air support."

"They're already on it. The first group should hit them in fifteen minutes."

"Good. Make sure we have up-to-date damage assessments."

"Yes, sir. Should I wake the rest of the men?"

"Not yet. Let them sleep. They are going to need it. The sound of tank tracks will wake them soon enough."

Armor was the only thing paratroopers feared. They were almost completely dependent on the Air Force and Navy fighters taking out an armored column. Bruno hated depending on anyone or anything. But armor was the great destroyer of paratroopers, even though they were highly trained to deal with it. He remembered what happened to the 101st Airborne at Bastogne during the Battle of the

Bulge. The Americans eventually won but were badly thrashed by German armor in the process. He didn't want history to repeat itself.

Brigitte stirred and said, "What's up?"

"Armor column heading our way," said Bruno.

Brigitte knew what that meant and said, "Oh shit."

"I've got to go and see to the men," said Bruno. "You stay here. When the shooting starts, keep your head down behind the sandbags. You're in a good position."

"Alright, Bruno. Good luck."

Bruno smiled and jumped out of the firing position at the mouth of the Western side of the bridge. In a strange way, Bruno lived for this kind of battle. It was like David facing Goliath. It's why he became a paratrooper. He had some of the most experienced soldiers in the world. They were aggressive and brave, like him. They trusted him not to waste their lives and would follow him to hell and back. He loved them for it. He and the men that were awake went to work repositioning their forces to face the threat coming from the eastern bank of the canal.

Radio reports of the air assaults were discouraging. The armored column had entered the outskirts of the city. The planes had done their best to destroy the column but it was difficult. The streets were narrow. While it made it difficult for the armor to maneuver, it also made it difficult for the planes to find a good angle of attack with their Hispano cannons. Bombs and rockets were even less effective as the surrounding building sheltered the column. They had destroyed three of the tanks and one tank destroyer. It was hardly a dent.

The air attacks on the armored column would continue all the way to the bridge. Each one would chip away at the Egyptian force. But still it advanced. Time was running out for the paratroopers.

One hour after the first report, the Egyptian armored column appeared on schedule from between two buildings on the southeastern side of the canal. They turned on to the street that paralleled the Canal. They were still a quarter of a mile from the bridge.

The French held their fire. They could not waste ammunition and it promised to be a long battle. The paratroopers hated to give up a position that they had bled for already.

The tanks and tank destroyers opened fire with their cannons as they progressed. They too were careful not to hit the bridge. They needed it as much as the paratroopers needed to hold it. The French firing positions in and around the surrounding buildings were another story. The Egyptian tanks pounded them with their guns. The Sherman tanks would advance, then stop to aim and fire. Although they could fire on the move, their shells would be terribly inaccurate and a waste of ammunition. After a brief barrage from the Egyptians, the buildings collapsed. Many paratroopers were wounded from falling debris. But they held their positions in the rubble.

Bruno's plan was simple. Simple was almost always best. The French would take out the lead tank creating a road block along the canal street. When the Egyptian column attempted to go around it the French would take out the next tank, further snarling the column.

When the Egyptians finally decided to find another way to the bridge, French bazooka teams would be waiting in the narrow side street and alleys. They would wait in their concealed positions until the first tank passed then hit it in the back or side with their bazookas vastly increasing the odds of a kill shot. Each bazooka team also carried a bag of grenades and Molotov cocktails. If they were successful at stopping the first tank, they would retreat and find another ambush position down another street.

The idea was not to destroy the column. That was too much to ask of even the paratroopers. They simply needed to delay the Egyptian advance until Allied armored reinforcements arrived.

With the Egyptian armored vehicles now out from the

narrow streets of Port Fuad and driving in the open along the canal road, the French F4U Corsair fighter-bombers had more luck in their air assaults. They swooped down and fired their 20 mm Hispano cannons, punching holes in the armored cars and killing the crews inside. Only bombs or well-placed rockets could penetrate the thick armor on the tanks and tank destroyers. The French aircraft unloaded everything they had on their hardpoints and took their toll destroying five Sherman tanks and three Soviet tank destroyers. It wasn't enough. They column advanced like a snake finding its way through the wreckage.

Bruno's plan was falling apart. The Egyptians kept advancing down the canal road and not moving to the side streets where his bazooka teams were waiting in ambush. The Egyptain armored column came within range of the French anti-tank guns on the bridge. The anti-tank gun where Brigitte was hiding had the best angle even though it was a longer shot across the Canal. It fired.

The shell missed its target – the lead tank – and plowed into a building where it exploded harmlessly. The column continued. The surviving armored cars in the column swung their turrets around and opened fire with their machineguns.

The anti-tank gunners reloaded and took aim again while dodging machinegun fire from the armored cars. They fired the gun again.

The anti-tank shell exploded on the side of the lead tank. The shrapnel from the explosion broke several teeth on the front sprocket causing the tread to slip. The experienced driver readjusted his steering. The tank continued to move forward, but at a slower pace. The driver looked for a place to position the tank so that it would not block the rest of the armored column.

The French anti-tank gun on the eastern side of the bridge fired. The shell hit the lead tank's front sloping armor below the main gun. The explosion damaged the front machine making it inoperable but did not penetrate the armor. The tank kept moving forward toward the bridge.

The French anti-tank gun across the canal fired again at the lead tank. The shell hit between the chassis and the turret. The armor on the turret held but the thinner armor on the chassis failed and the explosion killed some and badly wounded others of the crew inside. The tank swerved and crashed into a building. The wreckage blocked part of the street. The next tank went around the damaged tank and proceeded toward the bridge. The column slowed to a halt as the vehicles were forced to wait their turn. They didn't waste the opportunity. They turned the main guns on the anti-tank gun across the Canal and opened fire.

Bruno radioed the aircraft overhead and requested that they focus their attacks on destroying a second vehicle as it maneuvered around the wreckage. The planes pounded the armored vehicles with a mix of Hispano 20 mm cannons, five-inch high-velocity rockets and one thousand pound bombs.

Enemy tank shells exploded around the French anti-tank gun. The gunner and his loader were killed when a shell exploded right in front their gun sending a barrage of shrapnel over the top of the sandbags. The gunner fell on top of Brigitte. She tried to push him off and screamed. She couldn't help herself. His face was gone. She was alone and frightened. More and more tank shells exploded around the sandbags until one finally scored a direct hit destroying the anti-tank gun and launching the sandbags inward.

Bruno turned to see the explosion of the direct hit and the collapse of the firing position holding Brigitte. He knew his duty was to continue to direct his men in the desperate battle but everything inside him wanted to run to Brigitte. Images of her badly wounded flashed through his mind. It was gut-wrenching. He stayed with his men and continued to lead them but sent two men to check on the

Brigitte and the anti-tank gun crew. He told them to check the anti-tank gun to see if it was still operational.

The two paratroopers used the steel trusses for cover as they crossed over the bridge. As they approached the defensive position they could see that the sandbag wall had collapsed on one side. The sandbags had been blown inward and the gun was completely destroyed. They looked inside and saw the mangled bodies of the dead gun crew. There was blood and body parts everywhere. They were just about to leave and report back to Bruno when one of the men heard a faint gasp from inside the firing position. "Hang on," he said to the other paratrooper. "Did you hear that?"

"Hear what?"

The paratrooper jumped over the sandbag wall and cleared away the sandbags and debris. The second paratrooper jumped in to help. "You really think someone could survive this?"

"Just dig. I know I heard something," he said.

The lifted ten sandbags and found the body of the gunner. They lifted him up to find Brigitte underneath gasping for breath. The dead gunner's body had saved her from the impact of the explosion. They pulled her out and set her down against one of the bridge's support beams so she was protected against enemy fire. One of the paratroopers gave her his canteen. She gulped down the water and coughed spitting out sand. "Are you okay?" said the paratrooper.

"I've been better," said Brigitte.

"We'll get you a medic."

"No. I'll be okay. They're needed elsewhere. Just let me catch my breath. My ankle's messed up. I'm gonna need some help."

"Of course. Bruno's going to be glad to see you. He says you're his lucky charm."

"I don't feel lucky."

"Well you are. It's a miracle you survived."

Machinegun fire ricocheted off the streel trusses. "We should get out of here," said the paratrooper. "You should let us carry you. It'll be faster."

"Alright," she said. "Let's go."

The paratroopers lifted her up and used one of their machineguns as a seat that they each held on one end. She put her arms around their shoulders and they carried her across the bridge at a trot. One of the paratroopers called out as they approached Bruno, "Hey, Boss. Look who we found."

Bruno turned to see Brigitte alive. He desperately wanted to run to her, hug her and kiss her. He couldn't. He was the commander. He had to look beyond his personal needs and desires and direct his men as they fought for their lives. He gave Brigitte a nod and smile, then said, "Find her someplace safe. She's had enough for one day."

The paratroopers set her down on the north side of the bridge behind the concrete anchoring foundations. It was the safest place while the battle raged. They left her to return to their firing positions and continue the fight.

Brigitte was disappointed in Bruno's reaction. Her heart wanted more but her mind understood. Bruno was a patriot. He believed in duty above all else. But still it made her wonder. *Coyle would have sacrificed anything to see that I was safe and protected*, she thought. She wondered if she had made the right decision. *Had things progressed too far with Bruno to turn back? Would Coyle understand?*

On the street paralleling the Canal three Egyptain tanks and one armored car had already made it past the wreckage and were advancing quickly toward the bridge. Another tank maneuvered around the wrecked tank. A French F4U Corsair flew down from the heavens in a steep dive. It had already used the rockets that it carried. It fired its four 20 mm cannons into the top of the tank where the armor was thinnest. The shells had hardened tips that made them armor piercing. The closer the pilot flew the more accurate his aim. The shells pounded the top of the tank's turret and chassis. Each round that hit created an immense amount of heat, weakening the steel armor. The pilot expended all of his ammunition in the one dive, leaving nothing to protect him on his return to the aircraft carrier. It didn't matter. The Egyptians had no aircraft in the area. With his cannons emptied, he pulled out of his dive and flew over the rooftops of Port Fuad.

As the smoke above the tank cleared, there appeared three holes in the top of the turret and one on the top of the chassis where the driver sat. The shells that pierced the armor had created a spray of molten metal that showered the interior the tank. All the crew members inside were either dead or badly wounded. The tank turned wildly and wedged itself against the other wrecked tank pushing it farther into the building. Its treads kept moving, digging into the street until the engine overheated and seized.

The pathway to the bridge was blocked. The next tank in line attempted to push the two tanks out of the way. It was no use. They were wedged tight and didn't budge more than a few inches.

The paratroopers on the bridge cheered. They still needed to deal with the four armored vehicles that had made it past the wreckage but at least the rest of the column had been stalled. They focused their fire. They were able to damage the wheels on the armored car, halting its advance but the tanks were still approaching the bridge.

The rest of the armored column turned into the narrow streets of the city to attempt to find a new route to the bridge. The paratroopers were waiting in ambush. The streets were too narrow to maneuver and even traversing the tanks' turrets was a challenge that usually ended up with the main gun crashing into the front of a building or shattering a window. Paratroopers were hidden in the upper floors of buildings and would open fire through the windows as the column moved passed. They focused their fire on the support troops that accompanying the armor.

The bazooka teams were at street level, hidden in alleyways too narrow for the armored vehicles to enter. They would simply wait until a tank was passing the mouth of the alley before firing. The armored-piercing bazooka rockets had a deadly effect on the hulls of the tanks. At close range the paratroopers could accurately aim their weapons. Not one rocket was wasted. A dozen tanks and tank destroyers were burning within the first thirty minutes of executing the ambushes. The streets were clogged and vehicles could not turn around to find an alternative path. Their only chance at survival was to back up. When the paratroopers took out another vehicle on the street, the vehicles between the two wrecked vehicles were trapped. The Egyptian crews knew that it was only a matter of time before the paratroopers dealt with them too.

The battle became so one-sided that the Egyptian crews abandoned their vehicles and fled, searching for cover wherever they could find it. The paratroopers used grenades thrown through the open hatches to destroy the abandoned vehicles.

The machineguns on the three tanks that had made it past the wreckage were within accurate range of the paratroopers and were taking their toll. Paratroopers were falling dead and wounded as the assault grew more heated. Once the tanks were close enough to aim their cannons without risk of damaging the bridge, they would stop and fire their main guns and wipe out the paratroopers. Bruno and his paratroopers had fought bravely but they were simply outgunned. Their time had run out.

It was Brigitte that first saw the three French AMX-13 tanks appear on the northwestern side of the Canal. They were from the amphibious landing at Port Said. They could not fire for fear of hitting the bridge but they were about to enter the battle. The AMX-13 had a 75 mm gun with an autoloader. There were twelve shells in two magazines that fed the main gun. Once those shells were fired, the crew would need to go outside the tank to reload. The idea was to make those twelve shells count and end the battle fast. It's rate of fire made it a powerful adversary. It was light and maneuvered well but its armor was lacking.

Brigitte crawled up the embankment and shouted to Bruno, "Bruno, look!"

Bruno turned and looked to where she was pointing. He smiled and his expression became more determined than ever. He turned back to one of his men and said, "Go tell those tanks to position themselves across the southwest side of the canal and fire on the approaching Egyptian tanks.

The paratrooper ran across the bridge and flagged the lead tank down. He shouted up Bruno's request and the lead tank commander radioed the other tanks.

The French tanks rolled past the mouth of the bridge and stopped on the western side of the Canal. They swung their turrets around, took aim at the three remaining Egyptian tanks and opened fire. Their aim was accurate and their rate of fire deadly. Their shells pulverized the three tanks before they could swing their turrets around and return fire. One by one, the Egyptian tanks became still, their hulls pierced and their crews killed.

With the immediate threat to the bridge gone, the French tanks crossed the bridge in search of the rest of the armored column on the eastern side of the canal. Bruno and his men stayed with the bridge to tend to their wounded and in case another attacked evolved.

Once he had given his commanders their orders Bruno walked over to the edge of the bridge and climbed down to where Brigitte was sitting beside the concrete foundation. "You can come out now," said Bruno.

"All clear, huh?" she said.

"Clear enough. I doubt the Egyptians will give up but without their armor it is nothing my men can't handle."

"One more battle won?"

"I suppose. Are you okay?"

"Yes. But I think it's time for me to go and recuperate."

"Really?"

"You sound surprised."

"A bit. The Brigitte Friang I know never would leave the field until the story ends."

"Well... maybe you don't know me as well as you think you do."

"What do you mean?"

"Nevermind. I'm just sore in more places than I can count."

"War will do that."

"Yeah... it will."

"Come on. I'll give you a hand up."

Bruno reached down and helped her up. "Are you sure you want your men seeing you with your hand around my waist?"

Bruno looked at her confused. "Did I do something wrong?"

"No. You are just Bruno. Like you have always been and probably always will be."

"Is that so bad?"

"No. France needs more men like you. Willing to sacrifice everything for their country."

"Including one's personal life?" said Bruno probing.

"Especially one's personal life."

"You're mad because I didn't come to your aid?"

"Not mad. Just... disappointed. But I understand. I should not expect more from you beyond what you can offer."

"You're mad."

"No. But I will be if you don't stop putting words in my mouth."

"I think it is time to retreat and keep my mouth shut."

"You're learning. That's good."

"But I must ask one more question."

"Do so at your own peril."

"Last night in the shoe factory…Was that real?"

Brigitte thought for a long moment and said, "It was real at the moment."

"What does that mean?"

"I don't know. I am beyond tired and I need a bath. Maybe we should talk later when things are more calm and I don't have sand in my underwear."

"Of course. I'll see about getting you back to a French ship."

"Thank you, Little Bruno. I can always count on you."

"I hope that's enough."

Brigitte smiled in response.

Washington D.C., USA

Eisenhower was playing golf when Eden's call came to the White House. Eisenhower had been expecting the call and was even looking forward to it. Eden had insisted that someone find the president on the golf course and that his call be transferred to the club house phone. The call quality was poor with hissing and long delays. It was difficult to hear and they both spoke loudly being careful not to sound angry. "Sir Anthony, how can I help you?" said Eisenhower.

"I understand you denied our request for a loan from the IMF. I would like to know why," said Eden over the phone.

"Actually, we vetoed it and I think you know why."

"This is quite an unacceptable situation you have put us in."

"Really? What might that be?"

"This is no time to play games, Mr. President."

"I would agree."

"We must hang together or we will all hang separately."

"Did you just quote Benjamin Franklin to me?"

"You understand what I am talking about, Eisenhower."

"It's President Eisenhower, Prime Minister."

"Britain will fall without an adequate oil supply and with us, so go our troop commitments to NATO."

"I agree. As an ally, we cannot let Britain run out of oil. That's why I have already ordered several of our oil tankers traveling from Venezuela diverted to Britain. They should arrive within a week."

"You have?"

"Yes. But you are going to have to figure out how to pay for the oil once it arrives."

"We cannot do that without a loan from the IMF."

"That's quite a pickle you've got yourself into, wouldn't you say?"

"If you remove your veto, we would get the loan."

"That sounds like something a friend and ally might do… if you withdraw your forces from Egypt."

"That is extortion."

"I like to think of it more as blackmail, but potato, potato. Let's not quibble. Time is short and I've got a golf game to finish."

"This is no way to treat an ally."

"Do you really want to lecture me on the treatment of an ally, Sir Anthony?"

There was a long pause on the phone before Eden answered, "I do not, Mr. President."

"Good. So, think about my offer. Maybe talk it over with the Israelis and the French."

"I don't know what you are talking about, Mr. President."

"Oh, I think you do. And one more thing you might want to consider…"

"And what might that be?"

"If you do not call a ceasefire in forty-eight hours, I have instructed my Treasury Secretary to sell all British bonds currently in our possessions."

"You can't do that. The pound sterling will be worthless. It will bankrupt us."

"I can do it and I will. You see, Sir Anthony, I don't believe in using my big stick when a small one well applied will suffice. Good day, Prime Minister."

Eisenhower hung up. He didn't bother keeping score the rest of his golf game. He knew he had already won.

Port Fuad, Egypt

A fire team of four French paratroopers patrolled the Canal below the bridge. Their mission was to head off any attacks on the bridge from the water. Now that the Egyptians no longer had armor to retake the bridge, it was felt that they might try to destroy it to prevent the Allies from using it. A civilian boat filled with TNT could damage the bridge supports and render the bridge useless. They had orders to stop all boats from traveling near the bridge. They were to search the boats and turn them back the way they came.

Six Egyptian fishermen were sailing up the Canal toward the docks in Port Said's harbor. They had been fishing for the last several days in Lake Timsah near the city of Ismailia. It was safer to fish the lake than fishing in the Mediterranean where the French and British warships with their big guns were stationed. The fish were not as big, but their catch was still plentiful. Their boat was full of fish and they needed to empty it at the market before heading back to the lake. They had heard rumors of fighting in Port Said but they had little choice if they didn't want their catch to rot.

The paratroopers saw the fishing boat and waved to the pilot to come to their side of the Canal. The boat pilot saw their machineguns and was unsure of their intentions. He had been hijacked by pirates before but never from the shores of the Canal. The pilot yelled to the French in Arabic. He sounded angry but in reality he was frightened and wanted to know what the French soldiers wanted with his boat. "What the hell is he saying?" said one of the paratroopers.

"I have no fucking idea but he's not slowing down," said another paratrooper and yelled back to the pilot in French then in English. "Heave your boat to shore or we will fire."

Unfortunately, none of the fishermen understood French or English. The pilot kept sailing up the canal toward the bridge.

"Shit," said the team leader. "Henri, fire a warning burst."

Henri fired his machinegun at the water beside the boat but he let his barrel kick up from the recoil. He was no lover of Arabs. It was an intentional mistake.

Several bullet hit one of the fishermen. He fell to the deck and died. The pilot went wide-eyed and increased his speed. He had no intention of getting any closer to the French soldier.

"God damn you, Henri. I said a warning burst."

"It kicked up on me," said Henri with a shrug.

"Double shit! Bruno will have our guts for guarders if that boat gets near the bridge," said the team leader.

"Kill 'em," said Henri.

"Fuck," said the team leader. "Open fire."

The paratrooper fired their weapons at the boat. The boat's pilot house was riddled with holes, the windows shattered and the pilot was hit multiple times. He fell dead. The boat veered toward the opposite shore and rammed the earthen bank. Two more fisherman standing on the deck were hit by a spray of bullets. The two remaining fishermen dove off the opposite side of the boat into the Canal.

"Get 'em," said the team leader.

Two of the paratroopers borrowed a small row boat tied to the shore and paddled out to the fishing boat. The two fishermen in the water were nowhere in sight. The paratroopers waited. One of them saw some bubble toward the back of the boat. They paddled toward and readied their machineguns. One of the fisherman popped up and gasped for air. The paratroopers opened fire killing him. The other fisherman had made it to shore and was running up the embankment. The paratroopers turned and sprayed him with bullets. He screamed and fell dead. The two paratroopers paddled over to the boat and climbed aboard. They checked each one of the fishermen to ensure they were indeed dead, then waved a thumbs up to their team leader. "What do you want us to do with the fishing boat?" yelled one of the paratroopers.

"Burn it," yelled the team leader.

The paratrooper opened the engine compartment and cut the fuel line. Gasoline spurted all over the compartment and on to the deck. One of the paratroopers used his lighter to set the boat ablaze. They climbed back into their little rowboat and paddled back to shore.

The fire spread to the boat's fuel tank. It exploded sending a ball of flame and a black cloud into the sky. It took the rest of the day to burn the wooden hull to the point where it sank. Just another casualty of war.

Port Said, Egypt

Brooks and his platoon advanced into the broken city of Port Said. They were spread out in a staggered line to reduce casualties in the event of mortar attack or a machinegun raking their ranks. A grenade loaded on the end of his rifle, Ross stayed near Brooks whenever possible. Brooks didn't seem to mind. He liked Ross and wanted his grenadier nearby when a fire fight started.

Ross's grenades didn't have the punch of mortar or artillery fire, but they could be launched quickly and were enough to keep the enemy's head down while the platoon maneuvered into a strong defensive position. Those grenades were the only weapon in the platoon that could potentially take out an enemy armored vehicle.

There were bodies lying in the street; some contorted in the strangest positions and others with their clothes blown off by the concussion of an explosion. The stench of burned flesh mixed with the scent of charcoal. Bomb and artillery craters peppered the streets. Hundreds of houses and buildings burned out of control. The city fire department was too frightened to put them out.

The heat from the fires combined with the sun was like an oven. The soldiers' uniforms were drenched. They wiped their foreheads continually to keep the sweat from stinging their eyes. The sound of distant gunfire was a constant reminder that the war was still raging in the city.

Ross rounded a corner and saw a British pilot hanging by the straps of his parachute from the top of a palm tree. His body swayed in a gentle wind slowly dripping blood into the sand below. He had been skewered by a palm frond on landing. On the opposite side of the street, the tail of the pilot's crashed jet emerged from the side of a smoldering building like a bizarre piece of contemporary art.

As they continued deeper into the city, the paratroopers passed an entire block of houses burning on both sides of a street. The whole neighborhood was destroyed, leaving hundreds of Egyptians homeless and destitute. A terracotta roof collapsed into a weakened building, imploding inward as the heavy tiles took out the floor trusses.

Ross was next to Brooks when a rifle barrel poked out of a window just a few feet in front of them and fired at the paratroopers walking on the opposite side of the street. Nobody was hit. Brooks instinctively reached for a grenade to toss into the window. Ross reached over and grabbed the rifle barrel and gave it a good jerk to wrestle it away from the sniper. To his surprise, he pulled the rifle through the window with a young boy attached. The boy landed on the ground in front of the window. He reached for his rifle in Ross' hand. Ross pulled it away. Brooks leveled his STEN gun at the boy. Seeing that Brooks was about to kill the young boy, Ross picked the boy up by his shirt collar and gave him a swift kick in the butt. The boy yelped and tears came rolling down his cheeks. Brooks softened and removed his finger from the trigger. "Now what are you gonna do with him?" said Brooks.

Ross picked up the boy and threw him back through the window into the house. The boy landed with a loud thud and another yelp. "Problem solved," said Ross.

"Until he finds another rifle," said Brooks.

"He's scared now. I doubt he'll do anything but run under his mother's skirt."

"We're commandos, Private. Don't forget that."

"I won't, Staff Sergeant. But I have a little brother his age. I can't kill a kid."

"If that kid shoots at me or one of my men. I'm gonna put my boot up your ass."

"Fair enough, Staff Sergeant."

Brooks grunted as they moved on down the street.

Western powers had attacked a civilian population with their modern weapons in hopes of destroying its morale. It had the opposite effect on the Egyptians. Their families dead and dying from the bombardment, fathers and mothers fought for revenge unconcerned with their own lives. Even with the invading forces growing in number by the hour, the citizens of Port Said and Port Fuad vastly outnumbered the Allied troops. Nasser had given them weapons. They learned how to use them on the battlefield. They may not have been efficient soldiers but the sheer mass of the angry population was a threat to the Allied forces. Every open window or doorway hid a potential sniper as the Allies advanced through the streets.

The British troops had never seen anything like an entire city bitter and bent on revenge. They thought they were liberating the Egyptians from Nasser's oppressive regime and careless deeds. They were wrong. The civilians' irrational behavior frightened many of the soldiers and impaired their judgment. They saw their comrades dying around them and it stoked their wrath.

Many of the British and French soldiers no longer distinguished between civilian and soldier. They killed everyone they came across, tossing grenades into houses and buildings without looking inside, crashing through doorways and spraying a room with machinegun fire, killing the occupants, including women and children crouched in the corners. Those that tried to flee were gunned down in the streets.

The Egyptians fought back. They fired on the advancing allied troops from the windows and balconies as they had been instructed. They tossed Molotov cocktails into groups of soldiers and passing vehicles. The thought of burning alive was worse than being shot for many of the Allied soldiers. Anyone in an open window or doorway was fair game regardless of age or gender. British and French soldiers died, but Egyptians more… by the hundreds, then by the thousands. Bodies were wheeled away on carts used to sell fruit and vegetables in the market. Egyptian blood stained the wood. It was mayhem. It was murder.

London, England

Eden called Mollet by phone. Their discussion was frank. "The Americans have used their financial power against us and we have no choice but to comply with Eisenhower's demands. We must call a ceasefire tonight at midnight," said Eden.

"What about Nasser and the destruction of the Egyptian military?" said Mollet.

"I am afraid that will not be possible at this point."

"At the very least we must secure the Canal," said Mollet. "I am assured our troops only need forty-eight hours."

"In forty-eight hours, Britain will be bankrupt."

"You should have secured a loan from the IMF before the invasion, as we did."

"I don't think your financial criticism is constructive at this point, Prime Minister. What's done is done."

"All of this is for nothing?"

"I won't say nothing. We still have peace negotiations. We may be able to secure the right to operate the Canal and keep our troops in place as part of a UN peacekeeping force."

"Nasser will never accept those conditions. He wants foreigners out of his country, especially the British."

"The UN may not give him a choice."

"What about the Israelis?"

"They will make their own deal as always. They seem to be in a stronger position than us. I think they will fare just fine. In any case… what does it matter?"

"What if France refuses to accept a ceasefire?"

"Then you are on your own. Britain will ceasefire at midnight. I would suggest France does the same. Good day, Prime Minister," said Eden hanging up the phone in a huff, without waiting for Mollet's response.

Eden was beyond frustrated and in no mood to listen to Mollet complain about his shortfalls. He still wasn't sure how it was that the invasion had failed. It was a good plan. It should have worked. He wondered if maybe the Israelis had betrayed the British and had been feeding information to the Americans or even the Soviets. *One can never trust the Israelis,* he thought.

Eden wasn't looking forward to the calls he needed to

make, especially to the military commanders. They would be furious and threaten to resign. He would need their support when he faced Parliament and the Queen. *Oh, god... the Queen,* he thought. *That is a conversation I could do without.* There was much to be done and he needed to remain calm. He reached for the medicine in his desk drawer...

Port Said, Egypt

The company advanced toward the wealthier part of the city. There were Western-style hotels, restaurants and shops. It was strangely quiet. Sniper fire had all but vanished. Howard's platoon was on point. Major Tish, the company commander ran up behind with his radio man and two escorts. "What's the hold up, Lieutenant?" said Tish.

"What do you mean hold up, sir?" said Howard.

"Why are you still leapfrogging? We need to pick up the pace."

"It don't feel right, Major," said Brooks.

"I didn't ask your opinion, Staff Sergeant," said Tish. "What's it gonna be, Lieutenant? Do I need to put another platoon in the lead?"

"No, sir. We'll pick up the pace."

"Good. Keep me advised," said Tish, falling back with his team.

"Bad idea, Lieutenant," said Brooks.

"You heard the major. Let's pick up the pace, Staff Sergeant."

"Yes, sir."

Brooks obeyed and ordered the platoon to discontinue leapfrogging and advance in a staggered line. He sent a fire team forward as scouts. He would do what he could to protect his men.

The platoon approached the Palace Casino, a Victorian era four-story building with a large square in front of it. Its elegant archways and windows looked vacant and still. To Brooks' relief, Howard ordered the platoon to halt and take up defensive positions around the square. The fire team on point was sent in to scout the building.

Ten yards from the front door all hell broke loose. Every window and doorway in the casino came alive with Egyptian soldiers firing their weapons at the British troops. Two light machineguns and an anti-tank gun fired from the rooftop down at the paratroopers scrambling for better cover.

All four of the members of the scouting team were wounded and lay in the streets in front of the casino. The Egyptians did not kill the wounded soldiers. They used them as bait to draw the enemy out from their covered positions to save their comrades moaning in pain. Two more paratroopers were hit in the legs as they attempted to retrieve their wounded comrades and added to the four already wounded. Howard ordered no more rescue missions be attempted until reinforcements arrived and the area was secured.

As the rest of the company attempted to move up and support the assault on the casino, hundreds of Egyptian militia opened fire from second- and third-story windows in the buildings along the street. The Egyptians were bad shots but the sheer volume of rifle fire pinned down the company in a fierce urban-style battle. The paratroopers had to clear the buildings before they could advance and help Howard's platoon.

The militia had barricaded themselves inside the buildings, leaving fire teams on the ground floor hidden behind overturned desks and furniture. They would stay hidden, then ambush the paratroopers when they attempted to breach the buildings' entrances.

Howard was struggling to keep control of the situation at the casino as his platoon received fire from all sides. He was unsure what to do but he knew he needed to do something, and soon. "I'm gonna call for tank support," said Howard.

"Our wounded men don't have enough time to wait for tanks before they bleed out, Lieutenant. Besides, that place is built like a brick shithouse. We're gonna need something with more punch than a squadron of tanks. We should call in an airstrike and level the place," said Brooks.

"What about our wounded men in front of the casino?" said Howard.

"Look. They'll die if we just leave 'em there and the Gypos will pick us off if we try to go get 'em. Their best chance is for us to attempt a rescue during the airstrike. The Egyptians will be distracted."

"That's insane."

"Yeah, I know. I'll take seven guys with me while you and the rest of the platoon gives us covering fire," said Brooks.

"Wait… I'll go," said Howard.

"Dumb move, Lieutenant. The men need you."

"No, Staff Sergeant. The men need you. Those wounded men will stand a better chance if you direct the covering fire and I lead the rescue."

"It ain't your job, sir."

"No. But you know I'm right."

Brooks nodded. He had a new respect for the young lieutenant. He was leading from the front like all great officers. The men would respect him more… if he lived. Brooks barked out orders and organized the rescue while the lieutenant called in the airstrike.

Brook briefed the rescue team which included Ross and Howard, "You gotta move fast once the airstrikes starts. The Gypos are gonna duck for cover but they ain't gonna stay ducked for long once they figure out we're attempting a rescue. Everyone but Ross shoulder your weapon, grab a wounded man and hall ass back to our line. Ross, you see any movement in those windows you send a grenade through 'em."

"You got it, Staff Sergeant," said Ross.

Brooks could see that Howard was trying to hide his fear. He wanted to reassure him but knew better than to do it in front of the men. "Anything you wanna add, Lieutenant?"

"The air force is gonna do their best to keep their fire high. If anyone goes down, you leave them to me. Don't be heroes. Just grab the man you have been assigned and get back to cover. Don't pick your man up. Grab him by the vest and drag 'im. You're gonna want to keep as low as possible. Ross, you're gonna be last man, so you help me with anyone that still needs saving," said the lieutenant checking his watch. "We go when the first rocket hits in about three minutes. Good luck, men."

Brooks moved off to join the rest of the platoon. The lieutenant crouched behind cover with the rest of his rescue team.

A squadron of Westland Wyvern strike fighters swept in low from the Mediterranean where they had been circling until needed. The Wyvern was a strange beast with its eight contra-rotating propellers and the pilot's cockpit in front of the engine to allow for better visibility. It was designed by the Navy as a long range fighter with a big punch. Two Hispano 20 mm cannons were mounted in each wing. From there, air command could choose to arm it with sixteen rockets, a Mk 15 torpedo or three thousand pounds of bombs. It was not a particularly fast plane with a top speed of only 382 mph but that made it ideal for air-to-ground support. The squadron was outfitted with a mix of rockets and bombs. The warplanes with the rockets led the attack.

The pilot of the lead plane lined up by flying directly

over the boulevard where the company was fighting. As he approached the casino he took aim and unleashed his rockets at the upper floors as he had been instructed.

Sixteen rockets slammed into the front of the building and exploded in rapid succession. As expected, the Egyptians immediately took cover.

At the same time that the squadron fired its first rockets, Howard ordered Ross to fire a smoke grenade to cover their advance. The remaining platoon under Brooks's command opened fire, raking the casino's windows and doorways with bullets. With the rocket explosions as their cue, the rescue team took off, running as fast as possible with their guns slung over their backs.

Ross was a little slower than the rest of the team and trailed behind. He had chambered the next propulsion shell into his rifle but chose not to attach one of the four anti-personnel grenades that he carried for fear of the grenade falling off the barrel's adapter, hitting the ground tip first and blowing himself to kingdom come. It took him just under five second to load his weapon. By chambering a round he took two seconds off the load time when he would be under fire.

The next Wyvern fighter launched its rockets and pulled up. The rockets exploded against the front of the building. Chunks of stone from the building's facade pelted the members of the rescue team as they ran forward toward the wounded men. Several bullet ricocheted across the ground. "Ross," shouted Howard pointing to a window with an enemy sniper.

Ross ran forward, loaded a grenade and planted his feet. He lifted his rifle to his shoulder. The rifle was barrel-heavy with the grenade on the end and difficult to aim. He was using low trajectory firing in hopes the grenade would sail through the window or doorway at which he was aiming. He fired his first anti-personnel grenade. It flew toward the window and crashed into the wall to one side where it exploded. It was a miss and failed to kill the sniper but it had the desired effect of preventing the sniper from venturing too close to the open window. He would continue to fire at the British but with a much narrower field of fire, making it difficult to be effective.

Howard reached the first wounded paratrooper and ran past him despite the man's pleas. The lieutenant had assigned himself the farthest downed soldier. He ran to his side, checked to see that he was still alive and said, "Hang in there, trooper. I am going to get you out of here."

He grabbed the paratrooper by the top of his vest and pulled him back toward the British line. The other members of the rescue team grabbed their assigned men and pulled them back.

The rifle barrel from another sniper emerged from a window. Ross was ready with another grenade already loaded and a propulsion shell loaded in the rifle's chamber. He took aim and fired. This time his aim was true. The grenade flew into the open window and exploded, killing the sniper.

Another round of rockets hit the front of the casino and exploded. A wall crumbled, exposing several rooms on the upper floors. Brooks redirected the fire from the platoon toward the exposed occupants, driving them from the room or killing them.

Ross ignored the exposed rooms and looked for rifle barrels in windows. He saw another and fired his third grenade. Again the grenade found its mark and exploded inside the room. He heard the scream of the gravely wounded sniper inside, followed by silence. "I'm counting that one as a kill, he said to himself as he loaded his final grenade.

"Ross, get your ass back here," said Brooks.

Ross turned around to see that he was alone in the square. The rescue team was already back behind cover. The mission had succeeded. Ross realized that he was the only target in the square. Several shots ricocheted around him. He turned and ran back toward the British line. His rifle was still loaded with a grenade and it was pointed at his fellow paratroopers. Brooks waved him off and yelled, "Fire that damn thing."

Ross turned back to the casino and launched his final grenade high into the air in an unaimed shot. It exploded harmlessly twenty yards in front of the building. He continued to run back toward Brooks with bullet zinging passed his head. He dove for cover next to Brooks who said, "That was some fine shooting, Private."

"All except for the last one," said Ross.

"It wasn't in my direction. That makes it a keeper," said Brooks.

Over a hundred rockets slammed into the front of the casino, exposing more and more of the interior rooms as the façade collapsed. The final Wyvern fighter was armed with two one thousand pound bombs. The pilot pickled the trigger, releasing the bombs, and pulled up. The two bombs hit the base of the building near the front door lobby. The old building had had enough and imploded inward killing the remaining snipers and collapsing the roof where the machineguns and anti-tank gun were positioned. A huge cloud of dust rolled across the square and hit the paratroopers. Everyone hacked and coughed in between cheers. They had taken their objective... sort of.

NINE

London, England

Eden was on the phone in his office talking with Field Marshal Sir Gerald Templer, Britain's Chief of General Staff. "Sir Gerald, as of midnight you are to cease all military operations in Egypt," said Eden with disappointment in his voice.

"A ceasefire? But why? We are winning," said Templer.

"It is no longer a matter of winning. There are other diplomatic concerns outside the theatre of war."

"But the Suez Canal – we are so close to taking control…"

"I realize that and believe me, if I could give you more time I would. It's just not possible."

"I see. But we have until midnight?"

"Yes. And the more of the Canal Zone you and your men control, the better our position in the peace negotiations that will follow. Do you think it's possible to secure the Canal before midnight?"

"Before midnight? I don't. It's over eighty miles of enemy territory. The Egyptian army is still unorganized. I suppose it could be done."

"Then I suggest you get to it, Gerald."

"Yes, sir."

"We'll talk later. Right now you need to make a run for the Gulf of Suez."

"We'll do our best, Prime Minister."

Eden hung up with a burst of excitement. There was still hope. If the Allies could capture the Canal Zone in the time remaining, Britain... and Eden could claim victory.

Port Said, Egypt

Howard, Brooks and the platoon approached the Suez Canal. Dozens of bodies floated like logs jammed against boats and debris blown into the Canal from the Allied bombardment. When the bombing had let up during the amphibious landing, thousands of civilians ran for the Canal and tried to swim across. Those that didn't know how to swim or were too old or young crowded into small boats. Many of the overcrowded boats capsized as they attempted to cross the Canal to the relative safety of Port Fuad. Most of the passengers panicked and drowned. "Jesus," said Howard.

"Don't feel too much pity, Lieutenant. They brought it upon themselves when they elected Nasser," said Brooks.

"You really believe that, Staff Sergeant?"

"Doesn't really matter what I believe. We have a job. We do it. You can justify it however you need to."

Howard grunted and pulled out his map. "The French are about three miles down the Canal Zone at the Raswa bridge. We need to link up before sundown," said Howard showing Brooks the location on the map.

"Roger that, Lieutenant. Maybe we should give the men a quick break. They've been at it pretty hard all day."

"Alright. I need to report in to the major anyway. Ten minutes."

"You got it, Lieutenant."

"Make sure everyone takes their salt pills, Staff Sergeant. This heat can —"

A shot rang out from across the Canal and Howard stopped talking mid-sentence. The members of the platoon hit the ground and returned fire just as they had been trained. Brooks hit the ground too, but Howard kept standing. "Damn it, Lieutenant. Get down," said Brooks but Howard still did not move. He just stood there like a metal target in a shooting gallery. Brooks looked up and saw the reason- blood was spurting from Howard's throat. The sniper's bullet had torn a golf ball-sized hole in his neck and nicked an artery. Howard was in shock. "Shit," said Brooks as he swung his leg around and kicked the back of Howard's knees.

The Lieutenant collapsed to the ground. Brooks put his hand over the wound and applied as much pressure as he dared without strangling Howard. "Medic!" he yelled as more bullets dotted the ground around Howard. The rest of the platoon repeated the call for a medic until it reached the company medic.

"Ross, you see where the shots are coming from?" said Brooks.

"It's coming from the second story of that building at two o'clock, Staff Sergeant."

"Well, let go of your dick and get 'em."

"Yes, Staff Sergeant."

Ross knelt with his rifle and lined up the shot. He pulled the trigger and launched the grenade into the air. It landed on the canal embankment and exploded harmlessly. "Too far, Staff Sergeant."

"Shit," said Brooks crawling over to the radio operator. "I need you to call in an artillery strike."

"Can't, Staff Sergeant," said the operator. "The artillery is still not set up. They had trouble unloading it from the transport ships."

"What about an airstrike?"

"Sure, but it'll take a few minutes."

"We ain't got a few minutes."

"Everything in the air right now is supporting the troop and equipment landing in the harbor."

"Well, I sure as hell won't want to inconvenience them.

Alright. Try the Navy and see what they can do for us."

"Roger that, Staff Sergeant," said the operator and went to work calling in the strike.

The medic scrambled forward crawling on his belly. When he reached the lieutenant he went to work, spreading antibiotic sulfonamide powder on the wound and tying a field dressing with extra gauze pads around his neck. It slowed the bleeding but didn't stop it. Brooks kept applying pressure so the Lieutenant didn't bleed out. "We've got to get him back to a hospital ship or he's a goner," said the medic.

Brooks ordered the radio operator to call in and see about the evacuation of the lieutenant. "Go. I've got this," said the medic knowing full well that with the officer down the command of the platoon was now in the sergeant's hands. The medic swapped Brooks's hand for his own. Brooks took one last look at the young lieutenant and moved off, keeping low.

The French Navy had a light cruiser, *FS Georges Leygues*, eight miles off shore supporting the amphibious landing of their troops at Port Said. The commander was only too happy to oblige the British artillery request. He and his crew had seen little action and were starting to feel like the war was passing them by. The radio operator forwarded the coordinates and estimated wind speed to fire control which quickly calculated firing solutions for all nine of the 6-inch guns.

Receiving their targeting coordinates from fire control, the gunnery crews swung the massive turrets toward the shore. The cannons adjusted their angle. Only one of the guns fired, bellowing out a trail of fire and smoke from the barrel.

The first shell whistled in and landed in the canal displacing several tons of water, much of which ended up on Brooks and his men. "Fucking frogs can't hit the broadside of a barn," snarled Brooks.

Brooks barked out adjusted firing coordinates. The radio operator sent the adjustments back to the cruiser.

The cruiser fired another cannon.

The six-inch shell landed on the house next to the building which was actually very accurate for a naval vessel. The house exploded into pieces when the high-explosive shell detonated, shaking the ground. There was nothing left of the house but a pile of broken brick and roof tiles. The occupants inside were killed instantly. "Close enough," said Brooks. "Fire for effect."

Again the radio operator relayed the message to the ship.

On target, the cruiser fired all nine of its main guns within two seconds. The ship shuddered as the massive shells left their barrels.

The nine shells created a loud shrill as they rained down on the neighborhood across the Canal. The ground trembled. The explosions demolished four buildings and two houses around the building were the sniper was located. His building was unharmed and he continued to fire at the British troops across the Canal, wounding two more.

One minute later, another salvo of nine shells came down and flattened three more buildings including the one the sniper was in. There was no question that he was killed in the collapse. If the concussion from the explosion didn't kill him, then the falling debris and subsequent fire surely did. "Ceasefire," said Brooks.

But the radio operator didn't call it in. He was mesmerized by the sheer display of power from the bombardment. Another round of nine shells whistled in and slammed into the neighborhood destroying more buildings and killing more civilians. "God damn it. I said ceasefire," barked Brooks watching the unnecessary loss of human life and property.

The radio operator called the French warship and requested they ceasefire and added that the target had been destroyed. The skies turned quiet, as did the platoon. The soldiers watched the dust settle. Only the cries of children and the screams of people in pain could be heard from the rubble across the Canal. "Maybe we should help them," said Ross.

"No," said Brooks. "Our orders are to stay on this side of the Canal and link up with the French. That's what we are going to do."

"But we did that. We're responsible."

"You're damn right we are. Welcome to the war," said Brooks moving off.

Port Said, Egypt

Brooks led the platoon. He knew his command would be replaced by another young officer as soon as one became available. He had no desire to lead further than his role as staff sergeant. Officers had to fill out reports and Brooks hated writing. He liked being with the enlisted men in the platoon. It was brotherhood. He believed his job saved lives, especially the new recruits. He turned boys into men. That was enough. He sought nothing beyond. But today his job was to complete the mission they had been assigned.

The platoon was back to advancing in a leapfrog pattern. Brooks didn't give a damn about the major's desire to keep things moving. If the major wanted to put another platoon on point that was just fine with Brooks. He was already a staff sergeant and wasn't bucking for a promotion that would put him behind a desk in battalion headquarters. Port Said was still a very dangerous place and he wasn't taking any more chances with the men under his command.

The paratroopers worked their way along the Canal. Their mission was to link up with the French at the bridge creating one united front through the heart of the city. Resistance continued to be heavy with sniper fire from the buildings along the water's edge on both sides of the Canal. When a sniper fired from a window on the Port Said side of the Canal, the paratroopers would assault the house or building with grenades and raking machinegun fire from their STEN guns. They no longer distinguished civilians from soldiers. Everyone was the enemy. If they didn't want to get shot they should stay hidden inside their homes or businesses was the paratroopers' thinking.

Children were the exception. Many paratroopers went out of their way to protect children, even under fire. Others saw them as fair game. Bigotry or the lack of it were usually the deciding factors. Those that had served in the Canal Zone defense force before it was forced to withdraw were the most aggressive toward the civilians. Many of their friends had died from unseen sniper fire while on patrol or during rebel raids along the Canal Zone. They found no reason for mercy toward the Egyptians. Compassion was a casualty of unwanted occupation.

Brooks had two scouts on the forward flanks of the platoon. Their job was not to engage the enemy except to defend themselves but rather give the platoon warning of an attack, like canaries in a coal mine. It was the most stressful and dangerous job in the platoon and Brooks made sure that each scouts traded off after an hour on point. Everyone except Brooks and the radioman took their turn. Brooks would have preferred to take his turn on point but he knew that was idiocy especially with the lieutenant gone. His job was to keep the men under his command alive while completing their mission.

The paratroopers were often given the most dangerous missions. They were accustomed to fighting against insurmountable odds. They knew how to dig in quickly and defend themselves until reinforcements arrived.

One of the scouts motioned that he had seen something up ahead. Brooks gave the signal to the platoon to stop and take up defensive positions behind whatever they could find that might stop a bullet. The men were weary of using the doorways in the buildings and houses for fear of being shot through the door from a sniper or militiaman inside. It seemed like the occupants of every household or business had at least one rifle. The best defensive position was often just to stay spread out and lie on the ground.

The scouts crouched down and waited with their STEN machineguns at the ready. One of the scouts took out a grenade and slipped his finger through the safety pin pull ring. They heard an unseen voice calling out in French. "Speak English you bloody frog," said one of the scouts.

A French paratrooper stepped slowly out from behind the corner of a building and said, "Yes. Yes. English, my friend. We cannot expect a simple-minded limey to speak French."

"Bugger off," said the British paratrooper stepping forward and shaking the French paratroopers hand with a smile. "Good to see you."

"And you. We've been expecting you."

"Yeah, well… we had a little sniper trouble along the way."

"Yes. Snipers. Very bad shots but sometimes they get lucky."

Brooks watched the exchange and emerged from his covered position behind an empty vegetable cart. He could see that there were more French paratroopers staying under cover and keeping watch for the enemy. He motioned for his platoon to stay in their positions, then walked forward and greeted the French paratrooper. "How are you holding up?" said Brooks.

"Good now that the tanks are destroyed."

"You went up against armor?"

"Yes. Yes. Piece of pie."

"I doubt that. And it's piece of cake."

"Pie… cake… either way. I like them both. Where is your officer? My commander would like to talk with him."

"He was badly wounded. I'm in charge of the platoon. The company commander is a major. He should be along in a few minutes."

"No. No. You will do. Follow me," said the French paratrooper as he moved off back toward the bridge.

Brooks turned to a corporal and said, "Keep the men here until I return. Tell the major where I went once he arrives."

"Yes, Staff Sergeant," said the corporal.

Brooks followed the French paratrooper.

The French paratrooper escorted Brooks onto the bridge where Bruno was trying to use his radio, with little success. He was surprised to see the paratrooper with a British non-commissioned officer and asked for an explanation. They spoke in French. He turned to Brooks and said, "I asked to speak with the officer in charge."

"That'd be me, I guess. My lieutenant was wounded," said Brooks.

"I'm sorry. Was it a bad wound?"

"Bad enough."

"Will he live?"

"I think so. Maybe you'd feel more comfortable talking with our company commander?"

"No. No. You'll do just fine. Our radio is not working well. I was hoping for an update on the invasion."

"I'm not sure I'm the best one to give you an update."

"We are allies, are we not?"

"That we are."

"You are a paratrooper and fought, did you not?"

"Yeah."

"Then there is no one I would trust more."

Bruno pulled out a map. Brooks pointed out the different directions of the invasion and the points that they had captured, "We took El Gamil Airfield and the cemetery west of the city yesterday morning. By two o'clock we were ordered to dig in and wait for the armor support while Navy and the Air Force finished their bombardments of the city. The rest of our regiment arrived by helicopter in the afternoon and reinforced our position. This morning we advanced through the city and met heavy resistance near the casino."

"Regular army or militia?"

"A little of both I think. It's hard to tell anymore. The regulars ditched their uniforms and are fighting with the civilians."

"And the casino… did you capture it?"

"No. We flattened it."

"Ah. Better I think. Gambling is such a nasty habit."

"Not sure I agree with you but my ex-wife probably would. Anyway, we captured the Navy house, sewage treatment plant, customs house and the Suez Canal Company offices. We linked up with 40, 42 and 45 commando down by the fishing pier along with two squadrons of Centurion tanks. We advanced along the Canal Zone to link up with you. My lieutenant was hit by a sniper from a building on the east side of the Canal."

"I hope you killed the sniper."

"Don't know but I doubt he'll be doing much shooting after a building collapsed on him. Naval guns from a cruiser off the coast. Kinda flattened the entire neighborhood. Jack Tar aren't known for their accuracy but they certainly get the job done."

"You British like flattening things, yes?"

"When necessary."

"So, what do you think of bridge?"

"Kinda small."

"Really? You've captured a bridge before?"

"No, but we certainly tried. I was at Arnhem."

"Oh, bad luck that one."

"Yeah. We weren't expecting the two Panzer divisions stationed there."

"British Intelligence?"

"More like lack thereof."

"Yes. Yes. We have the same problem. I like you, Staff Sergeant. Join us for supper. Even in the field our cooks are known for their casseroles."

"I've heard that. But as much as I appreciate the offer, I need to get back to my platoon. Now that we've linked up we'll be heading to Ismailia."

"Make sure the tanks take the lead. We have reports of an armored build up north of the city."

"Good to know."

"Mind if I tag along?" said Brigitte sitting nearby with her ankle elevated.

"Staff Sergeant, this is Brigitte Friang. She's a journalist. She jumped with us."

"Is that how you hurt your ankle?"

"No. That's a long story which I would be happy to tell you as we head for Ismailia."

"Brigitte, what are you doing?"

"Finishing my story. I didn't come all this way to wind up without an ending."

"Ma'am, we are going to be moving kinda fast and…"

"Don't worry about me, Staff Sergeant. I'll take care of myself."

"She's right. Brigitte was with me at Dien Bien Phu."

"Really?" said Brooks, impressed. "You coming along ain't up to me. You'll have to talk with the major."

Brigitte climbed to her feet and used a walking stick the medic had found for her. "Lead on, Staff Sergeant," she said.

"Suit yourself," said Brooks, saluting Bruno and moving off.

"You're gonna leave me just like that?" said Bruno to Brigitte.

"You've done your duty, Little Bruno. But you are no longer the story. I'll find you when it's all done."

"I am sure you will. Good luck, Brigitte."

"Good luck, Little Bruno," she said. She kissed him on both cheeks to say goodbye and limped after the sergeant.

Bruno laughed and yelled after her, "The unstoppable Brigitte Friang."

The radio operator approached and said, "Bruno, you need to listen to this."

"You've made contact with General Massu?" said Bruno.

"No. But this is more important I think. It's the BBC."

Bruno listen to a faint signal from the BBC. The news anchorman reported that a ceasefire had been called for all Allied forces in Egypt at midnight. "This must some kind of joke," said Bruno.

"I don't think so, Colonel. I've been listening to the British radio chatter between units. They're making a run for it down the Canal Zone. They want to capture as much of the Canal as possible before the deadline."

"My God, the world has gone mad. First they pull us out of Algeria in the middle of a war and now this," said Bruno, clearly upset. "When will be allowed to win?"

Port Said, Egypt

The race was on. A company of fourteen British Centurion tanks rumbled out of Port Said and into the desert along the western side of the Suez Canal. They were flanked by a platoon of four tanks on the eastern side of the Canal. They advanced together down the Canal Zone along with a long line of vehicles of every make and type. The 16th Paratrooper Regiment had commandeered anything with wheels and a motor in order to keep up with the tanks. A squadron of Corsairs flew overhead to supply air-to-ground support if called upon.

Brigitte had found a home in a Bren gun carrier where she had her ankle propped up on the driver's rucksack. The universal carrier was part of a scout platoon that traveled ahead of the column and held the platoon's mortar crew. It would make first contact with the enemy and hopefully determine the size and nature of the threat. It was a more dangerous position than she was used to but she needed a ride because of her ankle and this was the only vehicle not fully loaded down with troops. Even so, it was cramped.

The carrier was open on the top which made it cooler than the interior of a tank but the dust that the vehicle kicked up when it came to a stop choked her and stung her eyes. Brigitte and the crew were lucky that the Egyptian air force had been destroyed or fled. An aerial attack could have been devastating to the vehicle's exposed occupants. The vehicle's armored walls formed a box. They were effective against enemy sniper fire but would do little against a direct hit from a tank or artillery shell.

The carrier's biggest threat was dust. Every ten to fifteen kilometers the carrier's engine would sputter then die a few minutes later. The driver who was also the mechanic would need to leave his cockpit and climb over the interior walls to reach the engine compartment in the back of the vehicle. He would pry open the covering plate exposing the engine, remove the air filter and give it a good couple of bashes against the side of the vehicle to empty out the fine sand that had accumulated in the mesh. Once cleared, he would put the filter back, restart the engine and button up the compartment. He would then climb back over the interior walls and into his diving cockpit where he would throw the vehicle once again into gear and take off. The procedure worked fine if they were no enemy units in sight but not so well during a fire fight or artillery barrage.

The platoon's orders were to move as fast as possible down the Canal Zone. The scouts kept a sharp eye out for the enemy. The Egyptians had been throttled badly by the Israelis in the Sinai and by the French and British in Port Said and Port Fuad, but they were still dangerous. They were armed with the latest Soviet weapons which in many cases were considered an even match with the Allied weapons. Superior training and leadership gave the Allies a strong advantage but the Egyptians still outnumbered the Allied forces by three to one. The war was far from over and, as the Allies had learnt from the Battle of the Bulge, a seemingly defeated enemy can quickly rise up and strike back without warning.

Several shells exploded around the carrier pelting its armor with rocks and clods of dirt. "Movement. One o'clock," shouted the Bren gunner as he opened fire.

The Egyptians had been playing a running game of chicken for the last two hours. Their infantry would occupy precut slit trenches and their tanks and mobile anti-tank guns would take up firing positions behind low sand dunes or manmade berms. As the scouting vehicles approached, they would open fire.

The scout vehicle commanders would radio the company commander. The Centurion tanks would form a firing line of seven tanks across, while the scout vehicle swung around in a big arc to secure the flanks and wait for reinforcements. The Egyptians would fire two barrages from their positions in a fast and furious exchange with the Allied forces then abandon their positions and retreat to the south before an airstrike could be called in. "Why do they do that?" said Brigitte as she watched the Egyptians retreat once again.

"Not really sure," said the vehicle commander. "It could be a stalling tactic to slow our advance but it could also be a way of saving their honor. If they put up a quick fight they can claim they did their duty and won't suffer any repercussions from their leaders when it's all over."

"So that's it; fire a couple of times then cut and run?"

"Pretty much. I image things will heat up quite a bit

when we reach El-Qantara and again when reach the outskirts of Ismailia."

"What about the ceasefire?"

"Don't believe it. We have unfinished business in Cairo. The generals will find some way to keep the war going. I'm sure of it. They want victories. So far all we've done is kill a bunch of Wogs."

"And how do you feel about that?"

"The way I see it, the Gypos brought this upon themselves. Frankly, I hope we go to Cairo and give the Wogs a walloping they won't soon forget."

Brigitte took notes of the conversation and took the commander's predictions with a grain of salt. She had been with soldiers long enough to understand their motivations. They were warriors. They wanted to win.

November 7, 1956 – El Cap, Egypt

It was twenty minutes past the ceasefire deadline of midnight when the British tank column rolled into El Cap. Resistance was surprisingly light, but then again there was little point in dying before a ceasefire. The Allied soldiers had pushed as far as they could and as long as they thought they could get away with. If anyone questioned the delay they would claim confusion as to whether it was to be Cairo or London time. They thought about claiming it was U.N. time which was many hours behind but nobody wanted to push too far. Nobody knew if the Egyptians would even keep their part of the ceasefire. There was only one way to find out. Stop fighting.

The distant gunfire and explosions fell silent. The Allies could see the lights in El-Qantara in the distance. The troops were exhausted and needed a meal. But there were firing positions that needed to be dug first. When the work was done, sentries were posted. The soldiers ate and visited one with another.

They had come up short of capturing the Canal Zone. If they had just had one day more everyone was sure they could have done it. Why not keep going? They were almost there. The blame was placed squarely on the shoulders of the politicians in London and Paris. Some blamed the United States for failing to side with their oldest allies. It would be a slight not soon forgotten by both the British and the French. There were those that were sure the war would start again and they would be allowed to continue until total victory was theirs. Others talked of going home in time for the holidays. And still others just wanted three fingers of whiskey and a fire to sit by on a cold November night.

El Cap, Egypt

As the sun rose the paratroopers and engineers were hard at work digging in and preparing fortified firing positions. French reconnaissance aircraft had reported a buildup of T-34 tanks and SU-100 tank destroyers in Ismailia.

Ceasefires were temporary in nature while peace agreements are negotiated. There was a very real possibility that peace talks could collapse and the war restarted. The Egyptians were no longer a fleeing rabble. They had reorganized and reinforced their forces along the Suez Canal Zone. They were ready and willing to once again take up the fight against the Allied invaders.

The British and French were not taking any chances. Engineers had torn up the track of the Egyptian railway that paralleled the canal. The railway ties that formed the foundation of the train tracks were carried to the Allied firing positions dug into the desert. The thick wooden posts could easily stop most bullets and shrapnel from nearby exploding artillery shells. A direct hit from a tank or anti-tank gun was another story. The posts would shatter and shower the troops behind it with shards of oil soaked wood. To prevent this hazard the stacks of posts were reinforced with interior slopes of sand, dirt and rock. It wasn't as safe as a concrete pill box but it was all that was available.

November 8, 1956 – El Cap, Egypt

It was late afternoon. Brigitte was wrapping up her interviews and hoping to get a ride back to Port Said where she could catch a plane back to civilization. She wanted a hot bath but would settle for a washcloth and a bowl of water to soak the sandy grit out of her underwear.

She found it humorous how low her expectations became after a few weeks in the field with a bunch of smelly paratroopers. They weren't a bad bunch, they just needed to brush their teeth. Many things went by the wayside when you were fighting for your life and those around you, she decided.

The British sergeant that had helped her get a ride with the column introduced her to some of the men in his platoon. He didn't want to tell his story. It wasn't important. But the story of his men might be worth reading he reasoned. For many of them, this was their first war and they were still impressionable.

She started with Ross who gladly accepted the offer to be interviewed for a magazine even if it was in French. He just asked that she take his photograph in hopes that it might appear in the article and he could show his girlfriend when he got back... as soon as he found one.

The sergeant helped her down into the private's firing position and then moved off to inspect the lines of his platoon. Brigitte sat down on a pile of sand next to Ross who kept his eyes focused on the enemy positions almost a mile away. "How did you hurt your ankle?" said Ross.

"Jumping off a roof with a crazy paratrooper," said Brigitte.

"You mean like a dare?"

"No. We were being chased by a mob of Egyptians."

"Bloody hell. That must have been scary. Maybe you should put that in your article."

"Maybe. It seems a bit mundane when compared with what you guys went through."

"Staff Sergeant told ya?"

"Yes. Quite harrowing."

"Yeah. This is my first war. Not sure I want to see another."

"You won't know until some time passes. You may miss it. I know I did."

"You've been in another war?"

"A few. Too many."

"Wow. What was the worst one?"

"Dien Bien Phu I think."

"What war was that?"

"The Indochina War in Vietnam."

"I haven't heard of that one."

"Enough of me. I'd like to hear about you. You are English, yes?"

"Yes. My family is from Yorkshire. My father worked for a small distillery outside of Harrogate."

"Whiskey?"

"No. Mostly gin and a bit of brandy. To be honest, I think he drank more than he bottled."

"So, why did you join the paratroopers?"

Ross ignored her question. Something had caught his attention. "That's strange," said Ross.

"What's that?"

"There's a group of civilians gathering by that tree a couple of hundred yards out."

"Civilians? Are they armed?"

"I can't tell. It's too far."

"Maybe you should tell your sergeant."

"Yeah, I think you're right."

Ross turned to look for Brooks who was kneeling next

to the adjacent firing position talking with a corporal. "Hey, Staff Sergeant. I think you should have a look."

Brooks rose to his feet and walked back to Ross's position. "What is it, Private?" he said.

"Two hundred yards out. 2 o'clock. Under that tree," said Ross.

Brooks looked out across the desert and saw the group. "What in the hell are they doing?"

"I don't know. They're just standing there."

"Nobody just stands in the middle of a war zone, son."

Brooks took out his binoculars and took another look.

"Are they armed?" said Ross.

"That they are," said Brooks. "Rifles and a few machine guns. One of them has a Russian RPG."

The leader of the group of Egyptians looked back at Brooks. He moved toward the British lines and ordered his men to spread out to form a skirmish line.

"No. You don't want to do that, buddy. Just stay where you are."

The group advanced.

The rest of the platoon was watching the sergeant and the group advancing. "Nobody fire unless fired upon," said Brooks.

"What if they don't stop?"

"I'd better go see what they want."

"I'm not sure that's such a good idea," said Brigitte propping herself up and looking out at the approaching Egyptians.

"I'll be alright. It's a ceasefire. They're probably just looking for some food or cigarettes. Whatever it is, I don't want them getting any closer to our lines."

Brooks walked out into the desert toward the approaching Egyptians.

Ross loaded an anti-personnel grenade on the end of his barrel.

Brooks made a hand gesture for the Egyptians to stop. The leader raised his rifle and shot Brooks in the face.

Brooks crumpled to the ground.

"Staff Sergeant!" yelled Ross as the British platoon opened fire.

The Egyptians hit the ground and fired back.

Ross fired his grenade, careful not to land it near the sergeant. It exploded several yards behind the Egyptians. Calm down, thought Ross as he loaded another grenade. He breathed in deeply, took aim and fired. The shell landed between two Egyptians and exploded. They both screamed, rolled over and died. The Egyptians pulled back and ran for the trenches back beyond the tree.

Ross shot another grenade at them to keep them running. They were already out of range and the shell exploded harmlessly. He removed the remaining propulsion shells from his magazine and loaded live rounds. "You're not going there, are you?" said Brigitte.

"Damn right I am. That's my sergeant," said Ross rising up and climbing out of the firing position.

"He could be dead."

"No. He's alive. I'm sure of it."

Ross took off running. The rest of the platoon saw that he was moving toward the sergeant and gave him covering fire. Ross could see that the Egyptians were jumping into their trenches. *They'll be returning fire soon enough*, he thought. He slung his rifle over his shoulder and picked up his speed. He slid to a stop next to Brooks. "Staff Sergeant, are you okay?" said Ross.

There was blood all over Brook's face. The bullet had him in the fleshy part of the cheek just below the right eye. There was no response. "Don't you die on me," said Ross.

"I ain't gonna die on ya," said Brooks groggy. "What happened?"

"Ya got shot."

"Where?"

"In the face."

"Ah damn. Not again."

"Don't you feel it?"

"My head feels like I got hit by a hammer."

"That's a good sign."

"Not from where I'm sitting."

"I gotta get ya back. Can you run?"

"I can run but I can't see too well."

"That would be the blood in your eyes."

"Heads kinda spinning too."

"I can lead ya. Just hang on to me. We gotta move now."

"Alright. Help me up."

Ross helped Brooks to his feet. More shots zinged past and pelted the ground around them. They trotted with Ross's hand around Brooks's waist and Brooks's arm around Ross's shoulder. They headed back to Ross's firing position, where Brigitte was watching, cheering them on. "Come on. You're almost there."

The leader of the Egyptian raiding party took careful aim with his rifle and fired.

The bullet hit Ross in the back and exited through his chest. They both fell a few yards short of the safety of the firing position. "Oh, God. No," said Brigitte.

"Ross, are you okay?" said Brooks feeling around trying to find Ross's wound. He felt the blood on Ross's back. Brooks raised up on his knees and turned Ross over. "It's gonna be okay, son. I'm here. You're gonna be okay," said Brooks reaching down to Ross's chest trying to stop the bleeding.

But the bleeding had already stopped. Ross was dead. Shots hit the ground around Brooks. A shot hit Ross' foot and blew a hole in it. "He's had enough, ya bloody bastards!" cried Brooks. "Let 'im be."

Brigitte pulled herself from the safety of the trench and belly-crawled to Brooks, keeping as low as possible with bullets striking the ground around her. She grabbed Brooks by the shirt and said, "We gotta go!"

"I ain't leaving him here."

"He's gone. He's gone. We've got to go."

Brooks nodded, resigned. Brigitte guided him back to the trench and they climbed inside. They were safe for now. Brooks cried. Brigitte joined him. Ross's war was over.

November 9, 1956 – Port Fuad, Egypt

Things had calmed down except for the occasional skirmish between Egyptian and Allied troops which included rock throwing and cursing but rarely involved actual firing of weapons.

Snipers were still a problem. The Egyptian military claimed that sniper attacks were just civilians venting their anger that the Allies still occupied Egyptian territory. Snipers would single out officers whenever possible. Saluting an officer in the open was banned by most units.

The Allies attempted to prevent civilians from crossing between their lines but it was difficult since most of the Allied troops didn't speak Arabic and the Egyptians didn't speak English or French. Most Egyptians just chose to ignore the Allied troops and continued on their way. It was difficult to keep a civilian population from carrying on their daily lives. The Allies made speechless gestures and threatened to shoot the Egyptian civilians but few wanted that type of thing on their conscience if it could be avoided. Eventually, the British and French commanders ordered that the civilians wishing to pass between the lines go through checkpoints so they could be searched for weapons. Life in Egypt was slowly returning to normal.

The French paratroopers had improved their defensive positions around the bridge, waterworks and along the Canal. There were several tanks stationed on both sides of the Canal and armored cars patrolled the surrounding neighborhoods for any militia activity. French warplanes armed with bombs and rockets flew overhead as a constant reminder of the Allies' ability to quickly punish any bad behavior on the Egyptians' part.

The Egyptians brought more reinforcements and armor to their positions as a reminder to the French that if the hostilities started again, they would not roll over as they did before. They were prepared and organized. The unit commanders ordered reconnaissance missions to map out the Allied defensive positions and developed plans to attack if the peace negotiations failed.

The French paratroopers were generally disgusted with the whole affair. They had fought and many had died to capture their objectives. Now politicians were negotiating away their gains like chips in a poker game. They believed they could defeat any Egyptian force brought to battle. They wanted to go to Cairo and destroy the Egyptian's military for interfering with the French war against the Algerian rebels. Nasser and his generals needed to be taught not to tangle with the French.

Bruno was never satisfied with the defensive positions his men had created and was constantly ordering improvements. In reality, he was just keeping his men busy. He did not like idleness and felt it affected morale. "Keep your men busy," he told his unit commanders.

He ordered the brigade engineers to repair the damage to the second bridge and supervised the work personally. It was his opinion that if he could get the bridge operational again, he and his men could count it as captured. He could claim he and his men had achieved all his objectives given to them during the campaign. Bruno hated to fail at anything.

Bruno stood on one end of a rope connected to a block and tackle. He helped the engineers lift an iron beam into place, so they could shore up a beam damaged by the Egyptians before the French arrived.

A small convoy of British vehicles rolled to a stop on the western side of the bridge. Brigitte stepped out of a truck cab and walked toward Bruno with a limp and a smile. "You survived," said Bruno.

"A little worse for wear but yes," she said.

"And your ankle... It was not broken after all?"

"No. Just badly sprained and bruised. The medic gave me some ointment to rub on it and I kept it elevated so the swelling would go down. Almost good as new. So, what's with the Tinker Toys?"

"We're repairing the bridge. When we are done, I will have my men leave the bridge and we will recapture it... intact as we were ordered."

"That is truly the stupidest thing I have ever heard."

"You are not a paratrooper. We don't like to leave unfinished business."

"Yeah, speaking of which... I think we should talk."

"I'm listening."

"The other night... we started something that we shouldn't have."

"And why is that?"

"You know why. I'm with Coyle."

"And that's what you want... to stay with Coyle?"

"I don't know what I want, but until I do... yeah, I'm gonna stay with Coyle."

"Play it safe?"

"Something like that, I suppose."

"You always do this, Brigitte. You are like a bath faucet running hot then cold then hot again whenever it suits you."

"You're right. I never should have..."

"I'm glad you did. I was beginning to wonder if I was wasting my time. Now I know I am."

"Don't be like that, Bruno."

"Go back to Coyle, Brigitte. I'm done," said Bruno moving off.

"Bruno, please..." she said, but it was too late. Bruno was gone.

November 15, 1956 – Paris, France

An Air France SE.161 Languedoc landed at Paris-Orly Airport. The four-engine commercial aircraft was French-built and had a long slender airframe. It was slow, with a maximum speed of only 274 mph but it had a good range and was comfortable.

It pulled to a stop in front of the main terminal. The ground crew waited until the propellers slowed to lazy spin before wheeling in the mobile staircase. The cabin door opened and the passengers began to disembark. Brigitte, because of her injured ankle, was the last to exit. She didn't want to tumble down the stairs from the careless bump of a passenger in a hurry to get off the plane. Her editor had sent a telegram asking that she return immediately so she could write her articles while the public was still interested. The Suez Crisis was fast becoming a topic to avoid in many social circles. The French had lost enough in recent years and were in no mood for more failure. She had caught the first available flight out of Tel Aviv after spending five hours soaking in a hotel bathtub.

Brigitte looked out from the top of the stairs and saw Coyle standing on the tarmac with a bouquet of her favorite flowers and a wide grin on his face. She wanted to cry but thought better of it. Instead, she just smiled back at him and made her way down the stairs. Seeing that she was limping, he ran up the stairs and met her halfway. "You didn't tell me you were hurt," he said, wrapping his arm around her waist to help her the rest of the way.

"It's nothing really. I'm just glad to be home," she said, and she meant it.

EPILOGUE

To everyone's surprise the ceasefire held, especially after Eisenhower insisted that both British and French troops withdraw from Egypt before peace negotiations could begin. Eden was once again incensed by Eisenhower's treatment of his allies. On December 23, Britain withdrew all its troops from Egypt. The French troops followed a short time later. The British and French lost all their leverage during the peace negotiations. It was the United Nations that took the lead.

The Israelis were another matter. They refused to withdraw from their positions in the Sinai and the Gaza Strip. They believed Egypt would attack Israel as soon as the weapons they had lost were replaced by the Soviets. The Sinai would be their early warning system and a buffer zone to give the Israelis time to prepare. The Israelis finally withdrew as both the United States and the United Nations threatened harsh sanctions. As part of their negotiations to leave the Sinai, the Israelis got the Egyptians to agree to give Israeli ships unimpeded access to the Straits of Tiran. It was a big win for Israel.

Nasser became a legend in the Arab world. He had fought the Western powers and survived. Under his leadership, Arab nationalism spread throughout the Middle East. It took the Egyptian engineers over eighteen months to clear the Suez Canal before ships could once again pass through with oil from the Middle East. Over the next ten years, Nasser made the fatal mistake of believing that Egypt had won a great military victory. In fact, he had barely averted the complete annihilation of his army and air force. On June 5, 1967 Egypt, Syria, and Jordan attacked Israel. The war lasted six days until the Israelis had decimated the invaders' armies and air forces to the point where they ran out of targets. It was a humiliating defeat for Nasser and the Arab world.

Eden never apologized for his role in the Suez Crisis and continued to insist it was necessary. On December 20, 1956, he spoke for the last time in the House of Commons. When asked if he had prior knowledge of the Israeli attack on the Sinai, he lied and said he did not. On January 8, 1957, Eden resigned sighting ill health. He was succeeded by Harold Macmillan, 1st Earl of Stockton and leader of the Conservative Party.

Eisenhower was reelected president of the United States and served another four years. NATO survived, although the French decided they would never again rely solely on the United States or Britain. Eisenhower was able to repair America's special relationship with Britain, especially after Eden had left office. Eisenhower decided that America needed to play a larger role in the Middle East after the Suez Crisis. After the Soviets launched Sputnik in 1957, Eisenhower authorized the creation of NASA and the space race was on. He also oversaw the planning and preparation of the Bay of Pigs Invasion which his successor John F. Kennedy would carry out… sort of…

LETTER TO READER

Dear Reader,

I hope you enjoyed Operation Musketeer as much I enjoyed writing it. The next book in the Airmen series is Battle of the Casbah. It's the conclusion of the Algerian War for Independence. Here is the link:

Click for Battle of the Casbah

Reviews for Operation Musketeer on Amazon or Goodreads are always appreciated. I read everyone and I believe they help my writing. Thank you for your consideration and I hope to hear from you.

In gratitude,

David Lee Corley

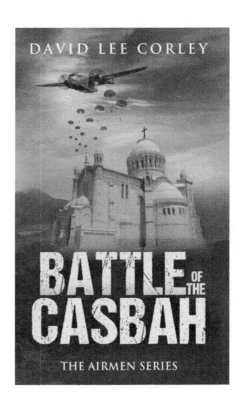

DEDICATION

I dedicate this book to my son, Cameron Charles Corley,
one of the nicest people I know. He cares about humanity
and the environment more than he cares about himself.
He has taught me the meaning of the word "selfless."

ACKNOWLEDGMENTS

I would like to thank Antoneta Wotringer for her excellent book cover design. She is truly an artist with a unique sense of style. I would also like to thank JJ Toner for proofreading and his wry sense of humor.

AUTHOR'S BIOGRAPHY

Born in 1958, David grew up on a horse ranch in Northern California, breeding and training appaloosas. He has had all his toes broken at least once and survived numerous falls and kicks from ornery colts and fillies. David started writing professionally as a copywriter in his early 20's. At 32, he packed up his family and moved to Malibu, California to live his dream of writing and directing motion pictures. He has four motion picture screenwriting credits and two directing credits. His movies have been viewed by over 50 million movie-goers worldwide and won a multitude of awards, including the Malibu, Palm Springs, and San Jose Film Festivals. In addition to his 23 screenplays, he has written three novels. He developed his simplistic writing style after rereading his two favorite books, Ernest Hemingway's "The Old Man and The Sea" and Cormac McCarthy's "No Country For Old Men." An avid student of world culture, David lived as an expat in both Thailand and Mexico. At 56, he sold all his possessions and became a nomad for four years. He circumnavigated the globe three times and visited 56 countries. Known for his detailed descriptions, his stories often include actual experiences and characters from his journeys. He loves to paint the places he has visited and the people he has met in both watercolor and oil. His paintings make great Christmas presents, though his three children may beg to differ.